Ask No Question

MARY HOCKING

Ask No Question

"I vow to thee my country, all earthly things above,
Entire and whole and perfect, the service of my love;
The love that asks no question, the love that stands the
      test,
That lays upon the altar the dearest and the best;
The love that never falters, the love that pays the price,
The love that makes undaunted the final sacrifice."

William Morrow & Company, Inc.
New York   1967

To
Pauline

Prologue

He had come at night and in too much pain to notice where they were taking him. "Don't worry about that," a voice had said, "there's no return journey." They had said that at Dachau, too.

It was an old building, not well-maintained and that at least was merciful because in this high stone wall there were chinks and one was wide enough for a glimpse of sky. Sometimes sound penetrated. Wind shrilling in wire, rain falling on stone. Most precious of all, men talking. The human voice, no matter how obscene the words, how rough the tongue, was a link with sanity; he asked for no bird song. As long as they never plugged this tiny breach, he felt he could survive, that the long solitude would not be complete. He believed in God, but he did not think that man, on earth, was meant to live with God alone. If they repaired that breach he would be so much alone with God that his mind would never again be able to establish a link with his fellow men. And there were two people for whose dear sakes he must preserve that link.

In the daytime, when they came to look at him, he lay

slack, his face vacuous. They thought that he was very ill. Perhaps they were right, sometimes it was difficult to tell. At night, when they left him alone, he exercised his body as much as his limited strength would allow. He did this because it helped him to go on believing that one day he would leave this place.

They themselves had told him that he could leave. All the time that they played their subtle, infinitely varied games with his body they explained how easy it would be for him to leave. There was always someone, squatting on the floor beside him, telling him in a quiet, reasonable voice that he had only to denounce certain men, men whom he had never met, with whom he had nothing in common except the misfortune of race, and he could be free.

That was a long time ago. Now they had wearied of him and the loneliness was more terrible than their brutality. He had tried to carve his name on the wall so that it would serve as a reminder if his mind began to lose its hold. His only tool had been a rusty nail and the words were scarcely legible. Every night he repeated his name as he tried to sleep, Mikail Kratz, Mikail Kratz, Mikail Kratz . . . He tried not to lose hope. Even at Dachau he had never lost hope. He would go on hoping here, as long as the breach in the wall remained.

Chapter I

The tunnel was closed. The Italian police were performing in comic-opera style; threatening fingers stabbed the air, gaping mouths blared incoherent orders. The delay might have been due to a landslide, a bomb, an earthquake . . . A bored Frenchman was telling a friend that a coach had broken down. He was probably right. Whatever the reason, the tunnel was likely to be out of use for several hours, if not all night.

Towards the end of the queue of cars, a gnome-like creature hunched beside a Fiat threw back his head as though imploring the gods to intervene. The gesture was worthy of the Italians, but the blasphemies that accompanied it were entirely Irish. When he had exhausted himself, he said, "Let's go see the doggies."

He eased into the seat beside the driver; in this position the ugliness of the body was concealed and one noticed only the surprising beauty of the long, thin face. His companion turned the car. Not an easy maneuver, the path being narrow and other drivers disinclined to give way, but he made it seem easy. One of the few good-natured drivers left in

Europe, the Irishman reflected. Perhaps one of the few good-natured men left in the twentieth century? Good-natured . . . an odd virtue for a man in his profession.

There was another delay at the frontier. Time was slipping by. As the car headed towards the Great St. Bernard Pass the evening star appeared between the peaks. The breeze had the edge of night. The men spoke only once. The Irishman said:

"I've been wondering all day why we were so suddenly instructed not to take the route through the Pass."

His companion said, "This is where curiosity leads you."

The Irishman looked ahead to where the rock bellied and the road seemed to swing into space with no barrier save an arc of stones like stumps of teeth in a massive jaw. No margin for error here. He looked at the hands on the wheel, firm, but not taut; he saw that the wrists were flexible, the shoulders relaxed. He looked up at the mountain peaks, glad that he was not driving. There was a lot of snow still; it had been a bad spring. As the car swung out he steeled himself to look down. Lights flickered here and there below. Other cars were following, but that was not important. The danger lay ahead, perhaps at the hospice, perhaps beyond it. He hunched down in his seat. It was not the battleground he would have chosen. His pale, sensitive face composed itself in lines more sardonic than usual; it was not in the least apparent that he was afraid.

It was nearly an hour later that they parked the car outside the hospice. The Fiat had negotiated the last few bends very slowly with the result that several cars were behind them when they arrived. There are times when it is good to have company.

"Do we go in?" the driver asked.

"I wouldn't relish a surprise encounter on the road down."

"And if they are here?"

"At least we shall know what to expect."

The two men got out of the car and walked across the yard. They paused for a moment, looking across the frozen lake. The wind was stronger now. The driver took off his gloves and flexed his fingers.

"I'm sorry Claus won't be here," he said. "I was looking forward to seeing him again."

The Irishman, thinking of Lausanne, its bright lights reflected in a kinder lake, said:

"Not as much as I'm looking forward to it."

They went into the small café. A couple were leaving a table near the door. The two men took their places, and the Irishman ordered coffee. The room was crowded, but not so crowded as to reduce its occupants to an indistinguishable mass. The driver, who had observed the recent arrivals getting out of their cars, had little difficulty in picking out the two men who had been waiting. Patient men with the indifferent eyes of the killer, they made little effort to pass as tourists. The Irishman said:

"I suppose the reason the coffee is so vile is that the water boils at a lower temperature." He put his cup down. "Where do we go from here?"

"Lausanne. The coffee will be better there."

He was thinking of Claus's flat, brandy and coffee and reminiscences. He slouched over the table, his dark head bent forward, the mouth slack beneath the dark mustache. It had been a long drive. Now was the time to relax tired muscles, rest the weary mind; so he thought of Claus who had been his friend in days more desperate but not so bleak. Opposite him, the Irishman's thin little body twitched, his face wrinkled with malign gaiety as excitement began to drive out fear.

"We'd better move before they move." He was always at his best when he could act quickly.

[11]

A dark, sweaty little waitress passed and the driver caught her eye; it was never difficult for him to catch a woman's eye. He ordered brandy. When she had gone, he said:

"Let them make the first move." Nothing ever seemed to him to be gained by trying to tackle a situation before it was ripe.

The Irishman bent forward.

"They know about our meeting here. Otherwise our orders wouldn't have been countermanded."

A man and a woman with a little girl were sitting nearby. The woman was saying, "It's too late to see them now, sweetie. They'll be all snuggled up for the night." The driver watched the little girl. The Irishman went on:

". . . and if they know about our meeting, they will think we're waiting for Claus. They won't expect us to leave yet."

The driver smiled at the little girl. "So?"

"You push off in the general direction of the *herren*. It's near the door. You can slip out without their seeing. They won't worry for a minute or two while they've got me in sight." The waitress came with the brandy. He waited impatiently until she had gone and then went on, "Drive the car to the far side of the lake. Take the road and go far enough down to be out of sight. I'll join you when I've shaken them off."

The driver picked up his glass. "It's phoney." He sipped the brandy. He was always a slow drinker: some said he was a slow thinker, too. "The whole situation is phoney."

The little girl was crying because she could not see a St. Bernard. One or two people went out. The crowd round the door began to thin. The Irishman said:

"It's going to be lonely here by the time you've finished that brandy."

The driver looked at his drink and saw a distorted image

[12]

reflected in the curved glass. Everything seemed unreal. The altitude, perhaps? Sometimes when you were tired it affected you that way. He didn't really care. He put the glass down without finishing his drink.

"We'll go," he said. "Both of us."

The Irishman began to argue; keeping his voice low he repeated his scheme. The driver repeated, "We'll go." They had to get to Lausanne and the way lay ahead; it was so simple, it irritated him that the Irishman didn't understand. He got up and went to the door. Outside it was cold and the lake looked desolate; it was not his kind of landscape, its statements were too uncompromisingly bleak. He walked across to the car, unlocked it and got in. The Irishman thrust a livid face down to him.

"You must be mad!"

"I'm tired of this." To him, it seemed a sufficient answer. His determination, if nothing else, communicated itself. The Irishman got in beside him; as they drove round the side of the lake the driver could feel his taut little body shaking with rage. On the far side of the lake they looked back. One or two people were getting into cars; they would have company on the way down. Suddenly something cut across their line of vision; a monk had leapt from a nearby mountain path, his habit billowing behind him as he ran. The driver laughed and eased back in his seat.

"A flying monk! That's all it needed."

The hospice and the lake disappeared as the car began to negotiate the first steep curve downwards. For a time it seemed that they had the whole valley to themselves. The scale of it was too vast for the Irishman's taste and he deliberately limited his awareness to the few yards of road ahead. He saw the arc of stones stand up in the car's headlamps. From his position, it seemed that the car swung out too far. He waited for the front wheels to grind against the stones.

There was one moment when there was nothing beyond the window; then the stones appeared again curving towards the safe shelter of rock. For a few minutes the road descended unadventurously, then swung out again. The arc of stones, the moment of darkness, shelter again. A pattern had emerged, a rhythm was established. The Irishman looked up at the peaks, the snow glimmering in the moonlight; it was always better on the way down, he thought. As the car swung out on the edge of a great buttress of rock, something else glimmered below the snowline.

"A car behind," the Irishman said sharply.

"Several, surely? There was a comfortable little caravan setting off when we left."

The road had curved inwards again. The Irishman turned to look back. After a few moments a ring of light moved round the rim of the buttress. He waited. No other light followed.

"Only one," he said.

The road dived steeply with high rock on one side and a shelf of scrub on the other. Now was the time to make ground before the next shoulder of rock loomed up and the path swung out again.

"You'll need to go faster," the Irishman said.

"Not on this path." Staid as a bloody coach driver!

"They're gaining on us."

"Let them! It's probably Mama and Papa and little Baby Bear."

"If it is, he'll put his fist on the horn and blast like hell any minute now."

He could feel the pull on the body of the car as the road curved outwards. This time he did not watch for the stones; he looked back and caught the full glare of headlamps as the other car thrust forward, eager to nudge them off the path. The driver wrenched at the wheel and the Fiat was clear, turning into the long slope downwards again.

"So now we know!" the Irishman said, and his body tensed, poised for the blind, ecstatic moment, for the wild plunge down released from fear and reason. But beside him the driver, steady eyes on the road, steady hands on the wheel, kept the car at a steady pace. Imbecile, this relaxed indifference! Now was the chance, now while the road ran straight and there was no room to overtake. The Irishman wanted to grab the wheel, to press his foot down on the accelerator . . . But already it was too late; the pattern was repeating itself. Another bend ahead, the other car drawing nearer as the familiar arc of stones appeared. It tried to ram them again and failed again, though metal grated ominously against metal as the Fiat rounded the bend and pulled in towards the shelter of rock. The driver said, "That's given them a taste of blood."

The road dived again, rock on one side, the shelf of scrub on the other. Far below, the road was a thin grey ribbon threading through the valley; if the tunnel had not been closed, the Irishman thought, they would be on that ambling road now. The valley disappeared as a great jaw thrust out ahead. The Irishman began to swear quietly. The driver glanced in his mirror, undismayed as the other car began to gain ground. Then, at the one moment when the maximum care was needed, he put his foot down on the accelerator and the car wheeled on the fringe of darkness throwing the Irishman hard against the door. As the little man clawed at the seat to pull himself up, he saw the other car coming on at a reckless angle. The headlamps blinded him. He heard the harsh conflict of wheel on stone but felt no impact, no sense of falling. The Fiat had stopped and the driver was saying, "Too fast this time." The Irishman looked round and saw the other car with its back wheels over the stones. It had a faintly foolish appearance. One of the men inside opened a door; weight shifted and the car tilted leisurely over the edge.

The driver got out of the car and walked back along the road. The Irishman came and stood beside him. A little avalanche of stones rattled down into the valley. Then it was quiet and very cold. The Irishman shivered as sweat chilled his body. They went back to the car. The driver sat hunched over the wheel. The eyes were bloodshot, the face lined with fatigue; but no tell-tale nerve twitched at temple or cheek. His was the tiredness of a man who has been driving a long time on a hard road. The Irishman, exhausted by exhilaration and despair, thought bitterly that, whatever doubts one might have about Mitchell, it was at moments like this that one had to recognize the quality of the man. Steadiness, patience, control, useful attributes in a bank clerk, but add to them this ability to reach one's peak at the moment of crisis, fearless, utterly relaxed, and you had something formidable. He said spitefully, "Are we going to wait here for another car to hit us?"

Wearily, the driver pressed the starter. "Strange, no other cars . . ." The Irishman did not answer. After a while, the driver said, "And why should they ever have suggested our meeting Claus in that God-forsaken spot when we can meet him in Lausanne, anyway?"

The Irishman said, "Curiosity will get you nowhere."

Not that one could accuse Mitchell of having an enquiring mind, he thought. He was beginning to feel ashamed of his own performance and this made him malicious. He wanted to find the weakness in the other man.

The road eased into the valley and soon they were driving across the plain where the glacial waters of the Rhône looked chalky in the moonlight. They came into Villeneuve before midnight and saw the lake and the great bank of distant

[16]

lights that was Montreux. The driver said, "Not long now."
They were coming along that part of the lake where the Castle of Chillon stands solitary, evoking memories of a darker age, when the driver said, "I hope Claus is in good form." The Irishman caught the slight inflection of anxiety in the voice, something of which the speaker himself was probably unaware. He smiled to himself triumphantly as he said:

"People mean too much to you. It's not a weakness you can afford."

Chapter 2

It was warm in Lausanne, even at two o'clock in the morning; windows were open on to balconies of flats, curtains moved in the warm night wind. As the car drove up the steep road from the lake towards the town's center, the Irishman said, "Eliot can't be expecting us now." They came to a crossroad where there were blocks of flats lofted high against the sky. Here and there lights shone. Mitchell looked at the nearest block, his eyes travelling along the fifth floor.

"We shan't need to wake Claus," he said, noticing the lamp glowing behind drawn curtains.

"And Eliot?"

"We'll let him sleep."

"I can't imagine Eliot asleep, but it's a fascinating thought. The last innocence . . ." He frowned, his mind moving from Eliot to Claus and Mitchell. He could imagine the sort of night it would be, the relaxed good fellowship in which he would have no part.

"Take me to the Suizerro," he said. "I'm too tired to be sociable. I'll ring Eliot—just in case he is troubled in spirit about us—and you can pick me up at nine in the morning."

[18]

Mitchell did not argue. Ten minutes later he was back at the block of flats, standing in the lift. He was aware, as the lift travelled upwards, of how much the light in the window had relieved his mind. Claus had been living recklessly lately. He was a large man with large virtues and large vices. There had nearly been an accident last year; he had laughed about it, but Mitchell had sensed the slackening of the climber's grip on life. The lift stopped and the door slid smoothly open; Mitchell walked along the dimly-lit corridor, knocked on a door, waited. He could hear dance music, intermittently interrupted by a voice on another station. "The damn thing isn't tuned in properly," he thought, and immediately realized that something was wrong. Even before the door opened, he knew his mistake.

"Stephen!"

The voice was warm, but the spontaneity of surprise was a lost art. She made the aloof gesture of drawing her wrap around her; later there would be the careless gesture when it fell from her. He knew these gestures so well, they had been the first things of which he had tired. He said foolishly, "I was just passing through."

"At two in the morning!" She held the door for him and he entered reluctantly. She closed the door and leant against it. In the half-light he could see that she had put on a lot of weight.

"You didn't expect to find me here." The gay unconcern had deteriorated into roguishness.

"No."

It took considerable control to leave the statement unadorned by explanation; he was miserably inept at finishing things, even statements.

She walked past him into the lounge, her bare feet leaving talcum powder imprints on the carpet. He remained in the hall for a moment, helplessly rebellious. Nearby a door

[19]

was open and moist, scented air puffed out; the hall mirror was misted over; the radio in the bathroom blared out an old jazz tune. He felt stifled. The lounge at least looked cool. She was sitting on the couch, leaning back, waiting. The room was ridiculously short of chairs, there was only one arm chair on the far side by the window. He joined her on the couch. She said:

"My brother is away. He said I could use the flat. I needed to be alone." Her face puckered with something of the old, clownish charm, inviting him to laugh at the idea. He was too dismayed to respond adequately.

"And now I intrude. I'm sorry."

She laughed, the harsh, guttural laughter that had come like a slap in the face in the days when he cared.

"Stephen! Don't be insincere. You know there is nothing I hate more than insincerity."

Only sincerity, he thought.

"Now that you're here, what will you drink?" She got up and went across to a cabinet in the far corner.

He said, "Brandy," feeling fatalistic.

She came back, swaying slowly across the thick carpet, the sash at her waist beginning to loosen. He felt very tired. She handed him the glass, letting the wrap fall open with the old generous gesture. Then she sat down and leant back, seeming to withdraw into herself as she stared up at the ceiling. It occurred to him that she did this kind of thing very well. He wished he could still feel something.

"Are you married again?" she asked.

"No." He hated direct questions; irritation made him unkind. "As you know, mine isn't the enduring kind of love."

She turned her head and studied him with that insolent, unashamedly sensual stare that he had always resented.

"You make marriage sound like some kind of test."

"Perhaps. In which case, it's a test I failed."

"How silly you are! You married a puritanical girl who made a ridiculous fuss because you were occasionally unfaithful . . ."

". . . because I came to the end of things. I seem to come to the end of things more quickly as time goes by."

She turned away, revolving the glass in her hand, staring down. The muscles round her jaw sagged a little and there were pouches beneath the bold, protuberant eyes. He sensed her fear. She was older, heavier, the years grinding her confidence down. He felt the betraying sweat of sympathy on his brow. Any moment now he would begin to explain why he had stayed away from her; he would try to avoid hurting her feelings and in the end he would give her the impression that he still wanted her. And then it would begin again. Another of his untidy, never-ending affairs. He looked up and saw the clutter of mountaineering photographs, all slightly askew, on the wall opposite. He said:

"Did Claus say when he would be back?"

"No. But he won't come tonight."

Not a very successful diversion. The silence lengthened; he was acutely aware of her unhappiness. If he went away now, she would cry a little and then forget; while he would feel guilty as long as he remembered her. If he did not go, he would feel just as guilty. How intolerable it was, not to care and yet to care! His hand moved along the back of the couch; she waited; there was that moment when the world seems to hold its breath and then the door bell rang. She remained quite still, and Mitchell remained still because he did not like to be the first to move. After a moment, she said without looking at him:

"Do you want me to answer?"

He did not reply. Her mouth curved bitterly; she got slowly to her feet, drawing her wrap around her as though she was

[21]

cold. In the hall, she fumbled a little opening the door, then a voice said:

"Is Mitchell here?"

The Irishman came into the room, dark and furious.

"It seems the bastard can't wait until the morning."

Chapter 3

There was no clutter of photographs on the walls of this room. The formal, uncomfortable furniture was arranged in the haphazard fashion of a hotel lounge. Indeed, nothing in the room was ordered to suit the needs of one person; its occupants, one would have guessed, were birds of passage, having no time to leave the imprint of a personality. Eliot had lived in it for twelve years.

The role of host had never been congenial to him; so now he left his guests to find chairs while he stood by the bookcase, a tall, uncouth figure, his dome-shaped head fringed with long strands of ginger hair. "You would think it impossible for a man with so little hair to look quite so sleazy," the Irishman had once said. Eliot, not unaware of this dislike, watched the Irishman, his amber eyes as devoid of human emotion as those of a cat. Dan Burke, he noticed, looked haggard. Stephen Mitchell, too. With Burke, the result was a suggestion of fiendish ill temper; with Mitchell, a weariness that was perhaps more dangerous. Burke's passion came quickly and went as quickly; Mitchell's was a slower fuse. Eliot wondered what these two men had been up to. It did not occur to him that they were tired; nor did it occur to him that they might be hungry or in need of a drink.

"You're late." A flat statement, inviting no explanation. Some men who have no feeling for their fellows affect a gusty good humour; it had never occurred to Eliot that feeling was necessary.

"We had to alter our plans," Burke pointed out. "We were going on leave if you remember. Stephen was going to Portugal and dropping me off in Madrid."

Eliot interrupted drily, "Now you are going to Tamaro on Lake Maggiore. You must be there before evening. That means an early start." He went across to a map on the wall and stabbed with a dirty fingernail. "Maggiore."

"I believe I know it," Mitchell murmured.

Eliot amused him. He would sacrifice his own mother to save a few minutes and waste an hour over a map, studying its contours with rapacious interest. No doubt he had stood in front of this map yesterday, calculating how long it would take them to reach Lausanne. Calculation was the bread of life to Eliot.

"If only I had known I could have taken my leave on Lake Maggiore!" Burke said.

"It was fortunate you were near enough to be diverted."

Eliot dismissed their lost leave and turned reluctantly from the map. He leant against the bookcase, his outstretched arms embracing the sides: a ragged carrion crow surveying his own particular battlefield.

"A man will arrive at Tamaro tonight. He will stay at the Hotel Pescatore, where you will also stay. From the moment he arrives, you must be near him. He is supposed to be on holiday, and this may be true. In which case, you will be able to have a holiday, too, Burke."

"Let's hope our tastes are similar."

"He is a scientist."

Burke closed his eyes and Mitchell said, "Oh God! We still have some left?"

Eliot, who was not in the least patriotic, gave a wolfish smile. "A diminishing species. They either emigrate to America, in which case they are ambitious, or to Russia, in which case they are traitors."

"And our man is going to Russia?"

"We have no proof. And less in the way of speculation than usual. Simply a gradual slackening of interest. It isn't that he has made any preparations for leaving the country, but rather that he has failed to make preparations for staying. For example, a paper that he has to read at Cambridge in the autumn not started yet, and he is a methodical man. Urgent repairs to the central heating system in his house not put in hand, and he is not unbusinesslike."

"He could be tired and in need of a rest," Burke suggested softly.

"He could indeed."

"Politics?" Mitchell asked.

"He has never talked much. Lately, he has not talked at all."

"Idealist?"

"Not noticeably."

"Then?"

"Shall we say he is one of those who have missed the highest rewards."

"But valuable?"

"He will never make a great breakthrough. But once it is made, he will understand how it was done. He has an excellent grasp of other men's ideas and a remarkably retentive memory. And he is very well placed to exercise these particular gifts. He is a biologist and he knows quite a lot about current research in molecular biology."

"Sounds harmless," Burke said.

[25]

"On the contrary, its findings could be of much more interest to homo sapiens than those of the nuclear scientist. The results of manipulating the genetics of viruses could, in certain circumstances, be quite devastating." Eliot's smile was cruel as he looked at Burke. "The freaks would outnumber what we regard as the normal specimens. I could give you details, if you like."

"I'll take your word for it."

Burke's dwarfish body was rigid. It was astonishing that such an inadequate instrument should be charged with so much feeling, Eliot thought. An enlarged spleen, no doubt.

Mitchell, who had been staring at the map during this exchange, said:

"But why Maggiore?"

"A conference on experimental biology is being held in Montreux towards the middle of next month. Alperin is having a holiday in Maggiore, and then attending the conference."

"Will he be alone?"

"As far as we know. He isn't married, lives with his sister. And he isn't the kind who makes friends. So it should be easy to spot his contact—if there is one."

Eliot looked at them; an impersonal glance, but searching —like having a Geiger counter passed over your soul, the Irishman thought.

"You won't fail, will you?"

Eliot's voice at its silkiest. The Irishman closed his eyes and reflected that he understood some of the pleasures of being a traitor.

But it had not been an idle enquiry. As he gave more detailed instructions, Eliot was wondering about the two men. They were not people with whom he liked to work. Burke was quick-witted, intuitive, sometimes spectacularly audacious; but unsound. Some said his temper would betray him, but this Eliot doubted—Burke's tempers were theatrical and to this extent controlled; it was his lack of discretion that would betray him eventually. About Mitchell, Eliot was not so sure; Mitchell was the nearest thing to a human puzzle that he had encountered. Most people respected him— "One of the bravest men I know," a man who had worked with him in the Maquis had said. Eliot, not rating bravery high, accepted this but continued to wonder. As he described Maurice Alperin he studied Mitchell. A strong body, tough but relaxed, a machine that would serve him well for many years yet; the face handsome, the features not coarsened by overindulgence, the eyes . . . Yes, Eliot thought, the answer lies in the eyes; warm, brown eyes that had some quality which Eliot did not understand.

"It sounds simple enough," the Irishman said when Eliot had finished.

Eliot, for once, agreed with him. This particular case was not likely to give rise to any difficulties. He shambled towards the door, anxious to be rid of his guests now that business was completed. He had switched off the center light when a thought struck him and he turned back.

"Why were you so late?"

"The tunnel was blocked," Mitchell told him.

Eliot stood quite still, sensing that he had not had the whole story.

"So we came through the Pass after all," Mitchell said.

Eliot seemed to have stopped breathing and in the dim light from a table lamp his face was yellow as old parchment. "You came through the Pass." The grey lips had difficulty with the words. "This is beyond belief."

"There was no other way," Mitchell retorted. "We shouldn't have been here by now otherwise."

"You are fortunate to be here at all. Their people were waiting . . ."

[27]

"They were less fortunate."

Eliot stared at them. His eyes went from one to the other; in the withered face they were startlingly alive.

"When I give an order, I mean it to be obeyed," he said. "I can't work with men who question my orders."

"You can't work with puppets, either," Mitchell answered.

Eliot looked away. His eyes went to the blank wall behind Mitchell and remained fixed there unblinking. Had it not been so unlikely that he should lose them, one might have thought that he was trying to collect his wits.

"You had better go," he said eventually.

But something had occurred to Mitchell now.

"And Claus Hesselmann?"

"Hesselmann?" Eliot was irritated by this diversion. "Hesselmann is dead." He seemed to realize, looking at the two men, that something more was expected of him. "A climbing accident, I don't know the details." He shrugged his shoulders. "It doesn't matter. He was quite useless to us lately; he drank too much."

They left after that. As they went through the warm, dark streets Burke raged against Eliot while Mitchell walked silent beside him. Later, when emotion had sweated out of him, Burke thought about the calm way in which Mitchell had taken Eliot's news. And only a little while ago, he had told this man that he cared too much about people! There was no end to the mistakes one could make.

Chapter 4

Maggiore was excessively coquettish in summer, mist veiling the shoulders of the hills, concealing the curving line of the shore. Its colouring was soft and deceptively gentle, but the lake glimmered with heat sparks sharp as broken glass. One sweated at every step. At Tamaro it was particularly exhausting; the town straggled up the hillside and some of the paths were almost vertical. Burke was glad that the Hotel Pescatore was by the quayside. Although this was the Swiss end of the lake, the Italian influence was strong; Burke made disdainful note of tiles missing from roofs, pink painted houses with plaster peeling off the walls, untrimmed vines darkening courtyards and windows. Not that he had any great respect for order. It was simply that he found this decaying lushness too much for his stomach, the relaxed acceptance of life irritating, and the insistent sensuality quite intolerable. Mitchell, of course, would like it; he flowered, or deflowered as the case might be, in this luxuriant Latin atmosphere.

When Burke had unpacked, washed and put another shirt on his already sweating body, the shadows were drawing across the bay. Darkness would come quickly. But it would bring no respite; night would be heavy, moist, scented, and one would not sleep for the breathless pounding of one's heart. He wished he was back in Berlin.

He felt rather uneasy about this assignment. Treat it as a holiday, Eliot had said, and Burke was resentfully inclined to do this. But he would never have chosen to go on holiday with Mitchell. Mitchell was good to work with, but there were things about him that irritated Burke, and on holiday there would be time for irritation to fester.

He went to the window to fasten back the shutters. Below, Mitchell was slumped on a bench overlooking the lake. He might have been a local inhabitant, staring across the water in the mindless way typical of these people; but Burke gave him the benefit of the doubt and decided that he was waiting for Alperin. And Alperin, unless he was a complete fool, would expect someone to be waiting for him. When he got permission for this trip abroad certain stipulations would have been made and he could scarcely have imagined that the authorities would trust to his honour alone to ensure that the conditions were met. Burke turned away from the window, frowning irritably. He had committed a cardinal error in thus imagining that other men's minds worked as subtly as his own. In fact, Alperin was probably convinced that he was beyond suspicion; clever men were often incredibly naïve. Burke took down his linen jacket and drew it on slowly, careful not to crease it. He studied himself in the mirror. As usual, he was too immaculate. But what could he do about it? Mitchell, with his strong, well-proportioned body, could afford to be casual in his dress; but when you were misshapen, you had to be careful. Burke looked at his face, the wide grey eyes, the fine, slightly hooked nose, the thin, well-shaped mouth; a beautiful face, mocked by the inadequate humped body with its disproportionately long arms. He turned off the light and saw for a moment the sky, deep purple pricked with stars, in the frame of the window. He wondered what life would have offered him if he had been wholly beautiful.

He went down the stairs slowly, longing for Berlin where the bizarre was accepted without question. In the dark, vine-covered bar he could hear women's voices raised in the endless, pulsing excitement of Italian conversation. He stopped at the reception desk to hand in his passport and to check again, in case Mitchell had overlooked it, that Alperin had not yet arrived. He strolled out on to the steps, the tips of his fingers resting lightly in the pocket of his jacket, and stood for a moment, his fine head raised, savouring the evening. It was theatrical and he knew it, but he could never move easily into the stream of life. There were a few people sitting at tables outside the hotel; one or two of them looked at him. His gesture made, he went down the steps into the street. There was a small, crescent-shaped esplanade lined with plane trees cut so that the branches fanned out like unlit torches. Behind, the hills rose steeply. The bay was small, intimate, too enclosed for his liking. He walked across the grass to where Mitchell was sitting. Mitchell did not move. Burke, seized with a sudden suspicion, asked:

"Has he come?"

Mitchell turned his head slowly. He looked at Burke as though having trouble in bringing him into focus.

"I don't know."

Burke sat down beside him, fighting a feeling of extreme exasperation. It was just as he had suspected, Mitchell was already besotted with the pleasures of this stagnant little backwater.

"A pity we had to come here instead of Locarno," he said. "I feel I might have found Locarno bearable."

"It isn't far away." Mitchell did not rise to the bait. "If it

[31]

wasn't for that promontory you would be able to see the lights."

That exhausted that controversy! Burke looked at his watch: it was seven o'clock.

"Should we have dinner? I don't think a reception committee is either necessary or desirable."

Mitchell did not seem to grasp the point, but he agreed to have dinner. The dining room was a courtyard with a glass roof overhead; vines clung to the walls and Burke discovered several insects crawling over the tablecloth. He picked up the wine list.

"Not Valpolicella, if you don't mind!" Mitchell did not argue. There were no French wines and in a fit of pique Burke ordered a Swiss wine, light and innocuous. He felt that he had rather overstepped himself, being extremely fastidious in matters relating to wine; but Mitchell drank it without protest. For the first time Burke noticed how tired he looked.

"You've damn near killed yourself," he said. "I'll drive on the way back."

"I'd rather die my own way." Mitchell pushed the cheese plate to one side. "I am terribly tired, though. And I have the oddest feeling that I'm not going to be able to take this business seriously. The whole thing seems unreal . . . dreamlike."

Burke said, "A night's rest will cure that." He did not sound convincing.

They got up. As they came to the archway that led to the foyer a quick, high voice was saying, "Alperin . . . no, no, no! Perhaps I had better spell it." It was dark in the archway, they were three steps down and Burke negotiated them carefully. Mitchell must have been too tired to notice them. The thin, high-pitched voice got to the letter 'r' and then stopped.

"Oh dear, oh dear!" He gave a nervous giggle, like an ado-

[32]

lescent who finds difficulty in reacting to an unfortunate situation. "Is it his heart, or . . ."

"It's his head," Burke said irritably. "He cracked it on the stone floor as he went down." He looked up from where he was kneeling to ask for water and got quite a lot of it in his face as the enormous proprietress lurched forward with a water jug. After that the staff descended, chattering like magpies, and Mitchell was borne away by a waiter and a porter even vaster than the proprietress. Burke was left in the hall with Alperin. He looked at him and saw a short, thin man with close, hazel eyes and a permanent smile that had no humour or friendliness in it.

"How very unfortunate!" Alperin gave another giggle. "I'm not sure that they should have moved him. He might have fractured his skull." He turned back to the desk and clicked his teeth petulantly. "There now! She's gone without telling me my room number."

Burke wandered round the far side of the desk. He studied the hotel register.

"What did you say your name was?"

"Alperin."

Burke glanced down the page.

"You seem to be in room 11."

He and Mitchell were in rooms 17 and 18 respectively. He hoped they were on the same floor as room 11, it would make things easier. Alperin was fussing over his luggage. Burke decided that he had done enough for the present.

"I must see about my friend," he said. "If I come across the porter I'll tell him to look after your luggage."

He went towards the stairs without another glance at Alperin.

Mitchell had a concussion; nothing very serious, the doctor said, but he must stay in bed for at least a week. For an active man, he submitted rather readily. He was feeling very

[33]

bad, and as the week went on he did not seem to get any better. He lay in bed and watched the bars of sunlight shift across the wall as day and evening came and went. He heard laughter in the street, the metallic voice over the loudspeaker as a passenger boat approached the quayside, the excited cries of children, the clink of glasses in the evening as people took their aperitifs at tables on the pavement below. He heard all this without interest; he felt no curiosity about the world outside.

Burke sweated after Alperin. He went on tours carrying packed lunches in brightly coloured paper carriers provided by the hotel; he drank Campari at cafés in the various towns and villages that Alperin visited; he bought endless picture postcards.

"I've sent you one!" he told Mitchell. "After all, I've got to do something to pass the time."

Alperin was a compulsive sightseer. After a time, Burke found some pattern in his movements.

"The bastard is doing the lake systematically," he fumed to Mitchell. "He started at the Swiss end with Ascona and Locarno and he has crept up the west side as far as Porto Ronco; and that's only a tiny part of it. Do you know the size of this bloody lake!"

Mitchell looked at him wearily. His sense of humour had deserted him and he saw nothing comical in the little Irishman's predicament. He made himself ask, without really caring, "Does he know you're following him?" Burke thought that by the time they had got as far as the frontier at Luino, Alperin would certainly know.

"But you can do the Luino trip since you're so fond of Italy. You'll be better by then, and I can have a breakdown."

He was getting very irritable and that meant he might be careless. Mitchell registered the fact without interest.

Another two days went by. The doctor seemed satisfied,

[34]

but Mitchell knew he was no better. Nevertheless, he got up on the morning following the doctor's visit and prepared to go out. He was surprised to find that his head did not hurt and that his body performed its functions as adequately as usual. His limbs were not stiff or bruised, although he was a little weak. He went down the stairs and out into the street. It was early; the hills were threaded with wreaths of mist, the lake was calm in a pearly light and the air was blessedly fresh. To the west, the mist had lifted and he could see the coast curving away in the distance, the wooded hills clotted with houses and tiny villages. A delightful scene; but it awakened no response in him. He walked slowly towards the jetty. A few fishermen were sitting in gently rocking boats doing last-minute repairs to their nets. The water slapped soothingly against the jetty. It was the most peaceful, innocent time of the day; yet he found no pleasure in it. He sat on a seat and stared across the lake, trying to come to terms with what had happened to him.

The adventure was over at last. It was natural that some of the zest should have gone after the war, that the years should have blunted the sense of purpose. One accepted these things. But it had not stopped there; it had grown colder and bleaker as blood drained slowly from the fabric of life. The last years—the years of Eliot and his kind—had been very bad. But some vestige of adventure had remained while Claus lived, some spark of inspiration could still be struck on memory's flint. Now it was over. There was nothing left, no anger, no pain, no fear. The water, lapping at the stone beneath him, dragged his mind back to the present. He hauled himself to his feet. The present was not going to be easy. But he had a job to do, a necessary job for a man who still believed in serving his country.

He walked along the esplanade. His pulse was steady and he was not short of breath, yet every step was an ef-

[35]

fort; he felt as though, far from losing weight while he had been ill, he had put on a stone. He tried to concentrate on the job. The job was important; as long as one believed in it, one could preserve some self-respect. Alperin was a scientist who possessed information which, in the wrong hands, could mean the destruction of the human race. A terrifying thought. Yet his mind accepted it almost indifferently; he had become conditioned to living with the threat of cosmic disaster. What surprised him most was that his reaction to Alperin himself was so mild. Traitor was a word which had meant a great deal to him at one time; now he found it impossible to regard Alperin as anything but a muddled little man. Or was it that the scale of Alperin's crime was too vast for comprehension? If he had been a dope pedlar, Mitchell would have been extremely angry; but Alperin was peddling something so overwhelmingly deadly that the imagination could not cope with it. Was that the answer?

Mitchell had come to the end of the esplanade; ahead was a brick wall surrounding the garden of a hotel. Perhaps it was as well to encounter a barrier at this point. He decided, as he turned to walk back, that it was time to bring an end to this unprofitable mental exercise. Eliot would have disapproved of it. He would have said that this concern with self-respect was nothing but pride; Eliot thought he had too much pride. And for once, Eliot would have been right. There was a job to be done. It was not for him to concern himself with Alperin's motives or with the possible results of his actions; all that concerned him was what Alperin was doing at this particular moment. Was he preparing to continue his slow progress round the lake? It was, as Burke had said, a big lake and the greater part of it was in Italy: Alperin had a lot to see yet. And Burke needed a break; he was getting restive and soon he would do something foolish. Mitchell quickened his step.

But as things transpired there was no cause for haste. Mitchell sat on the esplanade all the morning, keeping an eye on the hotel, while Burke went into Locarno. But Alperin did not appear; it seemed he had a stomach upset. Mitchell relaxed in the sun and refrained from taxing his mind any further.

The next day, the boat trips started again.

"I hope you enjoy it," Burke said sourly as Mitchell set off.

Alperin went to Isola Brissago and toiled round the botanical gardens. He argued with the guide, asking a lot of tiresome questions and making himself unpopular with references to Kew Gardens. The next day he went as far as Luino. He had a long argument with an Italian customs official whom he thought arrogant. A bright spot of colour fanned his cheeks. He was a man who bore resentment easily and nourished it carefully, Mitchell decided.

The boats were big. Mitchell soon discovered that he could avoid meeting Alperin by staying in the bar; Alperin was no drinker. The only time they met face to face was at Luino. Alperin seemed genuinely surprised.

"Are you better?" he asked.

"Yes, thank you. I think I'll stick to boat travel for a while, though. More restful."

Mitchell, who had decided that Alperin was the kind who would never remember a face, only an insult, was surprised that the man had recognized him immediately.

It was dusk when the boat arrived at Tamaro. Only a few people got off. Mitchell strolled across to a kiosk to buy cigarettes; he waited until Alperin was out of sight before he, too, turned towards the hotel. The street was empty and for a moment it was a lonely view, the evening light slanting across the bay, the plane trees casting long shadows, dust settling in the road. As he came nearer to the hotel, however, he could make out a figure standing on the pavement, head down, fists clenched in the pockets of a drab raincoat; something in the stance was familiar. Suddenly, he was in Berlin again, a thin drizzle of rain falling as he walked beneath the street lamps, enveloped in all the hopelessness of a grey winter evening. He had thought his spirits could scarcely be lower than during the last few days. He was wrong.

Chapter 5

Alperin watched the two figures meet and walk away; he watched until they were lost in the dusk. He was no student of human nature, but it was apparent even to him that they were not strangers. A surprising rendezvous.

Alperin turned away from the window feeling rather disappointed. For a time recently he had wondered whether the man, Mitchell might be one of their agents; he did not look like a spy, but then Lonsdale had not looked like a spy either. But it was surely inconceivable that if Mitchell had been after him, he would have turned his attention to anyone else. And his attention had been very much absorbed by his new companion. A pity; not many people come crashing down at your feet, thus demanding your attention. In his nervous state, it had seemed to him that it was some kind of sign. Absurd, of course. It was too much to expect someone to be installed at this hotel, ready and waiting for him. The approach would be up to him this time.

They had made one approach a year ago and he had rejected it. One does not readily accept the role of traitor. A naïve way of looking at things; but then one is so conditioned by national attitudes, it takes time and courage to fight one's way across the frontiers of conventional thought. But all that was behind him now; the battle of the mind had been fought and won.

The room was stiflingly hot and somewhere below a radio was throbbing out one of those odiously sentimental Neapolitan songs. It reminded him that the physical frontiers had yet to be crossed. When the great decision was made and he emerged from the dark tunnel, it had been surprising to find that he was still at Cambridge. Then came the conference at Montreux. Sir Harry should have gone, but he found these affairs boring. So once again Alperin was asked to substitute for him. Alperin prided himself that on this occasion he had handled matters with some subtlety; he had protested, said it wasn't convenient, that he hadn't had sufficient time for preparation. Sir Harry, predictably, had insisted: he thrived on opposition. It had seemed something in the nature of a miracle. So much so that Alperin had taken no initiative himself, had made no plans for a journey further east. His attitude had become fatalistic: events would take their course, the decision had been made and that was all that mattered.

Waiting had been trying, though. He was excited and found it difficult to maintain his air of sullen resentment. He decided to go abroad earlier. He needed a holiday, Sir Harry would vouch for that. Sir Harry would also be glad to have him out of the way as soon as possible; he was waiting to carry out reorganizations which Alperin would oppose. Alperin would lose the battle, of course, he always lost. Sir Harry Gethryn was friendly with the P.M. They didn't talk much about work, it wasn't necessary—a word over a glass of port after one of their exclusive dinner parties was enough. Just the same, Alperin could delay matters, he could make the operation work less smoothly; Sir Harry would be glad to have him out of the way.

[40]

It had all worked out. Sir Harry had even recommended that he should go to Maggiore for his holiday and Alperin, who had no ideas of his own, had agreed. All he wanted was time to think. He had the feeling that if he could get away to some lonely spot and be very quiet, the next step would be made clear to him. At Montreux there would be scientists whose loyalties were known to be suspect; there would also be observers from Eastern Europe. It should be possible to indicate his position. He was rather vague as to exactly how he would do this, but he was sure it would be possible. And they were very efficient. What was more, they wanted him. After all the snubs and insults, the honours given to other men while he did the hard, grinding work, the fact of being wanted was quite overwhelming in its impact on him. It represented his own private miracle.

It had come just in time for him. He had lately been a little obsessed with the injustices done to him and his sister, Dorothy, had hinted that he should see a psychiatrist. A brutal unimaginative suggestion, but then she was an insensitive woman. He had begun to feel quite ill at the effort required to stifle his resentment; sometimes it burst out in rather undignified scenes at the research center—there had been a ludicrous drama over the fact that his tea never came at the right time. He was glad that now he would be able to strike strongly, with blows that would hurt them and would also relieve this intolerable pressure within him. It excited him. It excited him a little too much, one did not want to give the impression of being overwrought. A calming down period was desirable.

And so Maggiore. But it was not at all what he needed. He had realized this in dismay as soon as he arrived. The air had not the desert purity, nor was the landscape sufficiently harsh; this was not a place in which the still, small voice would speak. Tamaro, in the fold of the hills, made him feel

[41]

more stifled than ever. He would like to have walked, but this was no place for walking; to the left was the esplanade which was not extensive, to the right was the road to Brissago along which cars hurtled at murderous speed, the hills rose vertical above and even if one tried to climb them there was nothing beyond but more hills. There remained the lake. He began to take daily trips on the lake. The boats were crowded with tourists and there was a loudspeaker which continually blared announcements in four languages. It was hard to relax. He went to Isola Brissago, thinking that an island would be peaceful; but it transpired that one was compelled to go on a guided tour of the botanical gardens. He complained to the guide about this restriction on the freedom of movement. The specimens were not even good; in one of those unreasonable throwbacks to nationalism he informed the guide that the gardens were nothing to compare with Kew Gardens.

At night there was little peace. The floors in the hotel were stone-flagged and a regiment marched up and down the corridors each night, the water for the whole hotel was piped through his room, and the toilet was next door. There was one hour in the middle of the night when there was peace, and then a man came out on the terrace and began to sweep it with an incredibly hard broom. Soon the man was joined by a maid; the two held excited conversations punctuated by moments of silence which were almost more disturbing. The heat pulsed and he could hardly breathe.

But in that one hour of peace he came to realize how much his decision meant to him. It was his last chance, his last hope of sanity, respect . . . The more he looked back on the world he had left, the more he saw that he must never return. Power was all that mattered in that world. Everything was subordinated to the need to dominate, there was hardly a man there with the genuine scientific curiosity, the disinterested thirst for truth. Those, like himself, who were not equipped for the power struggle, were crippled. He must get away to a country which still tried to live by an ideal. And if the ideal was harsh and alien, what did that matter? The climate would be one in which he could breathe, where results alone counted. And he could bring results enough! Other men's results. But, who knew, might he not recapture in this new, sympathetic atmosphere something of the promise of his early years? They had thought he would do better than he had done. Now, he would surprise them all by fulfilling that early promise.

Night after night in that one hour of peace he had comforted himself with this thought. But now he could think only of Mitchell outside in the dusk with someone who was of more interest to him than Alperin. His spirits spiralled down. Soon he was aware only that his head ached and his mouth tasted foul. He went across to the wash basin to brush his teeth before going down to dinner; the water was lukewarm and there was a cockroach in the basin. He would be glad when he could leave this place.

After dinner he strolled along the esplanade. It was hotter than ever, the air pressed on every nerve in his head. There would be a storm in the night. He went back to his room feeling sick. It was no use trying to sleep. He must do something to relieve this intolerable pressure on his skull. Perhaps there were certain steps he should take? The gods, they say, are kind to those who help themselves. He decided to write to Professor Schaffer at Bonn saying how much he was looking forward to seeing him in Montreux. He tried to think of subtle ways of hinting at his commitment. "Cambridge has become intolerable, I feel I must make a break." He was uneasy about that. Finally he wrote, "Cambridge no longer suits me. I feel the need for a change." As he read the letter through, wondering if he had said too much even now,

[43]

he realized that he had accepted the fact that he was bound to be watched by his own people.

While he was addressing the envelope he heard the first heavy spots of rain hiss on the hot stone of the balcony. The curtains billowed into the room. He went to the window and looked out. Lightning scrawled a strange pattern and for a second a fantastic, skeletal figure danced across the bay. He decided not to go out, but he stayed at the window for a few minutes. The man, Mitchell, and his new companion were sitting at a table. As he watched, Mitchell got to his feet and went indoors. An abrupt leave-taking. The stranger remained sitting hunched over the table. Another flash of lightning ripped across the bay. The lights in the hotel flickered and went out, the lake disappeared; there was only the wall of rain and the one figure sitting unmoving, the head bowed, the hands clenching the sides of the table. Alperin watched in amazement until the rain came down like a blind across the window.

Chapter 6

Mitchell said to Miriam Kratz, "How did you get here?"

"By train."

"But the fare?"

"I took some money."

"From that café where you work?"

"Yes."

"I see."

But he didn't see. The fact that she had stolen money did not surprise him; honesty was not a luxury Miriam Kratz could afford. What puzzled him was that she should steal in order to come here. Her raincoat was threadbare, but she would still be wearing it in the bitter Berlin winter; no doubt it would hang even more loosely then. If you deny yourself the essentials of life, you don't fritter money away on travel.

"When did you last eat?" he asked.

"In Berlin."

He turned towards the hotel and she spat at him, "I don't want to eat, I want to talk."

"After you've eaten."

He didn't care what she wanted, he wanted time. Miriam

Kratz's problems were no concern of his; there were many separated families in Berlin, it was a commonplace situation. Nevertheless, he had always found her rather disconcerting: born in a concentration camp, reared in a displaced persons' camp, she was a reminder of things it would be more comfortable to forget. Her arrival in this lazy, sun-bright town had a quality of nightmare. He went into the bar and automatically used his charm on the waitress who quickly produced salad, cold meats, a loaf of French bread and two bottles of lager. He insisted on carrying the tray himself.

Miriam was sitting at one of the tables. She had taken off her raincoat and in her straight, black shift she looked like a schoolgirl—the sullen, unwashed kind. The ragged dark hair added to the illusion; but the sallow face was dominated by eyes that were old as her people's history. Big, dark eyes, fringed with thick lashes, eyes that must always have drawn attention to her: even as a child she would never have been able to escape a man's attention. Those dark eyes aroused dark things. Even Mitchell, who hated hurting people, could imagine the intense pleasure some men would have found in hurting Miriam Kratz. Whenever he looked at her he felt the need to expiate something—other men's guilt or his own indifference.

Now, as he put the tray down in front of her, he wished her many miles away. In spite of this, good nature prompted him to say:

"Take your time. We've the whole evening before us."

She tackled the food obediently, but without relish; it was a long time since she had shown any interest in the material side of existence. A man passing glanced at them; he walked on, turned, looking at Miriam, his eyes exploring the black shift. Mitchell had known Miriam Kratz for a long time and had never lusted after her; it was as though for him despair had cloaked her in a nun's habit. But now, sitting here in the

[46]

close, violet dusk, his interest was quickened. She was thin, but not frail; and though the face had little animation, the body did not lack vitality. Not feminine, he thought, but definitely female. He wondered how often she had been raped in her long journey through the camps.

When she had finished the meal she sat passively, staring at him, waiting permission to speak in a way that disgusted him. A passenger boat on an evening trip approached the jetty. The sky was dark and bruised and the water was green. Only a man and a boy boarded the boat. Mitchell watched it move away, the prow cutting into water smooth as coloured glass. He wanted to say to Miriam Kratz, "Go away! You are no concern of mine." It had been bad enough in Berlin; but in Berlin there were so many desperate people, one gained a certain immunity from their contaminating despair. Here he felt alone and vulnerable. But he was always weak against this kind of emotional pressure, so instead of telling her to go away he offered her a cigarette. They smoked for a while in silence while the clouds massed over the lake. Eventually he said:

"Now, tell me."

"A man has said he will help Mikail to escape." Her hand was unsteady and ash dropped from her cigarette on to the table. "He says I must pay him . . ."

"And who is this man?"

"Curt Lesser."

She would not look at him; perhaps she was afraid of what she might read in his eyes.

"Curt Lesser!" he repeated. "But . . . why are you here?"

"I must know if I can depend on him. It is all the money I have."

"But you could have asked anyone," he said angrily. "You have friends."

"No!"

[47]

"But you know people . . ."

"Yes." She nodded her head wearily. "I know people. That is why I had to ask you."

He stared at her incredulously and she said, "You are different." There was no flattery in the dry statement. He felt as angry as though she had told him he had leprosy.

"This is beyond all reason! You mean to tell me that you stole money, lost your job, travelled all this way, just to ask me if you could trust Curt Lesser?"

Her face was blank, but he could understand only too well what this meant to her. All the money she had saved, all her hope . . . He felt himself engulfed in the great darkness which seemed to possess her. Perhaps this was why she had said he was different, because he understood too much. He looked across the bay. The boat was quite a long way out now, riding rough; the surface of the lake was combed with tiny waves, but here on the esplanade the air was taut as a stretched nerve. He said with uncharacteristic crispness:

"You can't trust Curt Lesser."

Her lips trembled and her voice had a wheedling quality which was not pleasant.

"But other people escape . . . every day someone escapes . . ."

"Not from prison. Curt Lesser can't get your husband out of prison. He hasn't the contacts, the resources, or the guts. He'll take your savings and that's the last you'll see of him this side of hell."

It was stupid of her ever to have had dealings with the little rat! But then, in this trade across the border, who but the rats would bother with Miriam Kratz? It was probably the only hope she had been offered in the four years since her husband had been arrested and she had been separated from her child. Even the Miriam Kratzes of this world can't live without hope. He said wearily:

[48]

"Anyone could have told you this."

"But I would not have known whether to believe them."

"Then why should you believe me?"

This unsolicited trust needed to be killed, for his own sake as much as for hers. He braced himself for the answer. Integrity? There were stories he could tell her; in Eliot's regime integrity did not rate high. Reliability? No woman had ever found him reliable. She was looking at him; the dark eyes nailed to his face. He said uneasily:

"Well? It's a long way to come without knowing why."

"I think perhaps you are . . . a little good."

"Is goodness something of which you have so much experience?"

"I have my husband."

The eyes shone with a fierce pride. Pride was something he had not expected in Miriam Kratz. He was too surprised to comment. He picked up his glass; the lager was warm and flat. Thunder rumbled in the distance and a gust of wind shook the plane trees and blew dust in his face. Only a green rim of water was visible, the rest of the lake was blotted out by cloud. How quickly these storms blew up! he thought. And then, with shocking irrelevance, another thought came to him. He said to Miriam Kratz:

"How did you know that I was here?"

"Dan Burke sent a postcard to Lotté."

"He did what!"

"He sent a postcard to Lotté."

Mitchell put his glass down on the table. The first spots of rain began to fall; he watched them gradually darkening the dusty road. It was a moment or two before he could trust himself to speak casually, then he said:

"I can't imagine what one would say on a postcard to Lotté."

[49]

"He said, 'Having wonderful time in this lovely little place'."

"And what did Lottë make of that?"

"She thought it was silly."

The rain was much heavier now, he could feel it stinging his shoulders; he looked at Miriam Kratz, the rain glistening on her bare arms, her head slightly bowed. His questions did not appear to be making any impression on her.

"Did Lottë know you were coming here?" he asked.

She did not bother to answer. No one in their senses would confide in a little fool like Lottë. Burke must be mad. Mitchell got to his feet and walked into the hotel.

The lights were out and the staff were scurrying about carrying candles. Mitchell went up the stairs and encountered a woman in a wrap peering from the bathroom.

"There aren't any lights in here," she told him accusingly.

"There aren't any lights anywhere."

She continued to peer at him.

"But I'm having a bath. Can't you do something?"

"For example?"

She retreated and slammed the door. There was no window in the passage where Burke's room was situated and he had to feel his way along the wall. Burke's door was unlocked and Burke was lying on the bed reading *The Brothers Karamazov* by torchlight.

"I trust you are keeping an eye on our problem," he said.

Mitchell shut the door and locked it. "I've been attending to your problem." He went across to the window. Burke watched him.

"How very dramatic! I hope you're not going to lock that, too? This is the first breath of air we have had in this place."

Burke's room had no balcony and the windows of the rooms on either side had been firmly closed against the

[50]

storm; the rain was sluicing down. Not a good night for eavesdroppers. Mitchell turned away from the window.

"One can't be too careful, can one?" he said.

Burke closed the book and laid it on the table; he snapped out the torch and laid that beside the book.

"You sound like a secret agent," he said. "One cryptic remark after another."

There was a pause. The darkness was disconcerting. Mitchell had the feeling of having lost command of the situation. Burke said rather edgily:

"What's all this about my problem? I rather thought that what was mine was thine—in this case, at least."

"How many postcards did you send?"

Burke's head moved against the pillow; Mitchell sensed that he was looking in his direction. Thunder crashed overhead and a gust of wind sent the curtains streaming into the room. Burke said:

"What are you getting at?"

Burke was fumbling in the darkness, too. Mitchell spoke with an authority he was far from feeling.

"Answer my question."

"Very well." A brilliant flash of lightning revealed Burke sitting up, his small body arched like that of a wary cat. In the ensuing darkness, his voice had a feline quality. "I'm afraid it's not a very interesting story—hardly worthy of the buildup you've given it. However, if you insist . . . I bought some postcards while I was waiting for our friend to come out of the gents at Porto Ronco. I started writing them on the boat because I was so bloody bored. I tried to see how many clichés I could record—an absorbing pastime, you should try it sometime, I feel you are developing quite a talent for it. I wrote cards to myself and to you. For some reason —the scenery probably, all that slovenly charm—I had been thinking about Lottë; so I amused myself by jotting down

[51]

a few clichés for her benefit. At Brissago, our friend went into the post office and produced a few clichés of his own. I tagged along in case he did anything interesting; but he is not very enterprising. Personally, I doubt whether he would ever make the journey East unless someone parcelled him up and sent him there! He wrote cards to his sister and Sir Harry Gethryn. As I had bought stamps it would have looked silly not to post my cards. Unfortunately, I forgot about the one to Lottë and that went, too." He reached out a hand, found cigarettes on the table, lit one. "Now. Perhaps you could tell me what this is all about."

"Miriam Kratz is here."

There was a long pause, then Burke said:

"Miriam Kratz! But why should she come here?"

It had not occurred to Mitchell until this moment that an explanation might be required of him. Burke repeated:

"Why should she come here?"

What was he to say? Because she could trust no one but me to answer a question that any of a dozen people could have answered? Because she thinks I am "a little good?" The lights came on again; they seemed very bright. Mitchell had not felt so helpless and exposed since the Gestapo had questioned him. Only this time, he had trapped himself. He said:

"Lottë showed her your card."

"And she came here, immediately, just like that?"

Burke looked at Mitchell. "Every mongrel bitch comes sniffing after you," the look said. Mitchell felt the palms of his hands becoming moist.

"I always thought it odd that someone who was so drearily devoted to her husband and child should choose to stay in West Berlin," Burke said.

"It's her only chance of getting help." Mitchell managed to keep his voice level. "You know that."

"On the contrary, I know very little about her." Burke's

[52]

eyes travelled over Mitchell's face and down his body as though he was stripping him. "That little Hebrew slut is not my style. Not my style at all."

Mitchell felt the blood throb in his face. "You surely can't imagine . . ."

"Then why is she here?"

"Because you sent Lottë a card."

Burke laughed. "You'll have to do better than that." He waited, poised between belief and unbelief, wanting to think the worst, still unable to credit it. Now, if ever, was the moment to explain. If he spiced the tale with sufficient ridicule, Mitchell could convince Burke. But he remained obstinately silent. They stared at each other, engaged in a strange battle; the feeling between them was intense, although neither knew what they were doing or why or, least of all, where it would lead them. In a brief, intuitive moment, Mitchell saw that Burke would like to destroy him. The realization helped him to control his temper.

"Don't make too much of this, Dan," he said steadily. "She wanted a rest, that's all."

"And she came to you!"

Mitchell dug his nails into the palms of his hands until the pain cleared his mind. It took quite an intellectual effort to decide to say nothing.

Burke shrugged his shoulders. "Oh well, we've been a long time in Berlin . . ." He got off the bed and strolled across to the wash basin; he washed his hands and face fastidiously. It was not often that he had the advantage of Mitchell where a woman was concerned and he meant to get the maximum pleasure out of it. He reached for the towel and said:

"I hope you haven't acquired a taste for depravity?"

"Don't worry about that."

[53]

Burke looked at him; in spite of his enjoyment he was still a little incredulous.

"There's nothing else? No other angle?"

Mitchell remained silent. Burke turned away and reached for his jacket. He eased it on slowly and stood looking at himself in the mirror, his thin face flushed, the eyes bright with triumph.

"I think dinner now, don't you?"

Mitchell answered, "Not for me."

When Burke had gone he sat down on the bed. His body was drenched with sweat and he felt sick and shaken, but not violently antagonistic towards Burke. He was a patient man, slow to anger. On the whole he blamed himself for what had happened. It had been unintelligent to attack Burke without realizing that his own role in the affair might be questioned. Well, nothing could be done about that now. It had been an unpleasant incident, but it was over; no doubt Miriam Kratz would be on her way back to Berlin tomorrow. The really disturbing thing was that he had discovered that Burke hated him. It was not his habit to analyze people, so he did not ask why this should be so; he simply noted Burke's hatred and accepted it as a factor to be taken into account from now on. He waited until he was sweating less freely, then he went along to his own room, washed and changed his shirt. He still felt rather sick and the thought of food was unpleasant. Nevertheless, it would be better not to leave Burke alone for too long. Even if it was not possible to cement the breach, some kind of short-term repair must be effected without delay.

Perhaps the same thought had been passing through Burke's mind for he greeted Mitchell warmly when he came into the dining room.

"You're just in time to choose the wine. What shall it be? Valpolicella?"

Chapter 7

Some time during the night the storm wore itself out. The temperature dropped and the air became fresh. Miriam Kratz shifted in her bed and the coverlet slipped slowly to the floor. Immediately she was awake, sitting up, her hands clutching frantically. Then, as she leant forward, she saw the pattern of moonlight on the ground and raising her head she saw through the open window a few rags of cloud strewn across a dark, star-pierced sky. The open window was a reassuring sight, but her nightmare was not so easily dispelled. She compressed her lips tightly and crouched forward, every muscle braced to control her body. But it was no use; the shaking began, as always, in her thighs and quickly spread like a living thing crawling across her body, agitating muscles in her stomach, her breasts, her forearms. She lay back, pulling the blanket over her, trying to get warmth to fight this terrible agitation. Every muscle in her body jerked now and her teeth chattered; the twitching of her thighs was particularly unpleasant. She turned over and lay face down, pressing against the mattress. For a moment, the shaking seemed to ease, then the violent twitching in her thighs started again.

She tried to think of her mother. Mikail had told her that her mother was the first human being she had known and that her mother had loved her. "Before everything else, there was love," he had said. Her mind accepted that this was possible, but her emotions told her that the first human being she had known was the woman in the top bunk at Auschwitz. She knew very little about her except that the woman wanted her blanket. At night, she would see an arm, thin as a withered branch, hanging above her face, the fingers clawing. When Miriam was ill, the woman took the blanket. She said, "The child is dead now." The others made her give it back. "They were good to you," Mikail told her. "They looked after you." But it was only the woman she remembered. Once, when Mikail had come to bed late she had gone for him like a madwoman when he pulled back the sheets, tearing his face with her nails. He had taken her in his arms then, eased the shaking of her limbs with the warmth of his body, comforted her with his love. But he was not here now.

Surprisingly, this thought calmed her because it reminded her that if she became ill there would be no one to work for Mikail. She had learnt to put him before everything, even before the child who at this moment would be asleep in Mikail's parents' house in East Berlin. Now, as she fought back the panic which made her body more agitated than ever, she repeated his name over and over again. Gradually warmth returned to her limbs and the shaking stopped. She could not sleep any more, but she lay for a while looking at the open window. Open windows seemed a luxury to her.

In the morning and in the evening, she always set aside a few minutes when she thought about Mikail. She told herself that, wherever he was, he would do the same thing. Although she knew that a stage could be reached when morning and evening were indistinguishable, she refused to consider the possibility that this had happened to Mikail. Now, as she watched the sky grow pale beyond the window, she told herself that he would be thinking of her. She closed her eyes. It had been very difficult at first to imagine that, although separated, they could still be together; she had missed the comfort of his body so terribly that no other kind of communication seemed possible. But as time went by, she sometimes felt his presence in the first morning freshness. After these quiet moments she usually felt better, as if she had drawn strength from him. Lately, however, it had begun to occur to her that it was she who should give to him. The idea of giving was new, she was not at all sure how to set about it. On this particular morning, she solved the problem by lying spreadeagled on the bed, a position in which she felt cold and unpleasantly vulnerable. In spite of her discomfort, she held the position for a quarter of an hour. Nothing spectacular happened. She heard the first footsteps in the street, the clatter of a dustbin lid, someone shouting at an alley cat. Alley cats had a bad time everywhere, it seemed. The sounds receded, the outline of the window blurred, her body seemed to be drifting somewhere beyond her reach. This feeling that her body had become separated from her was very real; she could see it lying on the crumpled sheet, a frame of bone through which only the morning breeze stirred to give an illusion of life. It seemed that she must make a tremendous mental effort to regain possession of her body. Her mind struggled across the ceiling, along the wall, down the iron post of the bed, and then at last the tension was broken by a long sigh. The rib cage expanded and contracted, the hands twitched, and somewhere in the distance, a church clock chimed six. Miriam sat up.

"I shan't do that again!" she grumbled.

Her limbs were stiff and her body heavy, in spite of the

breeze the room seemed airless and she could only draw breath with difficulty. She sat on the edge of the bed, hoping she was not going to be ill. There was no water in the bedroom. Normally this would not have disturbed her, but at this moment it seemed to matter a lot. She dragged herself to her feet and went to the door. In the corridor she saw that a jug of water and a bowl had been set down two doors away. She picked them up and returned to her room; the water was lukewarm and there was a dead fly in it, but nevertheless she felt refreshed when she had washed and stepped into her dress.

Her feet ached. She had walked a lot the day before, searching for the hotel where Mitchell and Burke were staying. She put the bowl on the floor and then sat on the bed, her feet in the water. She picked up her handbag and counted her money. As she had suspected, there was not enough to pay for her lodgings. She sat absently studying her feet, wondering what to do about money. It had been necessary to steal in order to get here, but now that there was no particular urgency she did not want to risk stealing again. It would not help Mikail if she was sent to prison in Switzerland. There was always Stephen Mitchell. If she asked him for the money he would probably give it to her, he was the charitable kind. But she was reluctant to ask him; she still had the feeling that he might be useful to her in more important ways. She thought about the proprietress. The woman was Italian and Miriam had a vague idea that this might be used to advantage, Italians having a reputation for being warmhearted.

She waited until seven o'clock, then she took the bowl and tipped the dirty water down the lavatory, replacing the empty jug and bowl in their original position. She padded swiftly down the stairs, wondering how she could ingratiate herself with the proprietress. But the big woman who met her in the hall and demanded immediate payment had the look of a business woman in her black, beady eyes. It would be no good appealing to her mercy.

"I have breakfast before I pay," Miriam said firmly. One should eat before battle.

"Breakfast is seven francs," the woman told her.

"That is all right."

Seven francs, seventeen francs, it made no difference when you weren't going to pay anyway. Miriam walked into the dingy courtyard where meals were served and settled herself at a table. As it might be a long time before she had another meal, she told the waiter that a friend would be joining her and ordered breakfast for two.

Burke was tired of the continental breakfast. Apparently this was something that had been coming over him for years but he had not told anyone about it until now. He waxed eloquent on the subject. Mitchell listened with more attention than would have been necessary in the days when their relationship was casual and easy. They were condemned from now on to a meticulous consideration of each other's feelings. It was a relief when Alperin came in.

After Alperin had ordered breakfast and his coffee had been brought to him, Burke left the dining room and made some loud and rather ill-tempered enquiries at the reception desk nearby. Eventually he was given a boat timetable to study. There was a longish pause before he returned.

"Find anything?" Mitchell asked him later when they were waiting for the nine o'clock boat.

"Only a letter waiting to be posted."

At this moment Alperin reached the ticket office and they broke off their conversation to listen. Alperin bought a return ticket, stating that he was going as far as Stresa. Burke sighed: Stresa was a long way down the lake, a day's trip there and back. Mitchell diverted his attention by asking him about the letter.

"It was to Professor Schaffer at Bonn. I didn't read it all—there wasn't much time, the chambermaids were doing the rooms—but there was a reference to the need for a change of air. I told you he went in for clichés."

"I don't know how you work so quickly," Mitchell said. "There's no one to touch you in Europe."

Burke was pleased. For a time after they had settled themselves on the top deck of the boat, he was quiet. He had intended to needle Mitchell with occasional oblique references to his affair with Miriam Kratz, but the sun was gentle and the air still fresh after the storm, so he decided to make it a peaceful day. Peace could be pleasant in small doses: Miriam Kratz was not pleasant. In spite of his decision to say nothing about her, he found it difficult to get her out of his mind. During the war he had been involved in an unspectacular way with an escape organization that had not done as much as it might have done for the Jews. He told himself that there were good reasons for this, the European Jew was an undeserving specimen; nevertheless, he always felt on the defensive where the Jews were concerned. He shifted his position on the hard, slatted seat and his thin fingers tightened on the rail of the boat. Miriam Kratz was scum. It was presumptuous to the point of arrogance that she should be so persistent about her husband's fate. Mikail Kratz was neither politically significant nor scientifically useful; he was just an unknown doctor who practiced in a poor district and who had been foolish enough to attend to a wanted man. Who did she think was going to take up his cause? True, he had been in Dachau and there were still a few who remembered him and said that he was a good man. But the concentration camps had exhausted their emotional appeal and goodness was not a commodity of any interest to governments. Why didn't the woman accept defeat and return to her child instead of staying in the West, making a nuisance of herself? Sweat broke out in his armpits, at the backs of his knees. The morning freshness was giving way to the usual breathless heat; the mist was forming again and the water was very calm. Mitchell was taking snaps of a child who was waving from the quayside at Porto Ronco; he was snapping away with the wasteful enthusiasm of the tourist. Burke, reminded that he, too, had a part to play, unbuttoned his shirt and displayed white, reluctant flesh to the devouring sun. He hoped his next assignment would take him to the Arctic Circle.

The lake widened beyond Luino and the pattern of water, coast and island became more intricate. There were many inlets and the coast receded into haze and materialized again where one least expected it; solitary mountains reared up, seeming to have no base but the water; islands appeared and drifted by.

"This is nearly as bad as the Hebrides," Burke complained. "You can't tell where the coast stops and the islands begin."

Alperin seemed to know. As the boat approached Isola Madre they saw him on the deck below, at the front of the group waiting to disembark. Burke studied the guidebook. "Another botanical garden!"

"He can't get into much trouble there," Mitchell said. "Suppose we go on to Pallanza."

They landed fifteen minutes later and ate their packed lunches at a café overlooking the lake. Light glared from the stone promenade and the metal table was almost too hot to touch. Mitchell sat back in the canvas chair watching a Frenchwoman at a nearby table. She was very poised, sitting with her head tilted slightly, pensively watching the smoke rising from her cigarette. He appreciated the accomplished way in which, without once looking in his direction,

[61]

she managed to convey the fact that she was aware of him. Burke, too, watched the woman. She was the kind of woman he had dreamt of as a young man before he had learnt that he could not hope for much except the occasional kindness of a good-hearted whore such as Lottë. He picked up his glass of beer and drank; the beer was warm and flat. He was nauseated by everything; by the sweat of his own body, by the greasy paper bag containing the moistly buttered bread, by the strong-smelling cheese and, most of all, by Mitchell and the woman. He took the last roll and examined its contents without much hope.

"My stomach is beginning to rebel against salami."

Mitchell said idly, "Anyone can tell you've never lived rough."

Burke crumpled the offending paper bag and stuffed it and the roll back in the carrier.

"Are you about to recount your wartime adventures?"

Mitchell winced at the acidity of the tone. "For pity's sake, Dan! What's got into you now?"

"Don't be so damnably superior!"

Mitchell shrugged his shoulders. "I can't keep up with you; I'm much too slow-witted."

"But then you have your beautiful, strong body."

Mitchell turned his head away and looked across the lake.

"You do that kind of thing superbly." Burke's voice was amused, but his eyes were dark and his lips chiselled the words to a fine edge. "But as a gesture it's dated. In fact, you're a trifle dated yourself. Did you know that?" Mitchell continued to look at the lake; the sun was at its zenith now and the light glittered painfully. "You think I'm odd?" Burke began to peel a banana. "But it's you who are the odd one, my gallant Stephen. This is the age of the twisted, the deformed, the age of the pervert . . . you should know, you've lived in Berlin. But you don't look about you. If you did you

[62]

would realize that you are out of place. For one thing, your comfortable upper-middle-class background is hopelessly wrong; people aren't interested in you nowadays unless you've elbowed your way out of a council estate with enough resentment in your belly to keep it rumbling for the rest of your life. The world has changed a lot since you and Claus were the kind that mattered." Needles of light stabbed into Mitchell's eyes, a red mist blurred his vision; but he went on staring at the lake, forcing himself to concentrate on the pain in his eyes. Burke, exhausted and feeling suddenly rather foolish, finished his beer and beckoned to the waitress. When he had paid, he said:

"I think that's the boat coming from Isola Madre now."

They walked away without looking at the woman.

As they stood waiting for the boat, Mitchell wondered how much more of this he could stand. Burke's venomous bouts were not entirely new; in the past Mitchell had been one of the few men who could cope with him at such times. But now the poison had begun to sting. The boat came alongside. It was one of the small motor boats which ferried between the islands and there were not many people on it. Mitchell, however, was still thinking about Burke as he boarded the boat and it was not until a few minutes later that he noticed Alperin sitting in the prow talking to another man. Beside Mitchell, Burke swore softly, "Jesus wept!"

At that moment Alperin looked up and saw them; his companion saw them, too. Neither registered much pleasure. Mitchell, on the other hand, appeared to be as delighted as if this was the moment for which he had waited all day. He waved and pushed past the rows of seats to where Alperin was sitting.

"We seem to be following each other around." He put one foot on the bench beside Alperin, crouched forward and pointed his camera at the receding shore. "People tell me I

[63]

ought to get a range finder, but I don't think there's anything like your own judgment, provided you have a good eye." He took a few shots and sat down, folding his camera into the case. "I've been trying Agfacolor for a change. Friend got some good results with it recently and I thought the colours were very soft . . . just right here." He gazed over the water at the hills, pale indefinite outlines which would elude all but the finest camera lens. "Not like Southern Italy, colours are so much stronger there. Wonderful country, Italy, don't you think? Everything so warm and rich, and yet such tremendous contrasts. I mean, compare this with Amalfi." He turned to Alperin who drew back hastily. "You know Amalfi?"

"No."

"You *don't* know Amalfi?"

"No." Alperin's voice was high-pitched.

"Then you must go there! It's obvious that you're in love with Italy; I've noticed the way you want to see everything. I'm the same myself. The war did it for me, of course. Right from Salerno . . ."

"I was at Salerno," Alperin's companion said.

"Terrible weather, wasn't it?" Mitchell answered blandly. "Not the right month."

Alperin's companion smiled, a smile that flashed like a knife and was gone.

"I've been back every year since," Mitchell went on. "Never missed a year."

Alperin said, "Really!" He sounded winded.

"Speak Italian like a native."

Alperin's companion looked away across the lake. He had black, sad eyes that were full of the kind of wisdom learnt in the dark streets of big cities. His brown face was smooth and unlined but it had never been young. His hair was black and naturally oily and it stretched across his skull like the

[64]

sleekest of caps, no single strand ruffled by the faint breeze that played over the surface of the water. While Mitchell talked, he stared into the mist, the velvet eyes unexpectant, as though it would not have troubled him greatly if the journey had taken them all into eternity. Presently, however, the boat drew near to an island and he interrupted Mitchell to ask:

"Isola Bella?"

"No. Isola Pescatore." Mitchell turned back to the tormented Alperin. "It's Isola Bella you must see. Wonderful people, the Italians! In England we should say it was spoilt if one restaurant opened up; but here they turn it into a floating Petticoat Lane. Not an inch of land wasted . . . except for the grounds of the château." He tapped Alperin's shoulder to emphasize the advice he was about to give. "If you want to buy something in the market, *never* buy at the price they first name; they don't expect it and . . ."

Alperin said breathlessly, "I don't want to buy anything."

"You'll have to buy something—that's what it's there for. There isn't a bench you can sit on without it costing you something."

The other man said, "Your friend does not appear to share your enthusiasm for Italy."

Mitchell glanced at Burke, who was leaning over the side of the boat brooding in a rather Byronic fashion on the far shore.

"Too humid for him. He likes the mountain air. We're going to Montreux later. At least he'll have a view of a few snow-capped peaks there."

"I'm going to Montreux," Alperin admitted reluctantly.

"Really? It's not what it was. All the big hotels take in tours now—the place is full of people grumbling because they can't get a nice piece of haddock."

As the boat left Isola Pescatore Burke got up and came

[65]

across to them. He scarcely bothered to acknowledge Alperin and he did not look at his companion.

"I hope you've enjoyed this trip," he said sourly to Mitchell. "How many films have you wasted?"

"They're not wasted, boy!"

Burke stared morosely around him. "In this mist? Just like a bloody Turner, isn't it? You wouldn't be surprised to see the 'Fighting *Téméraire*' bearing down on you any minute."

"You'll see plenty here." Mitchell nodded his head towards Isola Bella, the blue canopied stalls already visible between the trees along the front. Alperin screwed up his eyes anxiously and his companion said:

"You might prefer a visit to the château."

"It's about the only place where you won't be trampled to death," Burke agreed.

When they landed they set off for the château, Alperin and his companion with Burke stepping out purposefully between them. Mitchell, who genuinely enjoyed the market, spent a couple of hours wandering from stall to stall. He bought several scarves and a cheap leather wallet and then found a café where he could have a drink at a reasonable price. The café was by the lake; all the cafés overlooked the lake because the island was long and narrow, like a small, overcrowded raft, and apart from a few crumbling alleys it had no hinterland. Mitchell sipped his Campari and listened idly to the conversation of two of the stewardesses from one of the bigger boats. The younger of the two was quite attractive, but her dark face was thin and there was, he decided, more than a hint of the shrew about the mouth. He found himself thinking of Miriam Kratz, who had no hint of the shrew about her mouth. He frowned and picked up his glass, the Campari seemed particularly bitter. All in all, it had been a strange day. He thought he had long ago learnt to take things as they came, but Karel Huber's appearance had surprised him. Alperin must have gone further than they had realized; but it was not this that surprised him, it was the fact that Huber should have been used as the contact. Even to the Communists, Huber, the ex-Nazi, represented the trash of the trade. Perhaps Burke had been right: the kind of life he enjoyed was indeed drained to the dregs. He found the waitress, paid and made his way down to the quayside. It was early evening now and colour was deepening as shadows encroached.

He studied the timetable and found that the boat was due in ten minutes; it was the last boat back to the Swiss part of the lake. A few exhausted tourists were already hanging about the landing stage watching the fishing boats, but Alperin and his companions were not among them. Mitchell lit a cigarette and watched a fair-haired German boy balancing precariously on the edge of the landing stage egged on by companions at a safer distance. An Englishwoman grumbled, "That child will fall in." What if he did? Mitchell thought; he could almost certainly swim, and it would be a tremendous adventure that would imprint the holiday on his mind for all time. A boy needed such moments. He walked to the edge himself; in the distance he could just make out the boat coming from the direction of Stresa. There were more tourists around now. The Englishwoman marshalled her brood and stood them in line by the landing stage. The other tourists, mostly German and Italian, stood back, preferring the last-minute onslaught to the tedium of the queue. The boat came alongside, nosing against the supports with a contemptuous disregard for the finer points of navigation. Mitchell, who always enjoyed this performance, wondered how often the Italians had to effect repairs to their landing stages. The gangway was trundled forward and attached with a few nonchalant twists of an inadequate rope. A few undaunted passengers disembarked. By the time that the English family was disputing the passage with the Germans, Alperin and his dark companion had come into sight, hurrying from the direction of the market. Alperin looked hot and uncomfortable, his fair skin burnt painfully by the sun; beside him, Huber was cool as a lizard. There was no sign of Burke; no doubt he had found it advisable to part company with them, sustained cordiality was not his line. Nevertheless, he was cutting it fine. Mitchell looked back towards the market, feeling annoyed with Burke who was given to theatrical effects. When he turned round, Alperin was already on board. Mitchell called to him:

"Have you seen my friend?"

Alperin shook his head and shrank back into the crowd. Mitchell was alone on the quayside now. The man at the gangway shouted, "You come?" Mitchell shook his head and the gangway clattered down. The engine started and the boat began to move, only glancing against one of the supports this time. Mitchell watched the dark gap between the boat and the quayside widen; he could see Alperin, now on the top deck, standing against the rail with Huber beside him. No doubt Huber was congratulating himself on an easy victory. As Mitchell turned and walked slowly back to the market he realized that this was the most unprofessional thing he had ever done. He turned in the direction of the château. The path between the stalls was in shadow, the stall keepers were sitting down, resting now that the main body of tourists had gone. For them it was a moment of peace: for Mitchell it was the beginning of uneasiness. There had been one or two inconsistencies in his behaviour lately that he had put down to the fact that he needed a holiday; but there had been nothing as bad as that moment on the quay- side when he had suddenly felt that he wanted to turn his back on the whole ridiculous charade. This was going to take a lot of explaining, he thought wearily. And what the devil had happened to Burke? He disliked this place too much to elect to stay on it of his own free will.

When he came to the château Mitchell saw that the door was closed. There was a notice that said that the château was open from eleven in the morning until seven in the evening. Mitchell looked at his watch. Five past seven. With any luck someone would still be around. He pounded on the door which was eventually opened by an old man who pointed peevishly at the notice. Mitchell said in Italian:

"My friend is in here."

The old man shook his head and pushed the door; Mitchell put one foot across the threshold.

"He came in here a couple of hours ago and he hasn't come out."

"There is no one in here now."

"I shall come back with the police."

The old man looked at him as if he had said a dirty word; he hesitated and while he hesitated Mitchell pushed his way into the dark hall. He was quite sure that Burke was here. If you are going to put someone out of the way for a couple of hours, you don't do it in a crowded market when you have a convenient château in which to maneuver.

"More than my job's worth to leave anyone in here at night," the old man said belligerently.

"In which case you had better hurry up and find my friend."

This seemed to convince the old man and he set off, muttering under his breath, in the direction of the main stairs. They went from room to room and down winding corridors with occasional glimpses through slim windows of the lake, burning crimson and orange as the smoking sun dipped towards it. It was dark in the château; the old man put on a few lights but the corridors were long and the lamps few. It was not a hopeful place and Mitchell was reminded that all

[69]

adventures must come to an end. They had been searching for twenty minutes when Mitchell heard a thumping from behind a door off one of the main corridors.

"That's the private part of the house," the old man said angrily.

As though to emphasize the fact, a bolt had been shot outside the door. Mitchell drew back the bolt and opened the door, revealing Burke sitting on the lavatory seat, his foot drumming incessantly against the wooden skirting. It was a relief to find one was playing in farce, after all.

"This is reserved for the family ghost," Mitchell told him. "What the hell are you doing in it?"

"That bloody salami!"

They tipped the old man and went out. As they went down the long flight of stone steps leading to the terrace, Mitchell glanced out of the corner of his eye at Burke. Burke was walking very stiffly and his face was set, but as Mitchell looked at him little cracks at the corners of his mouth began to undermine the masklike composure. They reached the balustrade overlooking the lake and Burke leant against it laughing convulsively.

"Locked in the lavatory by Karel Huber! That would really convince Eliot that I'm finished, wouldn't it?"

They both laughed, laughter so violent and uncontrolled that one or two old people sitting on the stone benches on the terrace looked at them with furtive disapproval, wondering if they were drunk. After a while, still laughing, they walked down to the quayside to study the timetable. There would be a boat to Stresa in a quarter of an hour. Mitchell looked at his watch.

"If we catch a bus from Stresa without too long a wait, we'll be at Tamaro a good half hour before the boat comes in. In the meantime, let's have a drink."

They made for the nearest café in a mood of extreme good

fellowship. When their drinks were before them, and they were sitting looking at the shadowed water, Burke said:

"Do you realize that at this moment Alperin is probably selling his soul to the devil?"

Mitchell raised his glass. "To hell with Alperin!"

They drank to this. Burke reflected for a while and then said:

"You know, I'm rather sorry for Alperin."

Mitchell looked at him in surprise. "Sorry for him! Why? He's a shoddy little creature."

Burke did not argue and they relaxed into a companionable silence.

Alperin looked at the dim grey line of the shore, the details of village, house and church, of wood, road and ravine, no longer distinguishable. He looked at it anxiously, his sandy eyebrows drawn together and his eyes screwed up like those of a sentinel who has been on duty for too many weary hours and no longer sees very clearly. Beside him, his companion had fallen asleep. Great turrets of cloud were building up to the west and the water was grey, flecked with tiny silver-tipped waves. There were few people on the top deck. It was the one time during the whole day when they could have talked undisturbed; but Alperin's dark companion slept and Alperin had no desire to wake him. When he met this man on Isola Madre and their conversation led smoothly from the subject of botanical specimens to more general scientific issues, Alperin's heart had pounded as he realized that this man's contacts included many eminent scientists in Eastern Europe. He had had one golden moment when he experienced the joy of fulfilment. Words would have spoilt everything; indeed they seemed superfluous since the man was himself a part of the moment and must surely understand. It was the way that Alperin had always wanted it to happen, a sudden transformation without the necessity for words which were treacherous tools, imprecise, two-edged, inadequate for delicate work. So he had not spoken then, but had enjoyed his golden moment. It had been a brief ecstasy. Exhilaration had dwindled rapidly thanks to the intervention of the garrulous Mitchell and his even more loathsome companion who had made uncouth comments as they were conducted round the château until he finally disappeared, presumably too bored to complete the tour. That was over now. But it had been very exhausting, so Alperin watched the shore in silence and did not wake his companion.

All his life, it seemed, there had been a distant shore, and always enchantment had faded when he drew near. It was the Kafka experience in reverse: the more one penetrated, the more the veils were stripped aside and the less mysterious and more bleakly comprehensible the world became. Sometimes he feared it would all end in one brightly lit stone courtyard, without shadow or conflict of colour, and he would know that he had reached the empty heart of the universe. But hope is essential to survival and on the whole Alperin wanted to survive. So he still longed for the distant shore. He had longed for it ever since he could remember, although his conception of what it represented had changed as the nature of his disappointments changed. As a child, ignored by parents exhaustively concerned with their own failures, he had longed to escape to boarding school; at boarding school where he was good at the wrong things, he longed to go to university where his intellect would be appreciated; at university, where his lack of audacity was condemned and his sharp, accurate mind was not appreciated, he longed for the maturer judgments of adult society. By the time he had been rejected by adult society, he had exhausted the possibilities of his own world. He had been born in the wrong age, of course; but that was something which

[72]

could not be remedied. But there *was* another world, a new Jerusalem waiting for those whose faith was strong. It was a fine, invigorating thought and already it had carried him a long way; but, just occasionally, there came a terrible moment when he felt very near that brightly lit courtyard and he asked himself: suppose this last enchantment were to fail? This was wrong, of course; the climber must not ask himself what will happen if the rope breaks, nor must the sojourner in the desert think about the time when the water supply has gone.

Weakness . . . weakness . . . Alperin buttoned his linen jacket and spread a plastic raincoat across his thin knees; the mist was beginning to penetrate. Beside him, his companion slept on. There was time, Alperin thought, there was time . . . After all, this trip to Maggiore had been intended as a holiday, a necessary pause between two worlds.

Chapter 8

The threatened storm blew over and it was a calm, warm night when the bus from Stresa reached Tamaro. The bus stop was in the higher part of the town—Tamaro Supra, as it was called. This part was old and did not attract many tourists except at night when they came up to see "how the people lived." On this particular night the narrow main street was crowded with tourists staring in dingy shop windows and exclaiming ecstatically as they gazed down dark, rank-smelling alleys. The "people" sat in doorways and watched these antics with tolerant good humour. Burke, not so tolerant, fumed:

"What bloody fools they are! They come to Ireland and hang around perfectly respectable cottages, waiting to photograph the family living with the pigs."

Mitchell did not answer. There was a girl in front, strolling hand in hand with a long, thin man with long, thin hair. The girl wore very brief shorts, her hips were slim and her legs were flawless. Mitchell watched her legs while Burke transferred his wrath to the bus service.

"The boat got in over an hour ago. And yet they have the

[74]

effrontery to advertise a round trip—go by boat, come back by bus! What they don't tell you is that you have a two hour wait for the bus."

"I didn't think time mattered to the Irish," Mitchell murmured. He wondered whether the girl's shape was as pleasing from the front as it was from behind. On the whole, he tended to keep away from the young whom he always equated with innocence despite many proofs to the contrary. Nevertheless, he was pleased when the girl stopped to look in a shop window, revealing for his inspection a narrow waist and small, high breasts. She turned her head slightly so that he had a glimpse of a gay, provocative face that was not so young as the body had suggested. Mitchell, his interest quickened, wondered how he could get rid of Burke. The other man's despatch could, he felt sure, safely be left to the woman.

"There's no frantic hurry," he said to Burke who showed a tendency to walk at a reasonable pace. "It's been a long, hard day and . . ."

"You're tired and you want to go to bed." Burke was mocking but not ill-humoured.

The woman and her companion had stopped outside a pension where there was a courtyard with tables amid some rather unkempt shrubbery. The courtyard was lit by a few dim lamps round the walls; it did not look very clean and there was a smell of bad drains. Nevertheless, the woman urged her companion towards a table. Burke said maliciously:

"I'll have a beer—just to keep you company for a while."

A sullen young man in shirt sleeves and tight black trousers came to serve them and then slouched over to the woman and her companion. The other tables were occupied by local people. Mitchell sat back and anticipated pleasure to come. He made no plans; he never planned this kind of encounter, it was something that happened, or did not happen. If the woman went on her way with her companion, it would be a pity, but it would not greatly matter; there would be someone else, somewhere else. A sudden tremor went through him, the sweat cooling on the body, no doubt; but it changed his mood and he felt, as he often felt as he waited at such times, a sense of loneliness and desolation. Perhaps failure cast a long shadow. He took a draught of beer and reminded himself that romantic despair ill became him since others suffered most for his inconstancy. He glanced across at Burke who was looking sombre and was no doubt working himself into one of his own despairs. I am no more whole than he is, Mitchell thought in a moment of rare insight, and I have less excuse . . . Then he heard the woman's voice raised in the corner and forgot Burke as he realized that she was picking a quarrel with her companion. How delightfully ruthless women were! Burke put down his glass.

"I'll leave you now." He looked round for the waiter and Mitchell, anxious to be rid of him, said:

"Don't bother."

"It is my pleasure to buy you a drink," Burke assured him and disappeared beyond the shrubbery. When he came back he seemed to have shaken off his sombre mood and he bade Mitchell a particularly benign goodnight.

Not long after Burke departed, the thin man left the woman and ran out of the courtyard; she laughed as he stumbled over the curb, a low, throaty laugh full of genuine enjoyment. Mitchell reflected sadly, as he walked across to join her, that she was cruel.

The table where she was sitting was in a dark corner— not that this mattered, the clientele were not censorious. She talked rather too much in her throaty voice, giving him an account of her stay in Tamaro—which he was glad to

[76]

note would be brief—until he placed his hand on the small of her back where the inadequate little blouse parted company with the inadequate little shorts. Her back arched as he slid his hand around her waist and he could feel her heart pounding against her taut ribs; as he caressed her breast she leant her head against his shoulder and gave a low moan, she was an ardent little creature; he whispered, "Where can we go?" He was waiting eagerly for her reply when the waiter came to collect their glasses. Only it was not the waiter this time; it was the waitress, and the waitress was Miriam Kratz.

He fumbled for money, feeling as cold as though he had just come out of the North Sea in winter. She said in her flat, unemphatic voice:

"Your friend paid for your drink."

Damn Burke! No doubt he was dancing back to the hotel, gloating like the malevolent pixie he was. Mitchell paid for the woman's drink. He watched Miriam Kratz walk away and then said:

"Will you excuse me for a moment?"

She was standing in the doorway of the hotel, leaning her hip against the wall, a tea cloth dangling from one limp hand. In the yellow light of the door lamp her face looked haggard. He felt angry with her for spoiling his pleasure.

"What are you doing here?" he demanded.

"Working." She did not dispute his right to question her, she was not used to thinking in terms of her rights.

"But why?"

"I have to work somewhere."

"Haven't you got the fare back to Berlin?"

"No."

It seemed quite imperative to get rid of her. He said, "I'll give it to you."

"Thank you. But it is better not to go back yet. After a while, they will forget that I stole the money."

[77]

She bent down to loosen the strap of her sandal. He watched her impatiently. When she tried to straighten up she swayed and before he could support her she was on the ground. He knelt beside her, feeling exasperated and faintly ridiculous. She was not quite unconscious and she moaned as he touched her. He raised her in his arms. She clutched at him and sobbed, "Don't let me go!" He said, "No, of course not." He was embarrassed, but her appeal touched him. She pressed her head against his shoulder and whimpered like a tired child. This, too, touched him. He shouted for the waiter.

"Get some water," he said when the young man appeared.

"For her?" The eyebrows were raised in insolent surprise.

"If you don't I'll give you a beating you won't forget!"

It was absurdly melodramatic, but apparently effective; the waiter strolled away and returned with a smeared glass half-full of tepid water.

"She's no good," he explained, anxious to remove any misunderstanding. "She works here because she doesn't pay her bill."

Mitchell gave Miriam the water while the waiter leant nonchalantly against the doorpost.

"We get all sorts here in summer." He spat to give point to the statement. Someone called from a nearby table; he waited for a moment, as though hoping that Miriam might rise to answer the summons, before slouching away.

Miriam had recovered; her face was white as lard, but she did not seem much disturbed by what had happened.

"It is just that I have not eaten," she explained indifferently.

There was a movement behind them. The proprietress was standing in the doorway.

"She makes this an excuse because she does not want to work any more," she explained.

[78]

"I've worked all day," Miriam said.

They both addressed their remarks to Mitchell as though the other was not there. The proprietress went on:

"She stayed the night and had two breakfasts . . ."

"Dry rolls and cold coffee!"

"How much does she owe you?" Mitchell asked, anxious to escape.

"Thirty francs."

"I don't owe her anything," Miriam hissed.

The woman swore at her. The waiter came back and said that Miriam had not worked hard; Miriam responded by saying that he spent his time in the cellar making love to the kitchen maid. They began to shout. Mitchell produced his wallet, but Miriam snatched it from him.

"Don't give her any money! I've worked all day. *She* owes *me* something!"

The proprietress grabbed at the wallet but Miriam clung to it with surprising tenacity. Mitchell found himself wrestling with the two women. It was a preposterous situation; he lost his head and his temper. The waiter tried to intervene and Mitchell knocked him down. Then he turned on the proprietress. He could express himself well in Italian and by the time he regained possession of his wallet, Miriam had lost her job.

"Go and get your case," he told her.

She scurried away down a dark corridor leaving Mitchell and the proprietress to pick over the bones of their quarrel. There were a lot of people standing up to watch them by this time, but the woman in the dark corner was not among them. Mitchell scarcely noticed her absence. Miriam came back very quickly; it was obvious that she had no intention of letting her protector out of her sight for long. They went out of the courtyard watched with friendly interest by the small crowd that had collected. Miriam glanced up at Mitchell anxiously as they came into the street. He turned unhesitatingly to the left, not because he knew where he was going but in order to give her the impression that he had the situation well in hand.

"You must have a meal and then we must find you a place for the night," he said.

"Yes." She did not sound enthusiastic. She kicked at a pebble and muttered, "She owed me money."

"Not much, surely?"

"It was a lot to me." She sounded more stubborn than pathetic; she had him at a disadvantage and she meant to make the most of it. "And there would have been more money if I had kept the job."

"I'm sorry about that." The knowledge that he had come badly out of this was galling to him. To redeem his dignity he went on, "You're better out of that place, though."

She did not answer.

"What you need is a rest, time to gather your strength."

She looked away and laughed; there was something contemptuously dismissive in the way she did it that stung him as much as if she had spat in his face. He said angrily:

"I'll give you money to stay here for a month or so. After all, I'm to blame for your losing the job."

"A month!" She took him up quickly before he could change his mind. He felt her hand on his arm, the thin fingers had a surprisingly firm grip. "That *would* be a rest, wouldn't it?" Her manner was conciliatory now, but she added, so that there should be no misunderstanding, "A whole month without having to worry about money!"

She did not question that he had the money. To her, having money was an absolute thing; you had enough or none at all. But Mitchell was thinking, as they walked slowly down from Tamaro Supra towards the lake, that money was going to present a difficulty. Pride forbade that he should

[80]

use the Department's money. He could draw his own money, of course; but the amount needed to keep even someone as undemanding as Miriam Kratz in Switzerland for a month would be considerable. Eliot might get to hear of it. Had it been another woman, Mitchell would not have minded, but he thought it better that Eliot should not know of his involvement with Miriam Kratz. He had no idea what he was going to do; he only knew, as he felt those thin fingers clinging to his arm, that it was too late to go back. Each time he saw Miriam Kratz he took another step down an unfamiliar road.

Chapter 9

Eliot stood on the balcony of his flat which overlooked one of the pedestrian bridges that arched like the thread of a gigantic spider's web across the lower part of the town. Lausanne was a tiered town and Eliot's flat was at the top of the top tier. This he liked. The microscopic view of humanity appealed to him. Many men who have no feeling for their fellows have other emotional outlets which are said to make them recognizably human and fallible. But Eliot was exceptional in this; he had no beloved cat, he was not fond of white mice, he was unmoved by the plight of hungry birds and he could view fishes gasping in inadequate tanks with equanimity. He liked desert places, not for their soul-purging purity but for the sparseness of life. If he had had a choice he would have been born a Bedouin—if he had had to be born at all. Life was a cross, he could go this far with the Christian myth; particularly, it was a cross if each time you drew breath a knife turned in your chest, a knife that would kill you one day, but very, very slowly.

He turned away from the window and the movement hurt him. They had told him he should go to a sanatorium;

there was a good one near Montreux, Sir Stafford Cripps had been there. But that would have meant mixing with fellow sufferers and being pawed by doctors and nurses. Eliot preferred the pain.

He went into the room and picked up the bundle of papers on his desk. There was a cutting from a local paper giving a brief account of an inquest. He was glad to see, from notes prepared by his assistant, that this incident had not been reported in any other paper. So that was that. At least no damage had been done, even if nothing had been gained. Nevertheless, it annoyed him to have to cut his losses; he preferred success and so did London.

London was agitating again. A further report on Alperin was wanted. What contemptible muddlers the London people were! If they felt so strongly about Alperin, why had they given him permission to leave the country? The answer to that, of course, was that Sir Harry Gethryn was a friend of the P.M. and Sir Harry had wanted Alperin out of the way for a while. Now the P.M. was getting worried. He was not concerned about what Alperin knew—fortunately the P.M. had only the vaguest ideas on this subject—what worried him was that he could not afford a security scandal just now. He had said a lot of harsh things about security arrangements when he was in opposition.

Eliot picked up the reports, few enough, that he had received from his operators. Alperin appeared to be taking things quietly at Maggiore. No doubt London's fears could be allayed for a time. London had a great respect for Stephen Mitchell; if Mitchell said that Alperin was taking things quietly then as far as London was concerned that was the end of it.

Eliot pushed the papers aside and sat back in his chair. He coughed and it hurt; he coughed again and it hurt still more. He went into the bathroom and found a glass. The basin was filmed with grey scum and there was a dead fly in the glass. He went along to the kitchen. The odour from the greasy sink did not offend him in the least, but nevertheless he ran the water for a long time; he was fussy about drinking water, he liked it to be very cold and fresh. That was one thing he would have found trying in the desert.

He went back to his room and pulled down the map. He looked at Lake Maggiore, trying to visualize what was happening there. He had noted from the reports that Huber had arrived. He wondered what he would do. Huber was a good operator, he had a mind uncluttered by taboos and inhibitions, traditions and principles. He was lazy, but not when he was being well paid and Eliot happened to know that he was being well paid.

Chapter 10

Alperin was indeed taking things quietly. The date of the conference was drawing near. He remembered the feeling he had had as a child at the end of the long summer holidays when the days ran out desperately fast. When he was very young he had believed that something would happen to save him from the ordeal of returning to his hated prep school. When he grew older he became wiser. It was the dreams that vanished when you rounded the bend of time; the ordeals were there, waiting for you. A curtain seemed to come down over his mind at this point, a great inertia seized him; he told himself that he had been doing too much, that the heat was considerable and getting worse every day. During the time that remained he must rest. He took to sitting most of the day on the esplanade, staring vacantly across the glittering lake.

The heat really was considerable now. It made Burke feel ill. He enjoyed staying in southern Spain; but there it was a fierce, angry heat that he found stimulating, a heat that stabbed at you, while here it sickened and suffocated. He woke at night, his head throbbing, his heart straining. He was glad to take things easily, to sit and read outside a café with a cool drink close to hand. He always had one of Dostoevsky's novels with him; this time it was *The Brothers Karamazov.* In his teens, when he had been hopeful and rather surprisingly pure, he had been enchanted by the love poems of John Donne; but when he discovered that this kind of love was not for him, he turned to Dostoevsky. He always avowed a profound respect for Dostoevsky, although he had never managed to finish one of the major novels. Now, as he turned the pages of *The Brothers Karamazov* he found the weight of the book rather daunting: his intellectual ardours burnt bright but not for long.

Huber slid in and out of the pattern, cool and quiet as a lizard. He was not much in evidence during the day, but sometimes in the evening he would appear at one of the tables outside the hotel, drinking an aperitif before returning to his own hotel for dinner. Occasionally he would ask Alperin to join him, but only occasionally; more often, he seemed quite uninterested in Alperin.

Mitchell alone was active. He had become excessively restless and was never content to stay long in one place. If the heat affected him at all, it showed only in the shortness of his temper; he was much more easily roused, particularly by jibes about Miriam Kratz. The Alperin affair, he treated with contemptuous negligence. Burke, who had himself decided that the whole thing had been dreamt up by someone in London who had to justify his appointment, was surprised at this change in Mitchell's attitude. He had always associated Mitchell with a rather tedious sense of responsibility in such matters.

"The time will come, and that right soon, when Eliot will feel that you are expendable," he said as Mitchell joined him one evening after rather a long absence.

"Eliot is the one who is expendable."

[86]

"I doubt if London would agree with you."

"He's expendable as far as I'm concerned—and London is a long way away."

Burke, who liked to think that he had a monopoly of the rebellious spirit, was shocked. The remark had been made in a way that invited no argument; there was no panache, no venom, just a statement dry as the end of a chapter in a dusty book. He wondered idly whether Mitchell had a touch of the sun or whether the concussion had been more serious than the doctor had imagined. Mitchell had not eaten so much lately and his consumption of wine had declined noticeably. His expense account, had he bothered to keep one, would have resembled the inverted triangle so familiar to tourists at the end of the holiday. Burke noted all this without drawing conclusions. It was too hot for conclusions.

That evening Burke sat at one of the tables outside the hotel and drank iced Campari. Alperin was alone and Huber did not appear. Huber was playing a waiting game; Burke doubted whether these were the right tactics to adopt with a tentative creature like Alperin. Mitchell went into Locarno. He had never evinced any liking for Locarno until recently, but now he went there often. Burke wondered whether he had a woman there.

Mitchell gambled at Locarno. He was out of luck and he had the sense to stop, but not before he had lost more than he could afford. Things were going badly for him. Of course, he could arrange to draw his own money, it was ridiculous not to do this; but he could not rid himself of the feeling that it would not be wise. It seemed he had lived so long in the twilight world of fear and mistrust that he had become infected without knowing it. Quite when this had happened, he was not sure. He worried about the money. He had been in many kinds of trouble in his life, but he had scrupulously avoided money troubles. This was a matter which deeply affected his pride and he was not in the best of spirits when he visited Miriam Kratz late one afternoon.

She was staying at a pension on the way to Brissago. To the front of the pension was the main road, overhung by a shelf of rock; to the rear, the land sloped steeply down to a clutter of stone cottages at the lake's edge. It was a pleasant place to be if you had a boat, but it offered nothing else in the way of entertainment. Mitchell wondered how Miriam Kratz occupied herself. On this occasion he found her sitting on a wooden bench overlooking the lake. There were deck chairs on the terrace at the back of the pension and one or two women were stretched out sunbathing. He had noticed before that she never sat on the terrace with the other guests.

"Do you talk to the people in the pension?" he asked.

"No."

"Why not?"

"They don't talk to me."

"What do you do all day?"

"I stay in bed in the morning."

"And in the afternoon?"

"I sit here."

"And in the evening?"

"I go to bed."

Rest had not done her any good; it had merely destroyed the rhythm of her life. She felt lost and useless, and she envied the pension staff who were too busy to notice the passage of time. She looked at Mitchell sullenly. He had cut her off from the current of life, and now she sensed that he was about to lecture her for apathy. To prevent this, she said:

"They want me to pay weekly."

"Why?"

"They don't like it that I don't have any luggage."

And no doubt they did not like it that she wore the same dress every day, Mitchell thought. He wondered what she did about underclothes. Very little, judging by her appearance. He found himself disturbed, not for the first time, by the peculiarly urgent appeal of her body. He felt that if he were to run a hand up the taut line of her thigh the exploration would be the most hazardous he had ever made; he could feel the repercussions of it now as though an electric shock had passed through his body. He was not usually one to let the act lag far behind the thought. Yet now he found himself moving a little further away, holding back from her with a constraint he had not known even as a young man when intimacy had presented more problems.

She misinterpreted his withdrawal, and said insistently: "I have to pay them today."

He took out his wallet. When he handed her the money she counted it and then said grudgingly:

"This is more than I owe them."

"But you must spend something during the day, surely?"

She folded the money and put it in her pocket; her fist went in after it. That small, clenched fist seemed a symbol of the whole person. They sat in silence, staring down the grass slope to the stone cottages hunched beside the lake. There did not seem anything to say; he had made the payment and it was obvious that as far as she was concerned the purpose of his visit had been achieved. It was a little humiliating; he could not remember the last time a woman had been so unaware of him. He said:

"Your husband must be a remarkable person!"

It was a careless remark, prompted by a rather childish jealousy. He was quite unprepared for its effect.

"Oh, you feel like that? Without even knowing him, you can feel that!" The taut lips relaxed in a smile that was sur-

[89]

prisingly tender, the guarded eyes softened. "If you had known him as I knew him . . ."

Mitchell realized wretchedly that she was going to confide in him. While she talked he sat still, seeing how the long grass on the sloping hillside quivered and parted as the first breath of evening stirred. He did not really listen to what she said. He already knew something about her husband. Kratz had worked at a rehabilitation center for the victims of concentration camps. It had not been a very successful venture and most of the organizers had given up; but Dr. Kratz, it seemed, was not interested in success and he had carried on. When someone asked him why he did this he was reputed to have replied, "What else is there to do?" One of his patients had been Miriam. Mitchell watched the colours deepen as the sun bronzed the lake and turned stone to rose. It seemed that Miriam Kratz could be counted as one of the doctor's successes; at least he had taught her something of love. Mitchell was not best pleased to discover that this unhappy creature had had an experience he had never known. He was glad when the flow of words ceased.

"He must have been much older than you," he said.

She brought that clenched fist out of her pocket; for a moment he thought that she was giving him back the money. Then he saw that she was holding a photograph. He was not good at this kind of thing—what could you say when you looked at the picture of another man? He rehearsed a few safe phrases in the seconds before he looked at it.

The man in the photograph was fair skinned, blond; only the slightly hooked nose and something about the full, rather sad mouth told one that he was a Jew. The eyes were what Mitchell noticed. The eyes looked out of the photograph fearlessly; they seemed to look straight at him, still retaining, against all odds, an unmistakable liking for the human race. It was difficult to believe that those eyes had

[90]

ever looked on the barbarism of a concentration camp. Mitchell handed the photograph back.

"Did he ever try to leave East Berlin?" he asked.

"No. He had his clinic and he would not leave that. He did no harm and he wasn't afraid."

"Were you?"

"Yes. I was always afraid."

"He has been away a long time." Some inner resentment made Mitchell brutal. "Haven't you ever felt like giving him up?"

"I shall never give him up."

Something about the look of her carried more conviction than the words. Mitchell was surprised at the change in her. In Berlin, she had seemed shadowy, her only asset the pathos of the waif. But here, under the harsh scrutiny of the sun, she appeared more substantial. He was conscious of the sinewy strength of the thin body, of the stubbornness underlying the passive features; there was something of the inflexibility of the peasant about her. He thought suddenly: she will weather suffering, even outlive it. Just for a moment, he was a little afraid of her.

"I have to meet Dan Burke in half an hour," he said abruptly.

She took him by the sleeve, those thin, strong fingers holding tight again. She thanked him with an intensity of emotion which embarrassed him.

"It means so much to talk about my husband, so much . . ."

She made no mention of the money, which she took for granted, it was his interest that mattered. No doubt he was the first person who had been rash enough to show any interest in Mikail Kratz for a very long time. "Show them even a flicker of sympathy," Burke had once said of the Berlin

[91]

unfortunates, "and you'll find them mewing outside your door for the rest of your life."

It was cooler that evening, but the next day the heat was intense. Waiters in the hotel quarrelled, there was a fight in the road leading up to the old part of the town, the tourists sat listlessly in the shade and the people coming off the passenger boats had faces like skinned tomatoes. Alperin was driven from his lakeside seat. His inertia was replaced by a feeling of claustrophobia; the town had become a small, tight oven from which he must escape at all costs. He decided to take a trip to the mountains. No one followed him this time. He took the postal bus to a small village in the Valle Maggia. When the bus stopped the driver said, "You have four hours here." It was not the kind of place in which Alperin wanted to spend four minutes. Here were no wooden chalets bright with window boxes, no cowbells ringing from green flower-canopied slopes, no cool, snowcapped peaks to refresh the eye in the distance. This was a shanty town, ugly, bare, speaking only of the utmost poverty. The houses, dark and rough-tiled, clung to the slopes of the hills and men laboured on terraces so steep that they had to work on all fours. Grass grew through the roofs of the ramshackle outhouses. The children stared at Alperin in his peaked sun cap and neat linen suit and one or two stones clattered behind him as he hurried along the rough path that served as a street. One should pity them, of course; these were the people who did not appear in the bright holiday posters, these were the oppressed of this complacent little country. Nevertheless, he was glad to leave them and their ugly village behind him.

Unfortunately, the prospect ahead was not encouraging. The valley was narrow and wooded; the mountain peaks were hidden from view. There were a lot of insects and it was much hotter than it had been by the lake. He felt more trapped than ever. He took out his map and studied it. The nearest town was five miles away and if he went there he would almost certainly have to walk back; he had no desire to walk ten miles in this heat. He put the map away and told himself that he must take a stroll and enjoy the natural beauty of his surroundings. The map had shown that a river ran through the valley, but when he fought his way to it through tangled undergrowth he found only a trickle of water running between stones white as bleached bones. In the wall of rock above blue and purple scars marked the passage of a staunched waterfall. He sat down on a boulder and ate his packed lunch. The thought of being trapped in this place for four hours brought him close to panic. When he had finished his lunch he walked for a while beside the stream, but the valley got narrower and changed direction so that the sun shone only on the higher slopes opposite. He lay down in the grass and tried to sleep, pestered by flies. Above him, he could see the mountains like blue shadows stencilled on the sky. He felt exhausted and so disappointed that he wanted to cry. On the way back in the bus he applied a little elementary psychology to himself. All this touring of the lake in search of the calm reaches of thought, this turning to the mountains for the release of the spirit, was a way of avoiding the agony of the final decision that alone could release him. So be it, he had learnt his lesson. Tomorrow . . . no, tonight, he would speak to the man, Huber.

Huber did not come to the café that evening. He did not come the next evening either and Alperin was driven to go in search of him. He found him sitting under a magnolia tree outside a scruffy bar in a square in the old part of the town. There was a boy with him. Alperin went up to Huber and said:

"I want to have a word with you."

[93]

He expected Huber to dismiss the boy, but he made no movement. Alperin, whose life had been sheltered by his own obsessions, was surprised at the coolness of his reception; although he drew up a chair and seated himself between Huber and the boy, Huber did not acknowledge his presence.

"You must have a drink with me," Alperin said.

He ordered coffee and brandies for himself and Huber; as the boy remained, he ordered a Coca-Cola for him. He decided to wait until the brandy arrived before he spoke, it would be a civilized accompaniment to what he had to say: it was very important to be civilized about this. Huber and the boy were very quiet. Alperin looked at the magnolia tree. There was something about the texture of the heavy petals, waxen in the moonlight, that repelled him. His preference was for frail flowers that bowed tremulous heads before the wind; the magnolia had fought its battle with the wind a long time ago and now it was still and very assured. The magnolia, Alperin decided, was one of nature's less innocent achievements.

The drinks came. The brandy did not seem to have any effect on Huber but the Coca-Cola had an extraordinary effect on the boy. Alperin had begun to talk generally about the unsatisfactory climate in which scientific research was carried out in England, when the boy stood up and emptied his glass over Alperin's head. Then he picked up Alperin's brandy and drank it. After that he strolled away across the square. Alperin, shocked and temporarily blinded, groped for his handkerchief.

"What an extraordinary thing!" he said, trying to sound amused. "Is he simple?"

When he had mopped his face he put the handkerchief down on the table and knocked over Huber's brandy. This did not matter because Huber had gone. Alperin went back to his hotel and had a very bad night.

The next day he hardly left the hotel. He made constant excuses to go to the reception desk; he bought postcards, enquired about boat and train timetables, made arrangements for his departure next week. When he was not at the reception desk he was sitting at one of the tables outside the hotel. All day he kept watch on the hotel in case Huber called to see him. But Huber did not come and by the evening an unpleasant thought had occurred to Alperin. Suppose they no longer wanted him? Sometime during the dead hours of the night the thought translated itself into fact. He was an outcast: it was not a role that was in the least attractive to him. He saw himself walking eternally down a dark corridor flanked by doors which were forever closed to him. There was no escape but suicide. Sleeping pills, which he did not possess but could surely obtain, seemed the best answer since he was rather squeamish and had no flair for the dramatic. While he was wondering how he could obtain the sleeping pills, he fell asleep. When he woke he felt so sick and his head was so heavy that the idea of making himself worse by taking pills of any kind was out of the question. He decided instead to make a determined effort to find Huber.

He searched for Huber all day and failed to find him. But the search itself, being the most purposeful thing he had done since he arrived, kept him in good spirit and he felt that at last he was getting to grips with reality. He had had a bad fright, but he had learnt his lesson: now he was ready to act. He slept well that night and found Huber the next afternoon.

Unfortunately, he lost him again a few minutes later. One moment, there was Huber strolling by the side of the lake, gazing at the sailing boats bobbing aimlessly up and down

[95]

in the water; the next moment, he turned sharply to the right and boarded a bus. Alperin began to run. He was not a good runner, but he was very determined; he put his head down, gritted his teeth and charged. He felled a small child, got entangled with a poodle, and fractionally missed being run over by a hell-bent Mercedes. He was in great distress by the time he neared the bus; he saw the door closing but had no breath to make a spurt so he flapped his arms desolately in the hope that passersby would attract the attention of the driver. The bus moved off fast. A man at the cigarette kiosk nearby, who had watched Alperin's performance with interest, said to him:

"Last bus today."

"Last bus! But it's only three o'clock."

The man explained, "Special bus for fair at Rossario. Only one bus there and one bus back at night." He turned to serve a customer.

Alperin stumbled into the hotel and made for the reception desk. The garrulous Englishman, Mitchell, was talking to the receptionist; she continued to give him her entire attention in spite of Alperin's frantic signals. Mitchell's companion, crouched in the one comfortable chair in the foyer, said pleasantly:

"You'll never make it.

> *She loves not you nor me as all we love her.*
> *Yea, though we sang as angels in her ear,*
> *She would not hear."*

Mitchell did hear. He turned and said rather irritably:

"I'm sorry, were you . . ." He stopped, staring at Alperin. "Good God! Has there been an accident?"

In the mirror to the side of the reception desk, Alperin

caught sight of his face, purple as though someone had tried to strangle him. He said huskily:

"I missed a bus."

The receptionist turned to answer the telephone.

"There's another bus in an hour."

"Not to Rossario."

"Rossario!" She looked at him, cradling the receiver beneath her chin. She was young and incapable of hiding her surprise. "You want to go to the fair?"

"Yes."

They were all looking at him now, the girl giggling, the man, Burke, with amusement that was not reflected in his eyes, and Mitchell with a return of the heavy good humour which Alperin found so painful.

"A fair!" Mitchell looked across at his companion. "I didn't know there was a fair at Rossario, did you?"

"No, I didn't know there was a fair at Rossario."

"But we must go! They do this sort of thing so well; they really know how to enjoy themselves—no inhibitions about noise and vulgarity. Yes, indeed we must go." He turned and strolled towards the entrance. Alperin called after him:

"May I come with you, please?"

Mitchell turned round. Alperin, who had never before foisted himself on anyone felt his flesh crawl as Mitchell glanced across at Burke. Burke shrugged his shoulders. Alperin said desperately:

"You see, I've missed the bus and I . . . I have to meet someone."

"You mean you want to go now?"

"Yes."

"I see." Mitchell looked thoughtfully out at the lake. Alperin's overtaxed heart thudded against his damp shirt. "I was thinking of going to the lido," Mitchell mused. "A fair is so much better at night . . ."

Burke said: "There's a gala at the lido."

"So there is! That's settled it." Mitchell turned to Alperin. "Come along with us by all means. You'll need your passport—Rossario is over the Italian border."

They reached the Italian border in less time than Alperin would have thought possible. He held tight to the sides of the seat; he dared not hold the strap in case Burke, who was sitting beside him in the back, mocked his temerity. As the car sped along the road across the valley towards Rossario, Burke mocked him about other things.

"Now I wouldn't have thought you were the kind to like a fair so much."

"I never went as a child."

It was an omission for which he was thankful, but he had got used to blaming everything on childhood deprivations.

"I didn't either. Isn't it dreadfully sad not to have done the right things at the right time?" Burke looked at Mitchell, who had been silent for a long while. To Alperin's surprise the mockery had a sharper edge when he spoke to his friend. "I expect you went to countless fairs when you were a child."

Mitchell said, "Yes." Alperin hoped that Burke would leave it at that. The car was travelling as though bound for the point where parallel lines meet and it hardly seemed the time to distract the attention of the driver. But Burke went on:

"How wonderful to have enjoyed the fruits of each season!"

"Forbidden fruits in my case. The local fairs were out of bounds and I always got a good thrashing afterwards."

"But being thrashed is a part of boyhood, isn't it? And then you grow into a big, strong man and no one can thrash you again."

The back of Mitchell's neck was red. He said quietly, "If you don't want to come to this bloody fair I can drop you

[98]

right here." He sounded as though at any moment he might jam his foot down on the brake. There was a vineyard to the left and an orchard to the right; Alperin wondered which side the car would land. Burke laughed, a soft, exultant laugh as though he was really enjoying himself.

"But I wouldn't miss it for anything! The noise and the vulgarity and the freaks. Particularly the freaks."

Mitchell did not answer, but it seemed to Alperin that the car went even faster. He closed his eyes and kept them closed until the car reached Rossario, a dusty little town stupefied with heat. All that Alperin remembered of it afterwards was the scorched main street lined with yellowing plane trees.

"No people!" he exclaimed.

"Gone to the fair," Burke murmured.

He was right. When they came to the rough, boulder-strewn ground on which the fair had been set up, Alperin saw something that resembled a gigantic honeycomb encrusted with writhing insects, some of which detached themselves from time to time and crawled away making aimless, exhausted movements.

"No place for the halt and lame," Mitchell commented as he stopped the car.

Burke opened the door and Alperin stepped out on to a broken bottle.

"This is going to be stupendous!" Burke said. "I suppose you do know just where you are meeting your friend?"

"At one of the stalls . . . I don't remember which one."

"A treasure hunt. Better and better!"

They walked one on either side of him into the crowd.

"No place to be alone," Mitchell said protectively. "We'll stick with you until you find your friend."

It was the thing Alperin had feared, but now he no longer cared; he would never find Huber, anyway.

Hell, a priest had once told Alperin, is within you, hell is you. He was wrong. Hell was other people: grunting, sweating, belching beer and garlic, hot hands clawing, wheedling voices luring you towards tents to see the two-headed monster, the naked man with the snake writhing round his loins, the fat lady and the dwarf, the fire-eater and the bearded woman; all the world's grotesques herded together in one brazen square mile. But worse than the freaks was Common Man, black, cavernous mouth blaring, fat thighs bulging in soiled trousers, open shirt revealing curling hair on the flabby pelt; Common Man, reeking, mindless, battering a passage forward with no idea where he was going or why. And flickering in and out of this stinking heap of flesh, the slim, whey-faced pickpockets and the smiling gang boys holding the razor ready in bent palms. An hour of this. Then a pause to watch an incredible rubber-limbed creature performing on a trampoline, twisting and contorting in the air, landing on elbow, chin, stomach; a pause to laugh while men from the crowd tried their skill and something went ludicrously wrong with the trampoline. Then on again to the shooting range, the bowling alley, the wheel of fortune. A drink from a bottle at a stall. Another pause to watch a wrestler with the body of a Michelangelo god and the face of a pig taking on men fools enough, or poor enough, to endure merciless pounding in the hope of winning a few lire as the "man who lasted longest against The Great Arturo." Then on again; a sickening ride in tiny cars attached to a maypole by inadequate chains, a cocoanut shy, the wall of death. Then finish.

Alperin crumpled on a bench near the arena where The Great Arturo was operating on another victim. It was the fag end of the day and The Great Arturo's performance lacked zest. The clouds were smouldering in the sky, great rods of gold and bronze; the sun had done its work, peeling away the thin layer of goodwill, consuming reason; now it was climbing down the sky, red and heavy, scourging tempers raw as an open wound. The Great Arturo sweated out his time leisurely and the crowd grew more restive, impatience festering in the heat. Burke said:

"They'll take it out on the promoter soon."

Alperin did not care. He did not care if they lynched the man, provided he could sit undisturbed and rest his feet. The promoter, less sanguine, clambered into the ring and proclaimed the latest victim winner of the contest with an endurance time of just under five minutes. The sum due to him was eight thousand lire. The crowd jeered. The promoter, a prim little man with sleek black hair neatly parted in the center, was saddened. He said that his honour was at stake, and that, just to show how honourable he was, he would offer one hundred and seventy thousand lire to anyone who could stay in the ring with The Great Arturo for ten minutes.

"Near enough one hundred pounds!" Burke murmured. "He must be very sure of Goliath!"

The crowd was sure of him, too. There was a roar of derision and a shower of apple cores, banana peel, tin cans and beer bottles whirled round the promoter's head. The winner of the contest was being helped out of the ring by his friends. "His prize money won't even meet the hospital expenses!" Burke commented. The promoter repeated his offer of one hundred and seventy thousand lire; Alperin eased off his shoes and flexed his aching toes and Mitchell got up and walked down to the arena.

Burke said, "Holy Mother of God!"

While Mitchell stripped, the promoter took his man to one side and Alperin put on his shoes and limped away, stumbling over the laces in his haste. Burke sat still. "You stupid, boastful braggart!" he thought. "You deserve a beating."

The desire to see punishment administered was strong and he stayed to watch. The promoter stepped back from the ring. No doubt he had told his man to give the appearance of a contest for the first five minutes at least; Mitchell must have realized this, because he did not waste energy. Burke waited with mounting impatience for the first five minutes to pass. He was conscious of a growing excitement in his body; the discomfort was so strong that he could not bear to be still, so he got up and pushed his way to the front of the crowd where, surely, the faithful friend belonged and where, incidentally, he had a good view of the contestants. He was well placed when The Great Arturo began to try. The crowd's mood changed. Now that he was being extended, The Great Arturo showed that he was something of an artist; he knew just where to exert pressure and for how long. The crowd was more appreciative. The promoter, standing near Burke, looked at his watch. Burke said to him, "He won't give up." It would not be right for Mitchell to give up; a man can't make this kind of gesture and then opt out when the screw begins to turn. Burke watched The Great Arturo floor Mitchell and then bring his great weight down on him, kneeling in the small of the back, twisting the arms behind, bending the wrists back, slowly, very slowly. A hot wave of excitement flooded Burke's body, his limbs throbbed, his mouth was dry. He tried to say, "He deserves it," but all pretence of moral judgment was swept away on the tide of pleasure. He pushed forward again; he could just see Mitchell's twisted face but he was too far away to hear him groan. But The Great Arturo could hear and it seemed to inspire him; he treated his victim respectfully, as though he had gained possession of a fine instrument which if played with imagination will produce an interesting range of effects. Time was passing. The promoter was getting worried; he tried to climb into the ring and was hauled back by the

[102]

rougher elements in the crowd. The Great Arturo turned Mitchell over and brought his knee down in the groin. The crowd bayed exultantly. Agony brought Mitchell to life and reminded him that he knew some tricks of his own; The Great Arturo, unprepared for counterattack at this stage of the game, was flat on his back for the first time during the afternoon. Blood dimmed Burke's eyes. When he could control his vision again, The Great Arturo was in command and the executioner had taken the place of the artist. Mitchell fell face down and Burke felt the jar in every bone in his body. The Great Arturo was astride Mitchell, levering the shoulders back until it seemed that spine and labouring ribs must crack. Burke found that his lip was bleeding. He turned away, fumbling for a handkerchief. There was a great roar from the crowd. Burke stood shivering as though someone had thrown a bucket of water over him, not daring to raise his head. The Great Arturo must have lost his judgment and exerted that fatal extra ounce of pressure. Beside Burke a man was screaming the same words over and over again; after a while Burke realized what he was saying. "Undici minuti!" Burke looked up quickly. The promoter was standing in the ring, brandishing a wrist watch and shouting "Otto minuti!" The crowd was pressing forward, someone snatched the promoter's watch and stamped on it. The promoter, much moved by the shattered watch, promised to go and fetch the money if people would only trust him. A man hit him and he fell on his knees, blood streaming from his mouth. The Great Arturo, callously uninterested, was climbing slowly out of the ring; Mitchell, not interested either, was lying face down in a corner. But Burke was interested. He got to his feet; he felt sick and exhausted, but very determined to see that right was done. He scrambled into the arena and pushed his way towards the promoter; he was not strong, but he was quick on his feet and agile as

[103]

an eel. The promoter, in fear of lynching, had discovered that he had plenty of money and a man in a check suit was offering to look after it for "my poor friend." Burke pushed between the two men.

"But my friend isn't going to be poor!" he said as he snatched at the money.

The man was twice his size, but Burke did not care; at this moment he was prepared to fight until they tore him apart. The crowd swayed and hesitated, befuddled with sun and violence. Then a voice at the back called out, "The little runt was sitting with him up here." Burke got the money. He put it away carefully in his pocket. It was a lot of money. When feeling cooled, calculation would oust sympathy; it would not be just the pickpockets and the gang boys he had to fear. He was glad to see a couple of policemen hovering at the back of the crowd; a little law was certainly needed. He went over to Mitchell, who was still lying face down snatching for breath.

"My friend is very ill," he said dramatically. "Someone will pay for this." His Italian was not good, but the message came across and the crowd edged back. One of the policemen was making his way towards the ring. No one tried to stop him, but he lashed about with his cane just to show that it would not be wise to make any false moves. His friend waited a few minutes and then repeated the performance. Burke went over his own performance again. "My friend is very, very ill." The first policeman bent down and examined Mitchell briefly; he wasn't a very attractive sight, the face disfigured with bruises, the features blunted and coarsened.

"Has he broken anything?" the policeman asked.

"No."

Burke was not sure that this was true, but he did not want them to fetch an ambulance. He was sorry for Mitchell; nevertheless, he felt that he had suffered so much that a little more pain could scarcely matter. He kept very close as the policemen dragged Mitchell away; it would be a pity if he was attacked while the police had their hands full.

There was another complication when they reached the comparative calm of the area where the cars were parked. The policemen wanted to take Mitchell and Burke to the police station. Burke could see that they were going to be insistent: fair ground duty was hard work and any excuse to head for home was welcome. Burke took out the prize money. They were realists, no need for wearisome subtleties; twenty thousand lire persuaded them that a visit to the police station would be an unnecessary formality.

Burke drove carefully across the valley, anxious not to jar Mitchell by a sudden movement of the car; he was solicitous, almost tender.

"Sure an' it's a brave, bloody fool that ye are!" The edge had worn off the mockery; he sounded exasperated but affectionate. "Though why you did it, is something I'll never understand. You're the most unexpected man I know."

It was only when they had crossed the frontier and the car was negotiating the high spiral of Swiss roads that he realized the truth of what he had said. He pondered this unexpected act as darkness came down, easing the strained eyes, cooling the brain. From time to time, when the road straightened for long enough to allow him to relax his attention, he glanced round. The face that he could see was, in spite of everything, civilized and aware; it reminded Burke that Mitchell was no devil-may-care, brawling Paddy. He had proved long ago that he could stand pain better than most men; but he had learnt to respect it and he would never court it needlessly. And so? Burke was very cold now; his body was drained of feeling and his mind of distraction. The answer came quite simply. One hundred and seventy thousand lire. And the only reason that Mitchell could need money so urgently was Miriam Kratz. As one did not spend money on people like Miriam Kratz voluntarily, that meant blackmail. It all fell into place. He would have to think rather carefully about the future.

But before he could think about the future there was something to be done. He had an account to pay. He could not have explained why this was so to anyone, least of all himself; he simply knew that some payment must be made for the afternoon's entertainment.

When they reached Mitchell's room, Burke did not offer to play the Good Samaritan; he could not have borne to lay his hands on the bruised flesh. He simply put the money down on the dressing table and added to it twenty thousand lire of his own to cover the amount he had paid to the policemen. Twenty thousand lire represented a lot of money to Burke, who was not rich. The debt was paid. He went to his own room and lay down; he did not want to think, but the only book he had with him was *The Brothers Karamazov* and, most definitely, he was not in the mood for that. He listened to the sounds in the street; usually the noise annoyed him, but now he was glad of the distraction. He heard the music from the pleasure steamer as it came in to the jetty to pick up people for the "surprise evening cruise." He wondered idly what the surprise involved; then he began to laugh. They had left that poor little bugger Alperin at the fair!

Alperin had not thought it at all funny. He had meant to get out to the car and wait there until Mitchell and Burke returned. But he had lost his way in the bewildering maze of stalls; and then he had been knocked down and robbed. It had been quite unnecessary to knock him down, he would never have resisted; but the youths concerned had wanted to hit someone and he had been close to hand. They had hit him rather hard and dragged him behind one of the tents. He did not come to until the evening.

It was dark. The crowd had congregated in the amusement park; he could see the bright, flashing lights of the merry-go-round and he could hear music and the sound of fireworks. But here it was dark and deserted. Alperin sat up. Immediately he felt very sick and dizzy. He let his head hang forward to stop himself fainting. As he crouched there he became aware of sounds inside the tent, odd, inexplicable sounds. It was a relief to know that someone was at hand. His experience of the last few hours had, however, made him cautious and he decided to investigate before asking for help. He tried to lift the bottom of the tent, but it was firmly pegged down; so he crawled round to the front of it and lifted up the flap. It was a very small tent; he did not have any difficulty in seeing its occupants. One was the boy on the trampoline; at close range, and the range was very close, Alperin recognized the boy for whom he had bought the Coca-Cola. He let the flap of the tent down; the boy had not recognized him and Huber had been in no state to recognize anyone. Alperin crawled away until he was out of sight and earshot of the tent, then he lay down, his head pillowed on his arms. He had no idea how he was ever to get back to Tamaro and he did not in the least care.

Chapter II

It was good when dawn came; not that it was any easier to breathe, but there was a faint sense of reassurance, a belief that the nightmare would pass now. Mitchell thought that he would look at the clock. Usually this was an automatic action and he was not sure at first why it required thinking out; then he realized that he could not turn his head. He tried to move his arm towards the clock, but this proved impossible too. Panic took away what little breath he had. His mind, which still seemed able to function, fought down the panic. He could feel muscles he had not felt for years, so he was not paralysed. He was just very stiff and it would take a long time to get up and dress; nevertheless, he was going to get up and dress. He looked down at his hands, resting on the crumpled sheet like two bunches of bananas. He moved the little finger of each hand, then the third finger, the middle finger, the index finger, the thumb; he repeated the exercise. It was encouraging, soon he might be able to bend the knuckles. This, however, proved more difficult; he tried bending the wrists, which was agony. He rested for a while and then started again. After a quarter of an hour he had some control over his hands, although he could not do anything difficult, like picking up the clock. He wondered what to do next. It was his back that worried him; the spine was as rigid as steel set in concrete. There didn't seem much point in moving hands and possibly feet if one could never sit up again. He thought about this and while he thought he raised his head a few inches and lowered it again on the pillow. He did this several times. The neck held under the strain, so he turned his head a few inches to the right and then a few inches to the left. He moved his legs; there wasn't any serious trouble there. He hunched his legs up and tried to roll to one side; his spine became a red-hot poker pressing against raw nerves. The time to rest had passed; he would never have the courage to make this move a second time. Ignoring the pain and sweat and his own involuntary protests, he managed to roll sideways and lever his weight on to one elbow; he swung his legs over the side of the bed and fumbled for the bedside table with his free hand. He knocked over the clock, but that did not matter; time was never more relative than now. He clung to the table as exhausted as though it was the pinnacle of Everest. What was it that Hillary was reported to have said? "We've done the bitch!" He would say that when he reached the wash basin. It was a long journey; halfway there he caught sight of himself in the mirror and laughed. A bad mistake. He hadn't breath for words when he reached the wash basin. It took him a long time to wash and even longer to shave. When he had finished he wanted to go to bed again, possibly for a month. Instead he ordered breakfast; they would be serving it now, his maneuvers had taken the better part of two hours. He dragged a chair on to the balcony and sat down. It was probably unwise to sit down if he ever wanted to walk again, but he was too exhausted to bother about that.

While he tried to eat his breakfast, his thoughts broke free of the ties of bodily pain and he began to ask why he was in this appalling condition. The last time it had happened to him there had been a very good reason for it; then he had been wise enough to avoid asking questions. But now his sense of danger had been blunted and the questions were more insistent. Why had he done this? Whatever inconvenience he had caused Miriam Kratz, a gesture of this order was quite unwarranted; the nature of his involvement with her scarcely justified his behaviour up to yesterday, and from then on his actions were beyond justification.

His stomach rebelled against the food; he looked at the half-eaten roll on his plate and decided not to struggle any more. He had struggled too much and for too long to digest the unpalatable. That was probably the simple answer to his extraordinary behaviour. He wasn't suited to the kind of life he had been living over the last years. He had done well enough when strength and zest and a feeling for adventure had been what were primarily required, but the climate of feeling had changed now. He had never liked an east wind. He supposed that he was soft, temperamentally if not physically; no doubt that explained why he fell such an easy victim to the desperate appeal of Miriam Kratz. He had always been prone to pity. But unless one intended to do something about alleviating suffering, pity was a useless thing, a way of making up to other people for one's own inadequacies. In all the years in Berlin, who had ever really benefited from his pity? And was pity the final explanation of his extraordinary behaviour? It would be nice to think so. But he knew that when he challenged The Great Arturo, he had not been moved by pity and he had not been thinking of money. He had wanted the pain. For some incredible reason, he had felt an urgent need to suffer for Miriam Kratz.

He moved uneasily in his chair, wishing that he had a cigarette, reluctant to fetch a packet because that meant starting on the agonizing return journey to the bedroom. He hoped Burke would not come in. Burke had a quite astonishing mental agility; he could sum up a situation with bewildering speed and the swiftness with which he made decisions and passed judgment was breathtaking. Much though Mitchell admired Burke's mental gymnastics, he had no desire to submit himself for judgment at the present time. There were things that he had to put right before he had another encounter with Burke.

He gripped the sides of the chair and levered himself to his feet. He must see Miriam Kratz and put an end to all this nonsense. It had been stupid to imagine that he could help her; with people like Miriam Kratz there could be no half-measures, one must leave them alone or travel with them to the end of their dark road. He went back to the bedroom, groped his way along the corridor to the toilet and was sick. He felt better after that. He took the rest of the day easily and late in the afternoon he went to see Miriam Kratz.

She must have seen him coming up the hill, because she came out to meet him. She stood in the dusty road, waving and laughing as though she was glad. The sun had brought her to life. If he had not known otherwise, he would have thought her an Italian; she seemed to have all the Latin warmth and vitality at this moment.

As he came closer, her eyes looked at him directly, expressing pleasure without fear of rebuff. The last time they met, a barrier had been removed; she had talked about her husband and felt that he understood. He had not realized how her imagination would feed on that moment so that the next time they met she would feel that there was a bond between them.

He stood beside her, one hand to his side, breathing heav-

[111]

ily; he looked down, exaggerating his exhaustion to give himself time. She laughed at him and spoke with a teasing familiarity.

"What is the matter? You came up the hill like a crab."

"I had a fight and strained my back," he snapped.

"You were attacked?" Fear snuffed out the laughter. She put out her hand and touched his arm. The gesture, and the concern in her voice, were exactly what he had craved a little earlier: now he was afraid to accept them. She felt him stiffen.

"I am sorry I laughed at you." The old anxiety crept back into her voice. "Come and sit down, there is a seat here."

She led him across the long grass to the bench at the side of the terrace where he had found her on a previous visit. When they were seated, she looked at his battered face but she asked no questions. On the terrace two toddlers were playing with an inflated rubber ball. Mitchell watched the children. The ball was too big for the girl, and every time she threw it she fell over on her back. What superb natural comics children were! And what a fantastic range of feeling they could command, passing without pause for breath from ecstatic pleasure to the blackest despair. Mitchell studied the children because he liked children and because he wanted to put off the moment when he handed over the money.

"Are they brother and sister?" he asked.

"I think so. They sit at the same table."

She answered abruptly and he noticed that she did not look at the children. He supposed she was annoyed that his attention had been diverted. He must give her the money now, before the situation between them became more difficult. He put his hand in his pocket; the movement jerked his shoulder and he winced.

"I am so sorry!" she said quickly. "Was it because of me?"

She looked at him. She was indeed sorry, but nevertheless

[112]

she wanted him to have suffered for her. Her eyes examined the bruises on his face, hating them and loving them; a pulse began to beat in her throat. He put his arm round her shoulder. She said softly, "You must not endanger yourself for me."

The danger was that she should think of herself as playing a central part in his activities. He said, "It's over now." He meant to add that he would not be coming to see her again, but he paused too long and she spoke first. She spoke in a voice he had never heard before, nor ever heard again.

"Oh, these last few days! You can have no idea how wonderful they have been. At first, I hated having nothing to do; I envied the hotel staff because they were so occupied. And then, I stopped hating or envying . . . I just dragged myself about feeling so tired, so desperately tired, although I did nothing. I could not think, I was too lazy even to ask the time or to turn my head to look at a clock. Almost, I forgot who I was . . . And then one morning when I woke I jumped out of bed at once, without any reason, except to make sure that the sun was shining and it would be a good day. I felt so eager as I drew the curtain, so hopeful. Hopeful . . ."

She leant her head against his arm, marvelling at the miracle he had wrought for her; while Mitchell cursed himself for leading her on until the way out was harder than ever.

"Have you made any plans?"

"Plans? No . . . I . . ." She was confused by the matter-of-fact quality of his voice.

"Haven't you any relatives?" he asked desperately.

"Mikail has a brother in Austria."

She sat up and Mitchell moved his arm; the movement hurt, but neither of them acknowledged the fact this time.

"Do you know this man?"

"No."

[113]

"But perhaps he would help you?"

"Perhaps."

Her voice was dull; he did not look at her face. Instead, he fumbled for the money and handed it to her.

"This will help you to get to him."

There was silence. Then she said in a tone that was utterly despairing, "I've never had so much money. I shan't know how to use it." She fingered the notes, counted a few, and cried out, "What shall I do with all this?"

He felt something hit his leg and looking down he saw the rubber ball rolling between his feet. He picked it up, glad of the diversion. The little girl was stumbling through the long grass towards him. When she reached the seat she lost interest in the ball, sat down and scratched at a scab on her leg. She had flaxen hair, well-brushed and expensively shaped; her clothes were expensive, too. Mitchell said to Miriam:

"Is she Swiss?"

"German."

Her hands clenched over the roll of notes; the knuckles looked sharp and cruel and he was suddenly concerned for the child. The little boy was crying desolately on the terrace. Mitchell rumpled the flaxen hair and said, "Your brother wants you." The child looked up and her face dimpled in a smile that was enchanting and quite heartlessly unconcerned; then she took off her shoe and threw it into the long grass. Her mother, Mitchell suspected, must get tired of that gambit. He looked at Miriam. Her face was like a stone. Mitchell did not like to leave her with the child.

"I'm afraid I can't pick up that shoe," he said. "I really have hurt my back."

She got up and walked across the grass. It was only when he saw her bend to pick up the shoe and stand for a moment looking down at it, that he understood. He went across to her.

"I'll put it on."

She shook her head. "You mustn't hurt your back, must you?" She walked past him and knelt in front of the child; she put the shoe on with hands that were firm and fingers that were quick and efficient, she pulled up the rumpled socks, smoothed down the dress; then, still kneeling herself, she lifted up the child, gave her a little pat on the behind and sent her back to her brother. She sat back on her heels, watching the child run away, the fat legs thrashing through the long grass. Just when Mitchell thought that all was safely over, she crouched forward, her breast pressed against her limbs tight as a closed knife; she made a noise that was like no crying he had ever heard.

He said, "I'm so terribly sorry."

Her grief appalled him. It was too deep for his understanding, something torn out of the ground on which she knelt, something beyond the range of his pity. While he hesitated, not knowing what to do, she looked up at him; the harrowed face had a terrible beauty, he was fascinated and afraid. He looked into her eyes and saw, not the dark well of her despair, but his own image pitifully stripped of its comfortable compassionate pretensions.

"What are you waiting for?" she cried. "What do you think you can do? Give me more money?"

He turned away. She jeered and shouted abuse after him; her voice was surprisingly strong, the litany of hate seemed to follow him for a long way.

The road was hot and dusty and after he had been walking for a little while he became very thirsty. He stopped and had a drink at a café on the roadside. He tried not to think about Miriam Kratz. He talked to the waiter about the heat. The waiter, who was a local man, said it was always as hot as this and that Maggiore had the best climate in the world. The topic of the weather occupied them until the bus arrived from Brissago. Mitchell decided to return by bus, he was in no mood for long, solitary walks. He reached Tamaro at seven o'clock. His limbs were still stiff; perhaps a hot bath before dinner would be a good idea. He concentrated on the bath, still a ceremonial rite here, as he entered the hotel; he hoped the water would be hot . . .

"Where have you been?" It was Burke, confronting him accusingly.

"I took a walk . . ."

"Never mind that now. I've packed your bags. We're leaving at once."

"Has something happened?"

"Alperin came back soon after lunch, looking as though he had slept rough; he packed and departed in great haste. His bags were labelled for Montreux. I've booked hotel accommodation there."

Burke seemed to have forgotten recent events. So much the better. Mitchell was glad to be on the move again. It would be a hard journey, but in any case he had not expected to sleep very well that night.

Chapter 12

Eliot read the reports on Alperin with a feeling of satisfaction. It would come to nothing now; although, as a gesture to London, the wretched man would have to be watched during the conference week. "But it's pleasant here at this time of the year," he said consolingly to Mitchell and Burke. In case they should be encouraged to take things too easily, he added, "And there are some interesting people around. Josef Novak, for example; do you know him?" They didn't know him: Eliot would have been irritated if they had. "Very little is known about him. But he turns up in interesting places at interesting times. I have been following his career —in so much as you can follow the career of a man who disappears for long periods of time—with admiration. He is very accomplished." This was Eliot's accolade, reserved for the truly great. Mitchell lit a cigarette and Burke, who had nothing to do, asked whether Novak was Russian.

"His passport would tell you that he is Austrian. He speaks German faultlessly, but when he speaks English he adopts a broken accent. Yet there have been reports of a man, not dissimilar, who speaks English perfectly. This man was in

South America for a time and caused us quite a bit of embarrassment—the Americans thought he was one of our people." Eliot smiled; it was obvious that he had not been personally involved in the trouble.

"Sounds like an interesting character," Burke said.

"You think so? Well, try to get to know him. It will help to pass the time."

"And Alperin?" Mitchell asked.

"Oh, Alperin! He will go home with his tail between his legs at the end of the month. But see that he and Novak don't meet."

They parted soon after this.

"A quick drink before anything else!" Burke insisted when they reached the street. "Eliot in benign mood fills me with a gloom that only whisky can penetrate."

He had his whisky and then they left Lausanne. Mitchell drove slowly along the lakeside road to Montreux. Lake Léman was not so beautiful as Maggiore, which twisted and turned, continually offering new delights; but the air was cool and a fresh wind stirred the water, the outlines of the mountains were sharp against the sky. There was a purity and precision about this landscape that was satisfying. A return to sanity. The two men talked easily, the rhythm between them restored. Burke had booked rooms in a small hotel in the village of Veytaux which was on the far side of Montreux, a little way up the hill overlooking Chillon. Although it was only a short climb from the main road, few tourists stayed there; it was quiet and unpretentious, and the hotel in which they were staying had a good view of the lake. It also overlooked the hotel in which Alperin was staying.

"How ever did you find it?" Mitchell asked as he stopped the car in the quiet square which was the only flat piece of ground in the straggling village.

[118]

"I stayed here once, long ago, when I was a student."
Neither of them moved; they had been travelling for a long
time and now it was pleasant to be still. Burke went on,
"We 'did' Chillon. It's worth a visit, if you don't know it.
They seem to have preserved a bit of the atmosphere along
with the usual relics."

Mitchell sat back, watching the sunlight filter through the
trees in the square.

"What did you read at university?" he asked.

"English. I wanted to be a writer and I was supposed to
have some talent."

"Why didn't you carry on?"

"I was influenced by one of those take-life-by-the-throat-
and-shake-the-guts-out-of-it gospellers. You know the sort
of thing—those who can, do; those who can't, write." He
looked sombrely across the square. "And so, I chose to
do . . ."

Mitchell could see that the choice had probably been a
wrong one, Burke had qualities which might have flowered
in a more sheltered atmosphere; but it was too late for that
now, so he said:

"It hasn't all been so bad, Dan."

"Not for you, perhaps."

At this moment, Burke badly wanted to talk about the
mess he had made of his life; but he could see that he had
lost Mitchell's interest. Mitchell was reflecting that it was not
actions but sensations that brought the past most vividly to
mind. He remembered walking down a lane in France, coming into a village where there was a square with a drinking
fountain, light slanting through the trees; it was very quiet,
every nerve in his body shrilled when he walked across to
that drinking fountain. Nothing had happened, he had had
his drink and gone on his way; an unimportant incident, he
had forgotten about it until now. Some quality of the light

had reminded him; that, and the fact that now he was very thirsty . . . He wished it was Claus sitting beside him, he might have said something about it. But it was Burke, morose, uneasy. He did not want to listen to another of Burke's tirades against life; there had been too much of that already, it was one of the things he intended to leave behind at Maggiore. He opened the car door and said briskly:

"I'll see if there's a garage if you'll cope with the bags."

They had dinner early that evening and went to their rooms, they were both tired. Mitchell pulled back the shutters and opened the window; the air had an edge to it, the temperature must have dropped sharply in the last hour. He sat on the window ledge and looked down at the lake. The hotel overhung the main road, only the chimneys of Alperin's hotel were visible through a screen of trees. It was late evening now, all colour gone, the lake grey and the mountains dark, except where the peaks of Les Dents du Midi pierced the sky. Harsher than Maggiore, less reconciled to man, there was nevertheless something comforting in this more majestic landscape; it was strong, uncluttered and it had no knowledge of half truths. He looked away from the mountains to where Chillon jutted out into the lake; it was astonishing how the castle preserved its remote quality in spite of the tangle of tram wires that half obstructed the view. He would go there tomorrow as Burke had suggested. He turned away from the window, undressed and got into bed. He fell asleep almost at once and woke feeling better than he had felt for a long time. Burke seemed in good spirits, too. He had met the owner of a vineyard near Villeneuve on a rather dull North Atlantic flight a few years ago and now he intended to renew the acquaintanceship.

"We drank a lot of brandy and made extravagant offers of hospitality. I told him, why I can't imagine, that my family had a distillery in Dublin."

[120]

"Perhaps he invented the vineyard."

"I rather doubt it. He was very intense about the excellence of Swiss wines and the need to break down the snob barrier erected by the French. Most certainly he has a vineyard. Come with me and I'll prove it to you."

"Thanks, but I think I'll take your advice and have a look at Chillon."

Burke winced. "I was in sentimental mood last night. Don't expect too much."

Burke took the car. Mitchell refused a lift and walked slowly down the hill towards Chillon. He stopped at Alperin's hotel and made a few enquiries. Alperin, it seemed, was not well and he was staying in his room; he did not, the receptionist informed Mitchell, want to see anyone. So far, so good. Mitchell went on his way convinced that his long-delayed holiday had begun.

He had breakfasted early and it was only nine o'clock when he reached the castle. There were a few cars parked outside, but no coaches had yet arrived. Mitchell stood for a moment on the far side of the drawbridge, watching a paddle steamer waddling through the water like a pregnant duck. It was pleasantly cool still and the light was clear; there were children playing in a sailing boat beached nearby, and out on the lake someone was water skiing, wearing the bizarre black outfit now thought so necessary. Water skiing would be pleasant, Mitchell thought; if only he was not so stiff still.

He turned towards the castle, paid his admission fee, and crossed the drawbridge, enjoying the unfamiliar sensation of being a tourist. There were two Americans just ahead, the quiet, earnest kind who would do the castle inch by painstaking inch. The woman, gazing round the small, cobbled court, said, "It's so peaceful, like stepping into another world." The man rebuked her, "A hard world for some." He was right, of course; one had only to look at the massive

[121]

stone walls broken only by the archers' loopholes to see that this was a world from which men never looked outward with much hope.

The Americans were moving towards the underground vaults, intent on inspecting Bonivard's prison. Mitchell looked up at the sky, blue, flecked with small, friendly tufts of cirrus, and decided that he did not want to visit the prison at this moment. The Americans would probably make very heavy going of it. Instead he went down to the crypt and from there quickly made his way to the second courtyard and on into the Grand Hall of the Governors of the Castle.

Burke had been right, the castle was well-preserved; and as Mitchell wandered from room to room he was conscious of some kind of atmosphere, though he doubted whether it was generated so much by the past as by the design of the place. A fortress is a prison for all who move within its confines at whatever time. He wondered, as he stood at a window high up in the Grand Hall of the Count, what the Governors had felt as they looked from this window at the view of the lake and wooded shore. Had they acknowledged unity with the men below in the dungeons, prisoners all in the Castle of Chillon? Probably not, those had been dangerous times, not conducive to self-analysis.

He went on through a torture chamber with a low window only a foot above the floor, through the museum where there were several models of the castle as it had been at different periods, to the treasury. From this room a wooden staircase led up to the keep. A middle-aged woman was coming down the staircase. She was saying, "All right, then! You carry on alone. I'm not going one step further." Her plump hand gripped the wooden rail and when she reached the bottom she leant against the wall, snuffling like a distressed bulldog. She was followed by a red-faced man protesting loudly; in spite of his protests, Mitchell noticed that the man made no attempt to return on his own. Interested, Mitchell mounted the stairs as soon as the couple moved away.

The staircase was steep and narrow, the treads badly worn, it seemed to go up indefinitely; not a venture for anyone with heart trouble or an overworked imagination. At the top there was a small room with sloping roofs and several recessed windows from which lookouts had once surveyed the surrounding countryside. The view was rewarding. Over the intervening roofs one could see the lake widening beyond Montreux and to the east, the green valley of the Rhône overhung by Les Dents du Midi. Below, the pattern of the castle unfolded; interesting, provided one had a good head for heights.

A youth and his girl friend had clambered up behind Mitchell. The girl peered down at the pointed roofs of the towers below.

"If you fell from here, you might be skewered on that," the young man said, pointing to a spike on one of the tower roofs.

There was a glimpse of a courtyard, far below, which looked a kinder, though equally final, resting place.

The girl said, "You say that kind of thing on purpose to upset me. You were just the same about the Pagoda at Kew." The freckles on her face stood out like cinnamon on milk. Mitchell left the young man to comfort her and threaded his way back to the first courtyard.

The American couple would have finished their inspection of Bonivard's prison by now. Nevertheless, he lingered in the courtyard where the sun glanced between the towers and he could feel its warmth on his back. He knew that it was not really the Americans who had made him avoid this part of the castle. He did not want to turn away from the sun; he dreaded the moment when its warmth was cut off and still more he dreaded the moment, at the turn of the stair, when even its reflected light would be blotted out. But one could not go round Chillon without seeing Bonivard's prison, so he turned reluctantly to the vaults. He passed through the first prison quickly and came to Bonivard's prison, a long, gloomy room with heavy stone pillars. Byron had signed his name on the third pillar and the signature was carefully preserved behind a glass screen. The fifth pillar, according to the guidebook, was the one to which Bonivard had been chained for four years because he was "favourable to the Reformation." Four years . . . What belief could a man hold so strongly that he was prepared to accept such a terrible deprivation of liberty? What kind of a man was he? Mitchell, who had been intent on getting out of this place, found himself imprisoned by his own fascination with these questions. He sat on a ledge near the pillar. Four years . . . Now, in a century when the edges of truth had blurred, it was difficult to conceive that any belief could endure so long a test. It was quiet in this place, a hopeless, stone-deadened quiet . . . How did the mind survive? While he thought about this, he realized that sound was not completely deadened; he could hear water lapping against stone. He looked up and saw, some distance from where he was sitting, a narrow slit of a window. So Bonivard would have heard this sound, gentle, caressing, inexorable, night and day, day and night. Mitchell wondered whether it had helped to keep him sane. He could not see out of the window from where he was sitting, but no doubt if Bonivard had crawled to the full extent of his chains he would have seen water, had a glimpse of sky, a bird in flight. When he was too ill to move, the sound would paint the picture for him; perhaps gradually it would ease him into sleep. Mitchell was nearly asleep himself; his mind strayed and he found himself muttering with a tense, desperate urgency, "As long as they never brick up that window!" His heart missed a beat, dust caught in his throat, he began to cough; he hurried to the window, absurdly close to panic. For some reason, as he stood there fighting for breath, he was thinking not of Bonivard but of Mikail Kratz. He had not intended to think of the Kratzes, man or wife, again. Gradually, the paroxysm of coughing ceased. Through the slit window the air came in fresh, with a hint of spray. That was the place to be, out there on the lake with the sun warm across your shoulders! He turned towards the stairs and left the castle more quickly than he had entered it.

It was good to be outside again. He crossed the drawbridge and turned at once towards Montreux, taking the path that descended to the lakeside. He did not turn back for a last view of the castle. As he reached the lake a water skier swung round in a wide arc and passed close to the shore. A pity he was so stiff still, Mitchell thought. The arc had been too wide and suddenly there was no connection between the skier and the boat; the engine cut off and the boat turned back. Mitchell walked on and after a few minutes the boat passed him, the skier riding the water again, black skin gleaming.

Ten minutes later, Mitchell came to the quayside from which the skiers were taking off; there was a group of them hunched over the lake looking like a Cocteau variation on the Rhine Maidens. Mitchell stopped to watch. The boat had set off on another trip; it was a long way away, the skier a moving speck connected to the boat only by the pattern of movement, the long graceful arc, the outward curve held at the boat's axis. The boat did not seem to be following its usual staid course this time; it, too, weaved, curved and frolicked. One sensed that they were enjoying themselves out there. As the boat came nearer it became obvious that the skier was something of a clown, tripping and swaying and

[125]

almost falling but never actually going down, his idiocies marvellously timed. It was inconceivable, watching him, that this was not his natural element; he seemed a creature born of boat and the pull of water. But he looked quite magnificently human male as he came closer, wearing only the briefest of bathing trunks.

When he climbed on to the quayside no one greeted him. The black-clad figures turned heads to look at him, their expressions a mixture of admiration and the suspicion which men feel when confronted with someone who lives outside the herd. The man did not even notice them. He walked past them and paused beside the bench where Mitchell was sitting; he was breathing heavily and one hand was pressed to his side. An older man than one would have thought, watching his performance out there; he would do this kind of thing once too often, but then he was not the kind to tiptoe into old age. Mitchell looked at him and saw a dark head, close-cropped, a strong-boned face with deep-set eyes and a mouth that would clamp hard on the bit of life. Not a disappointed man. There had not been much time, Mitchell guessed, for the seed of disillusion to grow as it only can when the wheels begin to run down. He has been more fortunate than Claus and me; he still trusts life to offer him the kind of experience he needs . . . As these thoughts formed in his mind, Mitchell realized that he had found Josef Novak. It seemed a pity to let him go, so he said casually:

"We've met somewhere, surely?"

The eyes that turned to him were a vivid blue; they seemed to be laughing and the laughter was only just this side of normality. He would look at you like this when he was going to kill you. He studied Mitchell for a long time and then answered:

"No, we have not met. But I think perhaps we should have done."

[126]

He sat down on the bench and began to rub himself vigorously with his towel. He talked about Montreux and water skiing. He had a slight foreign accent and a rather staccato delivery. His conversation was not as interesting as his personality; but there was something naïve about his enthusiasm which was rather disarming and his approach to the listener had a directness that could be disconcerting. A strange mixture; one would never be able to calculate one's moves with this man. When he had finished drying himself, he said to Mitchell:

"Perhaps we met in South America?"

"I've never been there."

"A pity. But since we have met now, perhaps we should celebrate."

They strolled towards the big hotels with long gardens bordering the lake. They did not exchange names or ask questions. They had several drinks in the bar of the hotel and lunched together. In the afternoon, they went out in the man's speedboat. He maneuvered it in a way that must have made others on the lake think that a madman was at the helm; but Mitchell saw that he was not really reckless, he simply calculated much quicker than most men. In a tight spot, he would make his decisions coolly and he would make few errors. They came back to Montreux in the evening, ripping a path down the sun's last beam. They had more drinks, and then to clear their heads they went on the lake again.

In all that time, they made no confidences. They accepted each other and a certain limited community of feeling which was best expressed in action. One of the joyous things about speed, Mitchell thought, was that all extraneous thought and emotion were pared away in order to achieve a supreme coordination of mind and body, an exquisite moment of balance. He could not remember when he had felt so confident, so refreshed in spirit. He went back to his hotel at five in the morning, and as he walked up the stairs to his room he was thinking that life was still very good, that it was all a question of balance.

The light was on in his room and Burke was sitting in a chair, waiting for him.

Chapter 13

Burke was sitting with his shoulders hunched, his head thrust forward so that it seemed to jut out from his chest. One hand hung down at the front of the chair, holding a piece of paper; the forward thrust of the arm made his whole body seem more twisted than ever. His face was haggard. Mitchell said:

"Your friend wined you well!"

Burke said, "I didn't stay with him. I've been to Lausanne." He was dead sober.

"Lausanne?" Mitchell sat on the corner of the bed. "Come on Dan, out with it!"

"He showed me over his vineyard; he took me down to the cellars where the wine is stored. It was damp and very unwholesome; not the kind of thing I enjoy. While he gave me a little lecture on wine storage, I flicked through the pages of some old papers someone had left there. Incredible that it should have been that particular page of that particular paper that attracted my attention, isn't it?" He held out his hand and Mitchell took the torn sheet of paper from him and read:

"The body of Claus Hesselmann, the well-known climber, was found by a monk at the foot of a slope close to the hospice in the Great St. Bernard Pass on Tuesday, 7th May. He had severe head injuries. Police are puzzled that an experienced climber should have had an accident in this particular place . . ."

The silence in the room lasted longer than it took Mitchell to read the short paragraph. Eventually, he said:

"The seventh May . . . that was the night we were there."

"Yes."

Mitchell looked up at Burke, waiting. Burke went on:

"I went to Lausanne and saw Eliot. He was ill in bed, a haemorrhage. He explained the whole thing to me, lying like a corpse having the last word from his winding sheet. He told me that London had a rather delicate operation planned just about the time Eliot recalled us from leave. It involved letting the East Germans get hold of some information; that information had to be believed, so it was important they shouldn't come by it too easily. Something had to be sacrificed. This problem was handed to Eliot at short notice. He solved it by arranging our rendezvous with Claus through a contact he knew was suspect."

Mitchell said in a dry voice, "But he cancelled those instructions."

"He cancelled our instructions."

Burke was losing control; his face twitched and his hands were shaking, he clenched them together to try to stop the shaking. His voice was pitched a little higher as he went on:

"He sent Claus to meet us, carrying the prepared documents. Claus, of course, thought they were genuine. Claus was murdered, according to plan, and the documents changed hands. But then we intervened and spoilt the murderers' get-away, to say nothing of Eliot's plan! The memory

[130]

of it made him so angry he had a coughing fit and brought up blood. It was like seeing a waxwork bleed. He said that the damage caused by that night's happenings was incalculable."

Mitchell sat looking down at the rug at his feet as though he expected it to tell him something; his eyes followed the outline of a faded pink flower, travelled down a brown stem, explored a stained green ivy leaf. What he was really seeing all this time was the figure of a monk running down a path, his habit billowing behind him as he emerged just in front of the car. "A flying monk!" he had said and he had laughed.

"This is really true, is it, Dan?" he said to Burke.

Burke did not answer and eventually Mitchell looked up at him, like a man hoping for a reprieve. Burke looked back, filled with his own longings, waiting for the storm to break at last. He was desperately lonely and afraid; like Claus, he was expendable. He wanted a gesture of solidarity now more than anything; he wanted a wild, extravagant, drunken night bitter enough to take away the taste of fear. He couldn't do it alone, he had to have companionship. But Mitchell, seeing the answer to his question etched deep in every line of Burke's face, said only, "I see." He looked round the room as though faintly surprised to find it unaltered.

Burke said, "Do you?" A little colour stained his neck, spread slowly along the sides of the jaw and upwards to burn bright on his cheekbones. "Do you really understand what I've been telling you? Claus went up to the Pass thinking he was going to meet friends, you in particular. Eliot sent him into a trap and he used you as bait."

Still Mitchell said nothing. Burke went across to the dressing table and picked up a bottle of whisky.

"I brought this along because I thought you'd need it."

He poured a good measure into Mitchell's tooth mug and drank, watching Mitchell with eyes that still implored a response. Anger was draining away and fear was encroaching; he took another gulp of whisky. Mitchell sat, his hands dangling limply between his knees, his face impassive as he gazed at the rug. Burke poured another measure, threw it in Mitchell's face and went out of the room.

Mitchell sat without moving for a time after he had gone. Then he got up and went out of the hotel into the street. He walked slowly down the hill to the main road. Cars were racing up from the direction of Villeneuve; he crossed without looking and horns blared angrily. There was a turning to the left which led away from the noise and lights; he went gratefully into the darkness. After a few minutes he came to the lake. It was very early, the water was black and still. He leant against the rail, looking towards Villeneuve. There was that strange breathless expectancy which comes at the moment when night has taken its last long breath. Soon, he saw the glimmering outline of Les Dents du Midi; he stood a long time watching the great fangs soften, the ivory turn to rose. When he looked away, he saw the curve of the lake vanishing into mist and nearby the furred outline of trees and shrubs. His eyes registered the scene with great clarity; but he himself was remote from it, as though it was a world seen at the wrong end of a telescope.

He looked down at the water, grey, scarcely moving between the dark boulders. He shivered and hunched forward; he felt drained as though he, too, had had a haemorrhage. But in the rush of blood something had been released. He had a feeling of freedom; the freedom that comes at the extremity of sickness when no one can expect anything of you any more. A breeze was getting up, the water moved between the boulders; he listened to it, gentle against the implacable stone. Gradually, the water, too, turned to rose. As he watched the day stealing, soft and beguiling, across the lake he found that there were tears in his eyes, but

[132]

whether they were for Claus or for himself he did not know.

He pulled a packet of cigarettes from his pocket. He lit a cigarette, crumpled the packet and then stopped himself throwing it on the ground. Leaving litter on the tidy Swiss promenade was a small gesture of insurrection, a gesture for a child; he was on the far side of that kind of rebellion. He put the crumpled paper in his pocket and walked slowly along the path in the direction of Villeneuve.

There were a few people about now, the day started early for Swiss workers. As he passed men, neat and industrious, women, stolid, purposeful, he had the same feeling he had had years ago in Paris when he strolled past German soldiers and thought to himself, "I am your enemy, although you don't realize it." Life had seemed precious then and he had been afraid of discovery. Now, in one stride, he had moved beyond the reach of fear. When he got near Chillon the path climbed steeply; he hadn't the energy to drag himself upwards, so he sat on a bench, thinking about his new-found freedom, wondering how to use it.

He did not even consider telling Eliot that he was through; Eliot had released him from that kind of obligation. So what did one do? He felt a need, after all these bleak, subservient years, to do something for himself; the need had been growing in him for a long time. But what did one do? This was not a time when the individual could make large gestures, the twentieth century had gutted the individual.

Hunger and weariness confused his mind. He felt colder than ever and a little faint. He got up and toiled up the path, turning away from the direction of Chillon at the first fork and making his way to the main road. He was out of breath when he reached it; he felt all of his forty-four years. He took a tram into Montreux. It was still early, the shops were shuttered; but he found a café that was open, an impoverished place in a narrow street.

[133]

The woman who served him was thin and querulous. She had a small girl trailing after her, a dirty, unsavoury creature with torn pants tumbled to her knees. The woman told the child to go away and emphasized the order with a furtive punch in the face which Mitchell was not meant to see. The child took no notice, accepting abuse as a spoilt child accepts endearments. She sat on the steps of the café, easing her naked behind slowly down from one step to the next, watching Mitchell all the time. She had an ugly face with a low forehead and a slack mouth; not an appealing child, but the dark, mongrel eyes were hungry for something. Mitchell drank the coffee, glad of its warmth, and ate one of the rolls. He wondered whether the child wanted food. There was no shortage of food in this efficient, well-ordered town, but perhaps humanity stopped somewhere short of this mangy little cur. There were barriers in every town. But if he made a gesture now, it would be the worse for the child later. If you can't see things through, you must stand aside. He finished his breakfast, paid and left no tip for the woman, no money for the child, no salve for his conscience. As he walked away, he saw the child crouching under one of the tables; the face peered up at him, the eyes still asking for something the dim little mind would never be able to put into words.

He walked on and turned into the main street. The sun was bright now; the shutters in the rooms above the shops were thrown back, he could see the bed linen draped across one balcony. The women were returning from the market, their bags laden, and the first tourists were strolling towards the quayside and the coach stations. There was a sense of purpose about the town. Days started hopefully here. But he could still see the child's eyes. Not much hope there. He had seen so many eyes like that, staring across barriers . . . It would be good to remove at least one barrier.

The idea came easily into his mind, as though it had al-

[134]

ways been there; but the reaction was sudden and tremendous. He realized, standing in the dazzling street, just what had happened to him in this last hour. He had become an individual again, no longer hemmed in by the old loyalties. The battle for the mind, the war of ideas, the conflict of ideologies . . . the phrases were drained of meaning; East and West had long ago merged into one vast wilderness of fear and hate. He was finished with causes. He was an individual, owing no allegiance to any power. The sense of release was exhilarating as the feeling one had going down a steep ski slope, the master of air and wind. He was an individual and he could take individual action. He could make that small, individual gesture that was the only thing that seemed important now.

He crossed the road and went up the street that led to the station; every now and then he stopped to look in a shop window. It was important to appear aimless. From now onwards he must always assume that he was being watched. There were several telephone booths at the station; he stood for a moment sorting coins in his hand, then he strolled across to a newspaper kiosk and got some small change. The telephone booths were engaged; he had to wait several minutes until a man came out of the far one. It was nearly nine o'clock when he got through to the pension where Miriam Kratz was staying. The receptionist told him she was in bed, but he insisted on speaking to her. When she came to the telephone, he told her to join him in Montreux. When she hesitated, he said:

"I can help you."

He did not regard himself as a traitor or a counter agent; these were labels one attached to other men, meaningless when applied to oneself. As for England, it was a green and pleasant land that he had not seen for quite a while; he bore it no ill will and did not think of it in relation to what he intended to do. The world had become very small, and the only people of any importance in it were himself and Mikail Kratz. Mikail Kratz was a good man; goodness was not a commodity of any commercial value, nevertheless it should occasionally be rewarded. He would give this good man an extension of time. It would be the most exciting assignment of all, the most dangerous, the most worthwhile. The current of energy flowed strong and steady through his body; he was supremely confident.

Chapter 14

Alperin looked at the bars of light falling across the sheet of paper. He traced the lines of light with his pen. It was the most positive thing he had yet done; but it didn't lead anywhere. Man, Alperin thought, was not meant to be free. He looked down at the parallel lines of light on the paper and absently joined them to form a parallelogram. That was that: he felt as though a door had been closed. His head began to ache and his body tensed again; the muscles at the back of his neck were rigid. He tried to send a message to his brain warning it against another bout of thought. But it was no use; already it was rushing like a panic stricken animal into one alley of thought, backing, heading blindly down another alley, backing again like a creature performing some terrible rite, moving frantically in ever-decreasing circles until in the end it would become a prisoner in the center of a web too intricate ever to be unwoven.

And this was freedom, this ultimate negation! He stabbed with his pen on the paper, saying through clenched teeth, "Stop it, stop it, stop it! Stop all this abstract mumbo jumbo and get down to the realities." Immediately, he was confronted with Huber and the Room. He could not go to Huber. He had freed his mind of the shackles of the Western world and he needed to cross another frontier, accept new limitations . . . But he could not do it through Huber; it was a physical impossibility for him ever to go near Huber again. It was equally impossible for him to go back to the Room.

He was annoyed with himself for even thinking of the Room. It was a small issue, quite unworthy of him. The Room was also small and quite unworthy of him; moreover, it faced east and was at the end of a long wing which meant that the heating system exhausted itself well before it reached this outpost. "I shouldn't survive in it for six months, let alone a year," he had told Sir Harry when it had first been suggested that he might change rooms. Sir Harry had said that he would not be in it for one month, let alone six. "You'd be in the lab most of the time." As though any of them could afford to spend time in the lab, now! They were reduced to the status of administrators. He had told Sir Harry that, and Sir Harry had offered to relieve him of some of his administrative duties. It never paid to argue with Sir Harry. Now he would be planning the reorganization, taking the more responsible of Alperin's administrative duties from him and giving them to the new young woman from Cambridge with her slovenly clothes and slovenly morals. She would have his room, too. While he . . . He pressed shaking hands against his lips and hissed, "The Room doesn't matter!" It was the work that mattered, the years of research into the means of destruction; it was this that was gradually corrupting him. He really must get his priorities right and remember that it was his soul and not his physical comfort that he was concerned about. He wanted to escape so that he could work on something creative; on soil improvement, on new ways of making the wilderness bring forth fruit, the desert flower . . . He would transform the virgin lands as Khrushchev had failed to do, he would devise a five year plan that would be the world's wonder. And he would never have to work in the Room.

He flung his pen down and bent forward, tears streaming down his face. He had been crying a great deal since he came to this hotel. The shock over Huber, the obscene affront to all his hopes . . . He screwed up the paper in front of him and threw it on the carpet. There were a lot of scraps of paper on the carpet, all blank. His speech for the conference remained unwritten.

He looked round the room. From a great distance, a voice was trying to reach him, telling him to go out of the hotel, to divert his mind . . . But it was no use. There was really no point in leaving the hotel until he knew where he was going. That made sense, didn't it? Unfortunately, at this moment his eyes rested on the mirror. The face that stared at him knew little about sense. The eyes were screwed up as though unable to bear even the dim light in this room, the mouth was slack, and everywhere shadows encroached, beneath the eyes, on each side of the mouth, around the jaw. He fingered the jaw. This, at least, could be remedied. It would not do to let his appearance go altogether.

He got up and went into the bathroom attached to his bedroom. He shaved with a shaking hand, cutting his chin and his left ear. He found sticking plaster and applied it clumsily, then he mopped up the blood. The blood made him feel faint and he had to sit on the lavatory seat and put his head between his legs. This stopped him fainting and seemed momentarily to clear his mind. He was more in command of himself when he went into the bedroom. Then there was a knock on the door.

His heart started to pound and panic had him in its grip again. It was only the chambermaid; she came every day to torment him with requests to do his room. He went to the

door, dragging his dressing gown round him. He opened the
door, looking down because he could not bear the bright
amusement in her eyes.

"I shan't be getting up today," he began, and then realized that he was staring at a pair of men's shoes. The shoes
moved forward. Alperin edged back.

"That's all right. We can talk in here."

As Alperin closed the door, he had the nightmare feeling
that although the voice was familiar, it was in some subtle
way different.

"It's hot in here," the voice said. "Do you mind if I pull
back the shutters?"

"It gets hotter then and . . ."

"No. It's much cooler here than at Maggiore."

The white, clear light invaded the room. Alperin put his
hands across his eyes.

"I came to see how you were getting on."

Alperin edged into a chair, keeping his back to the light.
He said:

"It's very kind of you."

But the voice had not been kind. There was a silence which
the man made no attempt to break. And yet, before, he had
always been so talkative, so overbearingly friendly . . .
Slowly, very slowly, Alperin raised his head. He saw a big
man, sitting easily in the armchair, his head slightly on one
side as he studied Alperin with an interest that was not
friendly. The eyes that met Alperin's were not friendly, either; they were the eyes of a shrewd buyer who will
not purchase an article that has been over-valued. Alperin
remembered that he had once wondered whether this
was the man with whom he would have to deal. His heart
began to beat very fast, his mouth was dry and his breath
whimpered through his lungs. The other man bent down

[140]

and picked up one of the crumpled pieces of paper. He unscrewed it, turned it over, raised his eyebrows.

"No inspiration?"

"It's not inspiration that's needed. Merely facts. Unfortunately, they have to be assembled in some form that can be presented to the conference next week."

"I thought you people always prepared this sort of thing months ahead?"

"Not always. Scientists aren't all efficient, you know."

"I would have thought that you were a methodical man."

"I . . ." Alperin looked at him again. It was as though the eyes were slowly drawing something from him. "My mind has been occupied with other things." As he said it, he experienced a sense of release, as though a boat had slipped its moorings and was slowly bearing him downstream. "You see, I am what I suppose you would call the dedicated type of scientist."

"Are you so different from other scientists in that respect?"

"Very much so! You mustn't believe everything you read about scientists, their single-mindedness, their disinterested curiosity . . . It's not true. They're as jealous as a bunch of prima donnas and quite as ruthless when it comes to upstaging each other."

Mitchell looked at Alperin's face; the features had sharpened and the eyes were keen as though a film had dispersed, the lips formed words carefully and expelled them with a snap of the small, even teeth. Mitchell said:

"You surprise me."

"Take Sir Harry, for example . . ."

"Sir Harry Gethryn? He's quite a personality, isn't he?"

"Personality!" Alperin rapped his knuckles on the arm of the chair. "Yes, precisely, he's a personality! Not a scientist."

"He seems to get results."

"Other men's results. Sir Lawrence Virnay, Maximilian Schmidt, Horner . . . myself."

Mitchell took out a packet of cigarettes. Alperin watched. His eyes went anxiously from the cigarette to the other man's face. Mitchell lit the cigarette and flicked the match away. He looked at the glowing tip of the cigarette, an expression on his face that seemed to Alperin to be quite terrifyingly judicial.

"Don't you exaggerate your own importance?"

"No." Alperin was ready for this. His words were chosen with precision. "I can assure you that over the years I have formed a good estimate of my own value. And if you do not think my judgment is sound in this instance, you must accept Sir Harry's judgment."

"He thinks you are good?"

"He wouldn't say so. But although he does everything he can to humiliate me, he has resisted every attempt to transfer me to another establishment."

Mitchell continued to study the cigarette tip. Alperin said quietly, "If you want proof of my usefulness, I can provide it."

"My dear man, I don't know enough about your work to know what would be useful." Mitchell's eyes met Alperin's coolly. "You must find some other way of convincing me."

"You're not a scientist?" Alperin spoke with authority, as though he was conducting an interview. Mitchell shook his head.

"And you have no scientific knowledge?"

"Very little."

"Then one must paint a picture for you in terms the layman can understand."

"If you please."

Alperin folded his hands in front of him, absently examining the freckled skin stretched across the knuckles.

"Do you know Kent?" he asked.

[142]

"Yes." For the first time Mitchell looked surprised.

"The part to the south east that is rather flat, where the eye travels a long way over the fields?"

"Yes."

"I sometimes visit acquaintances who have a farm in that region. I have stood in the fields on a still summer day, when the sky is blue and the sun is shining. You have probably done the same thing. You can see for miles. Cornfields, vegetables, a few small orchards, but mostly corn and vegetables." He clasped his hands and said with serene assurance, "I can turn that fertile land into a wilderness of stubble and rotting vegetation in which nothing will grow again during our lifetime." He smiled at Mitchell, a smile that might conceivably have been described as companionable. "I mention Kent as an example, you understand, because we both know it."

"I understand." Mitchell's voice was cool, his reaction to the smile was cooler still.

"You believe that I can do these things?"

"Yes."

There was a pause, then Alperin asked shyly:

"Have we progressed as far as that?"

"We?" Mitchell was angered by the familiarity.

"You must remember that one crosses the frontiers of the mind first." Alperin repeated the companionable smile. "For a long time, I have been thinking of myself as already . . . one of you."

Mitchell turned his head away.

"You mustn't imagine that I know much about this sort of thing," he said. "My concern is with people."

"But you must have some information, surely."

"On the contrary, the less one knows the better. I have merely to perform one task. Before doing it, I have to make up my mind whether the price is right."

"But how can you do that, if you don't . . . ?"

"I shall expect you to produce something of more substance than a word picture of rotting vegetation in Kent," Mitchell snapped. He was more on edge than Alperin now; he seemed to realize this, because he added in a more casual tone, "Incidentally, just to satisfy my own curiosity, how is this sort of devastation achieved?"

"Various ways. Do you remember a poem of Auden's, I wonder, in which there is a line, 'Something is going to fall like rain, and it won't be flowers'?"

"Auden isn't a scientist."

"But he has the right kind of vision for this century—a world in which something has shifted a little out of true. Don't you agree?"

Mitchell looked away again. Alperin, anxious not to lose his interest, went on eagerly:

"But there are other methods besides spraying, which is really a very unsophisticated method. Some of the latest discoveries have astonished even us. Do you remember a lot of fuss a couple of years ago about a farm where all the crops suddenly died of a mysterious disease?"

"I've been in Berlin a long time."

"You wouldn't know about it, then. The authorities were very puzzled. They decided that a team of experts should be sent to investigate. But before the experts arrived there was another catastrophe. Some petrol cans which had inexplicably been left in a shed on a piece of waste ground near to the farm were ignited and the whole of the farm land was ravaged. Nothing will grow there now." He looked expectantly at Mitchell, who responded somewhat woodenly:

"Are you telling me that this was some sort of exercise carried out by your people?"

"Good God, no! We wouldn't dare do that kind of thing."

"Then?"

"An accident. Someone dropped a capsule."

"A capsule!"

"Yes." Alperin glowed, delighted to have achieved an effect. "One small capsule, about the size of a cod-liver oil capsule and not at all dissimilar in appearance. It was a tremendous demonstration of success for us."

"And the fire?"

"Fire purifies. And, of course, we couldn't have allowed the investigation to proceed. Our establishment is very near that farm."

"Have you evidence of this?"

"I have newspaper cuttings about the disaster."

"And the capsule?"

Alperin touched his forehead. "I have that, too."

"I might arrange for you to talk to someone about the capsule."

"There have been improvements since then, of course. We are now able to produce micro-organisms of extreme virulence." Alperin leant forward, words coming fast. "Don't imagine that this is the extent of my knowledge, will you? There are other things, infinitely worse, I do assure you. You said that you were concerned with people; the devastation wreaked on the land is nothing compared to what we can do to human beings. We are on the verge of producing a virus so deadly that it could create an epidemic in which people would die as the rabbits died from myxomatosis; the whole population of a country could be wiped out."

Mitchell looked at Alperin with an expression on his face that Alperin could not understand.

"You're thinking how ghastly this is?" Alperin nodded his head energetically. "Don't imagine I don't realize it! Why do you think I'm trying to get away from it all?" His voice spiralled. "It's because I'm not the kind who can drug himself with platitudes; I can't tell myself that these dreadful discoveries will be kept in reserve, that we shall

[145]

never be the first to use them." He laughed bitterly. "I would have thought that Hiroshima had given the lie to that."

Mitchell said, "You needn't justify yourself to me."

"But I do worry about it." Alperin stared earnestly at Mitchell. "It's only natural, isn't it? People will call me a traitor. It's not a nice word."

"It's a word you will have to learn to live with."

"Yes. Yes, you're right, of course. I suppose one loses this absurd sensitivity after a time?"

An angry frown betrayed Mitchell's ragged temper. He got up and walked across to the writing desk where Alperin's notes were spread out.

"I don't think you will have much time for sensitivity from now on. This paper that you have to prepare for the conference should occupy your mind."

"Does the paper matter now?"

"Certainly it matters."

"But . . ."

"You wouldn't want anyone to get the impression that you were not returning to England, would you?"

Alperin looked sly and shook his head.

"And if you were returning, you would have to make a reasonably efficient job of this paper, wouldn't you?"

Alperin looked wise and nodded his head.

"So you must start working on it. And it had better be rather impressive."

Mitchell turned away quickly before Alperin could register agreement to this. Alperin watched him. He was longing for kindness, for a hand stretched out in the dark. But when Mitchell spoke again, his tone was more brusque than ever.

"Don't talk to anyone about this."

"No."

"Other people may approach you, but . . ."

"You mean that man, Huber?"

"For one."

"I can promise you I shall have nothing to do with him!"

"It isn't Huber with whom I am primarily concerned. You must not give any indication of this meeting, by word or action, to my companion."

"I thought you were working together," Alperin said, but not as though it really mattered. He was beginning to look rather dejected.

"No. We are not working together and you must be very careful of him."

Alperin said, "Yes, I'll be careful."

Mitchell went out of the room. Alperin sat staring at the closed door, doleful as a disappointed child. After a few minutes, he got up and went to the writing desk. He began to make notes for his speech at the conference; but every so often he looked up and his eyes moved uneasily round the room. It had been exciting to find someone to whom he could talk and he had experienced an extraordinary desire to form a friendship with the man to whom he had made this tremendous declaration. But now the excitement was draining away, leaving him exhausted and apprehensive.

Chapter 15

A scrap of paper twisted in the evening breeze on the platform. This unexpected hint of the slovenly combined with the greyness of late evening took him back to Berlin. He had expected that she would come transformed by hope, but the scrap of paper and the chill breeze dispersed this romantic illusion even before he saw her walking down the platform, stiff and straight, balanced on the razor's edge between hope and despair.

In front, a man and a woman greeted each other, arms encircled clumsily. Mitchell hesitated, shaken by a strong impulse to run away. Then, as she neared him she caught her foot in a strap trailing from a trolley and stumbled. He stepped forward and she was in his arms. He said, "Everything depends on this," and bending down, kissed her. It wasn't well done, but the other couple had been clumsy, too. He held her close to give her time to compose herself; he could feel her heart beating as though it must break free of her body, it was an uncomfortable sensation, but not without pleasure. When he released her, she did not look at him. The dark hair clamped across her forehead and formed dark furrows between her brows, the heavy lids pressed down on the eyes, the lips pressed inwards; she might have been willing herself a thousand miles from him. He said lightly, but with a trace of irritation he could not hide:

"You'll have to do better than that!"

He took her case, so small it made him feel ridiculous carrying it; he put his arm on her elbow and guided her forward.

"You couldn't manage a smile? It's important that people should think you have come here for me alone."

A taxi swung round in the yard in front of them; he pulled her back and she jumped violently at the sudden pressure on her arm. He said angrily:

"We shan't reach the hotel alive at this rate!"

She flashed him one of her most resentful looks. So far she had not spoken and her mouth was shut tight as though she never intended to speak. He hailed the taxi and bundled her inside. The sooner they reached the hotel and talked things over, the better. The taxi driver was watching them. Mitchell put his arm round her and drew her close; he bent his head so that the man could not see her stony face. She was very still, as though she feared that the slightest movement of the flesh might excite him. He whispered against her ear, "I won't hurt you. I promise I won't hurt you in any way." She moved her head and her cheek brushed against his mouth. She shivered. Her body became more tense than ever; it generated a current of excitement that made him wish that he had indeed asked her here for the conventional reason. It was a relief when they reached the hotel.

The hotel was large and impersonal and the staff were bored and incurious; it had seemed a good choice for his purpose when he booked the room. Now, seeing Miriam staring up at the heavy chandelier as though at any moment it might descend and blot out the universe, he cursed himself for lack of imagination. He brought her forward to sign the register. The receptionist gave her one brief up-and-down glance and looked away; she was not impressed, but she was not surprised, either. It was a long time since the hotel had had the kind of custom that went with the chandelier; now it relied mainly on bookings from the cheaper tour companies. Even the bellboy who relieved Mitchell of Miriam's inadequate case was not surprised.

"I'll see you settled in," Mitchell said as he stepped into the lift with Miriam.

He despatched the bellboy quickly once they were in the room. There was a light film of sweat on his brow; he had not been so ill at ease in such a situation since he was nineteen. He went to the window.

"You've got a nice view of the lake," he informed her.

He had chosen the room carefully. It was at the end of this wing of the building and it was separated from the next room by a linen cupboard. There was no balcony. Nevertheless, he closed the window before he turned back to the room.

"I like windows open," she said.

"There are times when I prefer them closed."

She was sitting on the edge of the divan, her knees pressed together, her head bent, her shoulders hunched forward; he could see the bones at the back of her neck where her hair parted, they looked brittle. The feeling of fear and excitement was almost tangible, demanding a physical response. One way and another, the chances of having a quiet talk seemed rather remote.

"Why don't you lie down?" he said. "You've had a tiring day."

For a moment she did not seem to hear; then she swung her legs on to the divan and stretched out. She was so taut she might have been on the rack.

He said, "Try to relax." He sat beside her and put one hand on her thigh. He was not quite sure what he intended to do and he was spared making a decision by the divan which gave slightly beneath his weight, throwing him against her. The next moment he was on the ground and there was blood in his mouth. He pulled her down beside him before her heels could gouge out his eyes. She used her nails after that, they were razor sharp; it was a good job there was no glass on the bedside table, he didn't like to think what she would have done with broken glass. She was remarkably strong, it took him all his strength to pin her down. Her face was ghastly, smeared with his blood, the eyes desperate as though reason was gradually being shredded away. "What do you think you're playing at!" he shouted. "There's no better way of rousing a man." She spat at him. He hit her hard across the face, twice; it was much more effective than shouting at her. When he was satisfied that the fight had gone out of her, he got up and went across to the wash basin. He rinsed his face, feeling shaken and very sorry for himself. He could hear her moving behind him; although there was a mirror over the wash basin he did not look in it, he did not care what happened now. He had thought that he could work a miracle for her; but she did not believe in him, and without her belief he could do nothing.

When he turned round she was lying on the divan, her hands folded across her stomach; there was a bruise across one cheek, but she looked quite calm and her eyes met his without resentment. He found a chair and placed it at a distance from the divan; he sat down, holding his handkerchief against his face which was still bleeding. He said wretchedly:

"Why did you come if you didn't trust me?"

She did not answer and he said angrily, "That was a stupid question, wasn't it? You can't pick and choose; you have to accept help wherever it comes from, even from rats like Curt Lesser."

[151]

He heard the divan creak as she slipped off it; he heard her feet padding across the room, the scrape of a chair as she dragged it across the boards. He mopped at his face again while she sat down and took a squashed packet of cigarettes from her handbag. She gave him a cigarette and lit it for him.

"You must not compare yourself to Curt Lesser."

She spoke more gently than he had ever heard her speak before; but she did not say that she trusted him.

"You said you could help me," she prompted.

"Only if you believe in me."

"I do believe in you." She accepted his rephrasing eagerly.

"Will you do what I tell you? It won't involve going to bed with me."

"Yes."

"Without question?"

"Yes." She sounded impatient.

"Think about that, it won't be easy."

She shrugged her shoulders. "If you ask questions you find out too much."

He finished smoking the cigarette in silence. It was stuffy in the room, he wished he had not shut the window. He felt uneasy, trapped by her calm acceptance. One moment he was helpless because she did not believe in him, the next moment he was frightened because she accepted too much. He stubbed out the cigarette and said:

"There are questions I have to ask. One in particular. You won't like it."

"Never mind."

"How can you be sure that your husband is still alive?"

She looked at him without flinching. "I know it."

He was not impressed by this kind of certainty.

"Do you mean you have heard from him lately, or that it is something you feel?"

"If he was dead, I would know . . ."

[152]

If he was dead, she would not want to go on living, so she believed he was alive. Mitchell said:

"That isn't proof enough for me."

"But I have no proof."

"Then we must find it."

"But that is impossible."

"On the contrary, it is quite easily arranged. Only I shall need your help. I want you to think very carefully tonight and see whether you can remember something that only your husband would know—some joke you had between yourselves, perhaps." Looking at her now it was hard to imagine they ever had jokes. "Whatever it is, it must be . . . one of the last things he would forget."

He did not want to put his doubt into words, but he saw by the expression on her face that she understood; she had, after all, grown up in a concentration camp. He said quickly to divert her attention:

"It must be something quite simple, a name for a doll your child played with, provided it is unusual enough, or the beginning of a sentence that he alone could complete."

"Yes . . ." She sounded doubtful. He guessed that now that the opportunity to find out about her husband's fate had been presented to her, she was a little afraid. In the morning he would help her, but he was too tired now. He said:

"There is one other thing I want you to do. It is important that people should think that you are my mistress. You understand that?"

"Yes."

He took out his wallet and counted out notes.

"Buy yourself some clothes. Act as though you are enjoying doing something you haven't been able to do for a long time. Be brazen about it. You understand?"

"Yes."

[153]

She took the money and stuffed it away in her bag. He got up and looked at himself in the mirror.

"And finally, I think you will have to go out and get some sticking plaster. I can't go out like this."

When she had gone, he opened the window. It was dark now. He could see a pleasure boat moving towards the jetty; the sound of music carried over the water. He remembered standing at the door of Claus's flat; it seemed a long time ago.

When Miriam came back she had sticking plaster, a bottle and a roll of cotton wool. She wanted to tend him, and although her hands were rather dirty he did not argue; they had hurt each other enough already. She shook a few drops from the bottle on to the cotton wool and dabbed at the scratches on his face. It hurt and he gritted his teeth.

"Oh, you are so English!" she chided. "Why don't you cry out, make a fuss? It will feel better then."

She took the towel and held it under the tap, then she bathed his face; she was more expert than he had imagined, and more gentle. She put the plaster on, one strip above the left temple, the other on the right cheek. She took time smoothing it out; and then, as though reluctant to finish their work, her fingers travelled lightly across the cheekbone, down the side of the mouth. He pressed his head against her breast like a child demanding comfort and she held him close. It was a long time since any demand had been made on her tenderness; she had thought the source had withered, but now she was filled with the longing to be a woman again. She let him go and backed away from him. He looked up, surprised, a little awed. She turned away quickly.

"You must go now."

The blood pulsed in her veins; she could hear nothing but the beating of her heart. Her body was rent with the bitter pain, the incredible, ecstatic wonder of being a woman again. The room seemed to be full of light. The curtains

[154]

swayed towards her, almost as though someone had passed through them, then the life went out of them and they fell limp against the window frame. She did not realize at first that the draught had been caused by the opening and shutting of the door. When she turned round, the room was empty.

"That is good," she said to herself. "Anything might have happened if he had stayed."

But she felt no relief. To occupy herself, she began to clear up the mess in the room. She picked up the bottle and screwed on the cap, then she cleared away the dirty cotton wool and washed out the towel. When she had finished, she hung the towel over a chair to dry in the night breeze. The pleasure boat was moving out, the lights winking in the dark water; she could hear music and she could see a few couples dancing. She leant against the window frame, listening to the pulse of the music that told her insistently that she had something to give, something to give, something to give that must be given soon. Surely she could not be expected to wait while she grew dry and cold again. It was hard on Mikail that he should sow this seed of tenderness for another to reap; but that was the way of life.

She reached up quickly and pulled the curtains across the window.

Chapter 16

Eliot had not slept. Life was a cunning device, its torments infinitely skilful; and one of the most skilful twists of all was the fact that the human sensitivity could only appreciate good fortune in retrospect. Who valued sleep when it came readily? He eased himself up against the headrest of the bed. He was glad to see that the curtains, which had seemed darkly substantial an hour ago, were now reduced to their natural threadbare state. The struggle for sleep could be abandoned. He pulled back the crumpled grey sheets and swung his legs over the edge of the bed; he sat breathing uneasily, studying the ivory of the shin bones, the purple veins that clotted the calves. How he hated the ugliness of the human body! When he felt able to make the effort, he got up and shuffled across to the window. The parted blinds revealed an ashen sky. It would rain soon, but as he was not in the least responsive to atmosphere, this did not trouble him.

He sat on the couch by the window, tugging his dressing gown round his thin body for warmth. There was so little to think about; the world had shrunk during this last illness and now it seemed nothing but an old, empty skull in which there lodged only a few particles of dust. But the dust irritated, and the irritation caused some kind of friction which set his mental process working again. He was annoyed about Burke. Behind the man's simulated anger, the studied scorn, there had lurked a more genuine emotion. The irritating thing was that Eliot could not define that emotion. He had been too concerned with himself at the time: a bad mistake, and one bad mistake had led to another. He did not like making mistakes and he found it difficult to tolerate the fact that a man like Burke should have teased him into making one. Now, sitting in this grey room, alone and undisturbed, he could not think why it had been so imperative to put an end to Burke's stabbing questions, to rid himself of that grating, overcharged nervous energy. He clawed at the dressing gown again and the collar rubbed against his face; the garment smelt of death. And that, of course, was why he had had to get rid of Burke. He had thought that he was dying and a man's right to die alone overrides every other consideration; so he had spat out the truth to Burke, knowing that this would get rid of him more effectively than anything else. Now, when death had momentarily evaded him, he was annoyed with himself. There was no knowing what a man like Burke would do with such a dangerous commodity as truth. One thing at least was certain, he would need watching.

It was tiresome, but it provided a way of passing the time. The alternative was to sever his connection with time once and for all. Since he had never valued life, this seemed the obvious solution; but he had become absorbed by the pain and was not yet prepared to reject it for oblivion. He got up and made his way to the desk where the telephone stood.

"I have some new information about Alperin," he told

[157]

Burke when he arrived an hour later. "He will need a much more careful watch than I had thought."

"And the new information?"

Eliot's fingers twisted the strands of hair that fringed his dome-shaped scalp, the movement went on and on, the unceasing, senseless fidgeting of a sick person. His eyes regarded Burke reproachfully, as though he had said something in bad taste. Burke, unimpressed by the performance, repeated his question. Eliot said:

"All I can tell you is that you must watch Alperin very carefully and report to me here every day."

"We shan't have much time to watch Alperin if we do that."

"Leave that side of it to Mitchell. You can report to me."

"I'll come twice a week."

There was a new authority about Burke. Eliot found this surprising since the man was undoubtedly afraid. He did not mind being surprised, provided he was confident of ultimate success, so he said:

"You may come twice a week."

It was going to be more interesting to break Burke than he had thought; there was an element of courage in the man for which he had not bargained.

"I shall look forward to seeing you on Thursday," he said as Burke left him.

It was eight o'clock when Burke left Eliot's flat. The rain had just begun. Miriam Kratz woke with the feel of it in her bones and decided to indulge in the unaccustomed luxury of a hot bath. The bathroom door was locked, but she had seen the chambermaid put the key on a hook in the broom cupboard so this difficulty was soon overcome. The real problem was how to get water. She studied the bewildering battery of shining round taps and decided to work from left to right. The first sent a shower down on her head and shoulders, blinding her; the second sent a gush of scalding water over her hand; the third merely increased the volume of water. As she now had no idea which tap was which she wrenched at the nearest and the top came off in her hand. By this time there was a lot of water everywhere. A lever operated the plug; she pulled hard in the wrong direction and it jammed. Obviously she would have to bathe quickly. She flung down the raincoat which served her as a dressing gown, and stepped into the water. It was uncomfortably hot and came up to her waist; the water in the shower was uncomfortably cold. She soaped her body rapidly. Someone had left a bottle of shampoo on the shelf at the end of the bath; it seemed a pity to waste it so she emptied the contents over her hair. She felt elated and hummed a coarse Berlin street ballad as she rubbed vigorously. Thanks to the rather too abundant lather, she could no longer see what was happening but she could feel the water creeping up her breasts. An agreeable sensation. When she had finished her hair, she lay back and let her legs float up. She lay there, feeling more relaxed than she had ever felt in her life, and watched the water creep up to the level of the taps. She supposed that eventually she would float over the side. She had a vision of the hotel corridor transformed into a canal and herself drifting down it. There was something extraordinarily pleasing about this idea and she abandoned it reluctantly. There would be a lot of unpleasantness when the water reached the corridor. She clambered out of the bath. While she groped for her towel and raincoat the shower sprayed her buttocks with icy water and a series of electric shocks seemed to pass through her body. A wave of water slopped over the side of the bath. She struggled into her raincoat without drying herself and hurried to the door. As she left the room, she had a glimpse of water, frothed with shampoo, snaking across the floor. She ran lightly down the corridor to her room.

She dried herself, put on her black dress and combed her hair. Her usually sallow face was pink, beaded with sweat, and rags of dark hair fell across her forehead; her eyes smarted, her heart was thudding and her skin felt as though she had been beaten with a bristle brush. Altogether, it had been a most stimulating experience. She found her shoes and put them on with difficulty because her feet were swollen. Then she went to the door. There was a lot of activity on the landing; someone was shrieking from the direction of the bathroom and she passed a porter carrying a mop and bucket. The porter apologized for getting in her way. She took the lift and went down to the restaurant where she had an excellent breakfast.

It was cold in the street and the rain stabbed painfully at the backs of her legs which felt raw and vulnerable after the hot bath. She hurried along, glancing quickly from right to left as the first shops appeared. On the corner of the street where the trams swung round on the way to Villeneuve, there was a shop which had a show window of dark mirrors with one brilliant twist of magenta in the center. As she stood staring at the bright colour a strong gust of wind swirled up between her legs and before she knew what had happened she was standing in the entrance to the shop.

The assistant, a thin woman with hair like rusty nails, looked at her as though the wind had blown a crumpled leaf across the immaculate threshold. Miriam said:

"I want to try on that dress in the window."

The assistant gave a bleak smile. "That is a slip, madame."

She moved across to close the door and seemed surprised to find Miriam on the inside.

"Then I will try on the slip."

The assistant hesitated, and while she was meditating

[160]

her next move, Miriam glanced around. There was a small bronze model of an emaciated nude on a stand nearby; the nude was leaning forward holding an absurd froth of a brassière between her teeth while an extravaganza of frills trailed from one hand. Miriam pointed:

"I will try those, too."

The assistant moved reluctantly across the floor. Over her shoulder, she said:

"They are very expensive."

"So," Miriam said, "I had supposed."

The assistant looked surprised. Miriam felt surprised, too. The assistant capitulated.

"This way, madame."

She pulled back a dark crimson curtain and touched a button so that light flooded a small cubicle. She stood watching, her nostrils pinched together, while Miriam unzipped her dress; after a moment she averted her eyes. Miriam took advantage of this to close the curtains.

The door of the shop opened. The assistant greeted someone in French which Miriam did not understand very well.

The brassière was no more than a ruched tape covering the nipples. The frilled extravaganza turned out to be a pair of briefs whose only purpose could be to titillate the imagination. Miriam prowled in front of the mirror, excited by the brilliance of the colour which heightened the attractions of her body. The slip was a heavy taffeta, it was tight and it pulled against her thighs as she drew it on. She looked at the price tickets; the figures were beyond belief, she would have kept her family for months on such a sum. She stood looking down, thinking how much she wanted these beautiful things and how much she would like to score over the thin-faced bitch outside. Beyond the curtains, it was quiet. She went across and peered through the gap. The thin-faced woman had gone and in her place there was a plump blonde

[161]

girl, who looked attractive but not intelligent. Miriam scrambled into her dress. She zipped it up and then parted the curtains.

"I am waiting for the underclothes," she said plaintively.

The blonde looked surprised. "I thought you were trying something on, madame."

"No. The other one said she would bring me a slip, brassiere and briefs." Miriam smoothed her dress down and added sedately, "Nothing very expensive, of course."

The blonde brought tailored cottons. "We do not stock any cheap lines, madame."

Another customer came in. Miriam drew the curtains and examined the price tickets; the garments were certainly not cheap, but the total figure was one with which she could come to terms.

"These will do," she said, emerging from the cubicle. She paid and went out. She could feel the taffeta slip moving against her thighs. It gave her a feeling of extreme physical satisfaction.

Inspired by success, she bought a brilliant orange dress and a turquoise coat. She also bought a pair of patent leather shoes and a handbag to match. While the assistant was packing the handbag, Miriam appropriated a gilt Catherine-wheel brooch. She felt she owed it to Mitchell to make what economies she could.

She hurried back to the hotel and put on the new clothes. The effect was flamboyant but not ineffective. But as she stared at the mirror, it was not the clothes that most surprised her. It was a long time since she had really looked at herself in the mirror and it was disconcerting to find a stranger there. The face, a little browner, was familiar enough; but a different person looked out from it. Miriam said defensively, "Mikail would understand." But the eyes that met hers were not satisfied. She realized in surprise that it was no longer enough to say that Mikail would understand; there was someone else with whom she had to reckon now. She wondered how long that other person had been there.

She turned away from the mirror. What harm could there be in finding pleasure in new clothes? Especially as she had not even paid for the expensive underclothes. She picked up the brooch and pinned it on the lapel of the coat; it looked very well there. She went out of the room.

The rain had stopped and the clouds were tearing apart, revealing ragged fragments of blue sky. Miriam walked towards the quayside where there were a number of cafés fronting the lake. In the distance, the outline of the mountains hardened as the mist began to clear. She did not like mountains. She crossed the road near the coach depot, stepping carefully over the puddles. She was so anxious not to dim the brightness of the shoes that she did not hear the car approaching until someone shouted. A wave of water broke over her and she was in the gutter. A man ran forward to help her. The last time she had been in the gutter was when the police broke up a bread queue in East Berlin; a policeman had beaten her and no one had come forward to help her. But she had not cried as now she cried for the turquoise coat and the shining patent leather shoes. She brushed aside the man who had helped her to her feet and rushed back to the hotel. The staff, shaken out of their indifference, gathered round her convinced that she had suffered some terrible injury; but she thrust them aside and raced up the stairs. In her room she gave way to a paroxysm of rage that petrified the chambermaid who was sorting linen in the adjacent cupboard. Conflicting emotions tore her body, anger, bewilderment, disappointment, and most provocative of all, guilt.

In the end, guilt won. It was a comparative newcomer in her range of feeling, but it seemed nevertheless that it had come to stay. She sponged down the coat. There was hope for it, the water had not been dirty; but it would never seem so gay again. The bright shoes had cracks across the toes now. Her leg was bruised and her ankle was grazed, but this did not bother her. She ran cold water in the basin and plunged her swollen face into it; when she looked a little better, she went out again. She did not want to stay in her room, thinking about the clothes which had looked so splendid and would certainly have excited Stephen Mitchell when he came to see her.

She looked carefully both ways before she crossed to the quayside. She went into one of the cafés and ordered coffee. The waiter asked if she wanted cream and pastries, but she said no: she had had her extravagant moment. She was sipping the coffee when Burke came in. His eyes went to her table immediately, no pretense that he had not been following her.

"It was you in that car," she said when he joined her.

"I thought I recognized you. But you looked so different that I had to come rather close to make sure."

She made no protest; protests, in her experience, never served a useful purpose. He ordered coffee and cream and pastries. After that he studied her thoughtfully, his eyes taking in the coat, the orange dress, the new handbag, the shoes. Eventually, he said:

"A long way from the Brandenburg Gate."

"There's no point in waiting there for ever."

The waiter came with coffee. Coffee was a ritual with Burke. He handled the jug as though he were celebrating mass. When he took sugar he seemed to stop breathing while the long, fastidious fingers held the spoon delicately poised over the cup; even one granule in the saucer would offend him. When the ceremony was completed, he said:

"Is there any point in waiting here?"

"I have to pass the time." Mitchell had told her to be

brazen. "So why shouldn't I enjoy myself? After all, I'm a woman."

She might have said something blasphemous, the way he reacted; his hand tightened, the cup shook and coffee slopped into the saucer. He sat staring at the spilt coffee as though it represented a personal outrage. She was surprised, but not displeased. She leant forward. The dress had a scooped neckline, even the assistant had raised her eyebrows when she saw the effect: Burke went white. Miriam said:

"I *am* a woman, you know."

He drew back in his chair, his thin little body looking incredibly frail. She threw back her head and laughed, a strident laugh that made people turn to look at them. Burke's face seemed to wither. He would be more careful how he spoke to her another time; she was sure of this because she had had to be careful all her life. Refugees can't afford to take risks, and neither can cripples. She finished her coffee and got up.

"You can pay the bill," she said loudly.

She walked slowly along the promenade. The incident had excited her. She did not often take the offensive and win. There was no knowing what she could do, where she might go; for a moment, life seemed to open out before her. She was still young, it was wrong to allow herself to be shackled by the past. But that other person who had stared at her from the mirror believed otherwise.

Chapter 17

Mitchell did not come to see Miriam until the middle of the afternoon. It was hot and airless; petrol fumes hung in the air mixed with the aromatic smell of the shrubs as he walked through the garden to the hotel. Inside, the shutters were down and the hall was dark. It was the least active time of the day; the guests were out and the hotel staff were about their own affairs. Mitchell's footsteps echoed hollowly on the marble floor as he crossed to the lift.

Miriam was sitting by the window and she did not turn her head when he came into the room.

"Don't you usually lock your door?" he asked.

"I don't like being shut in."

She still did not look at him. The shutters had not been drawn and the window was wide open, but there was no breath of air in the room. Immediately below the window the bright awning over the sun lounge was still and in the garden the leaves on the trees did not move; this was the dead hour of the afternoon. He looked down at Miriam. She at least was vividly alive in a tangerine dress; but her attitude had changed, she was quiet and withdrawn. This in no way detracted from her appeal. Tangerine and olive skin, black hair and blacker eyes . . . All this planning and plotting, what was it worth? There was more satisfaction to be gained in one hour here than in the whole of the hazardous scheme to which he had dedicated himself. There was a tiny hollow of shadow beneath the broad cheekbone, as though a sculptor had pressed his thumb lightly into the flesh . . . While he was examining this delightful discovery, she sighed and said:

"I've tried so hard to remember."

"Remember?" he repeated blankly.

"About my husband." She turned her head, her eyes puzzled. "Something to tell you . . . but it's so difficult."

She looked away again, baffled by her inability to remember. For years the world had been Mikail; he had grown within her until there was no reality but him. Yet now, when another person was concerned with him, when she was asked to talk about him as a man among men, she found that there was a blank space where once he had been. Behind her, Mitchell said:

"There are so many memories. It must be difficult to select."

He did not sound as though the words meant anything in particular. When she looked at him again, she saw that his eyes were examining the brilliant dress, the soft folds of material falling away from the scooped neckline. It was the eyes that had drawn her to him, long ago when she first met him, kind eyes that brought a brief warmth to the mean winter afternoon; now the eyes were hard and their brightness hurt. She said sharply:

"Can't you help me? Tell me the kind of thing you want to know."

He said woodenly, "What is your daughter's name?"

"Naomi."

"Did you have a pet name for her?"

" 'Pet' name?"

"Never mind. Tell me about her. Is she like you?"

He was rapping out questions savagely now. She stared at him, unable to express her feelings and he shouted at her:

"What's the matter? You want her back, don't you?"

"Want her back!"

"Well then, you must learn to think about her again, talk about her . . ."

"It's no use!" She was shouting, too. "How can I talk to you about her? You have no children."

His head jerked back as though she had hit him; his complete unpreparedness touched her more than anything else could have done because it made her realize how much he was at her mercy. She said, "I'm sorry."

"She might not want to come back. Had you thought of that?"

He could not get control of himself and his voice shook. She was too sorry for him to be angry. She said quietly, turning away from him:

"It's no use asking questions about Naomi. I can't answer them."

"But when you see her? What then?"

"I shall have to begin from there."

Mikail had said that every day is a beginning. In the hot, dry room she could hear his voice, husky with fatigue, and she had a glimpse of the real man, quieter and less masterful than the godlike creature memory had created. A tired man, the clinic had always been under staffed; but now, sitting beside this other man and seeing her husband as a stranger, she suddenly understood that there was another reason for the tiredness. He was lonely. She saw it very clearly now that she stood apart from him; there had been no one with whom he could share his burden, he had had to have courage for both of them. Her lips moved, she scarcely realized that she was speaking aloud.

"He said once that 'one should never make decisions in the evening; the evening is for despair.'"

"That doesn't sound the kind of thing he would remember." Mitchell's voice was a long way away, much further away than the voice of Mikail.

"He would remember," she said.

He would remember because the words were branded on his spirit. She had always been grateful to him for all that he had given her, but she had never asked how much it cost him; he had seemed to have an inexhaustible well of strength within him and it had not occurred to her that he might drain himself to give to her. She sat still, looking across the bright summer garden, trying to comprehend how much she owed him. Mitchell, watching her, noticed how strained the eyes had become, as though they were trying to penetrate beyond the natural limits of vision. He remained silent, knowing that he had lost her and could only wait now. After a while she turned and began to speak calmly about her husband and child, telling him everything she could remember that might be helpful; she named the child's dolls, described the few treasured toys, told of her first meeting with her husband. When she had finished, she sat back in the chair, withdrawn from Mitchell; she asked no questions when he got up to leave. He said:

"You won't speak of this to anyone, will you?"

"Who would I speak to?"

"Burke, for example."

"Oh, Burke!" She shrugged her shoulders. "No, I shan't speak to him."

"Try not to worry too much about all this. Don't think or make plans or . . ."

But she was not listening. She was sitting with her hands

folded in her lap, her face turned so that the light from the window fell on it. He noticed again the way that she was changing. There were cracks in the smooth brown flesh of the face and the bones were more prominent; the woman was taking the place of the gamin. In a few years she would look gaunt, but durable. He thought about her as he walked down the stairs and made his way into the street. When he first saw her, enigmatic in the exotic dress, he had been so physically excited that he could scarcely trust himself to look at her; but now, the physical excitement had been replaced by something more irrevocable than desire. It would be more difficult than he had imagined to go through with his plans.

Chapter 18

Huber had arrived. Mitchell saw him that evening strolling along the promenade between the brilliant shrubs bordering the lake and the smooth green lawns of the hotels; he looked sad and alien in his flashy blue suit, a creature more at home in an Arab market, one would have thought, although in reality he would have been equally out of place there. Huber belonged to places that had lost their distinctive flavour, to a landscape reduced to shadows and rubble; it was strange to see him here in this calm, self-satisfied town, a reminder of the dark side of the world's coin.

He knew that Mitchell was watching him and he stopped to light a cigar. Over his shoulder Mitchell saw the waters of the lake, still as glass in the evening light, the mountains massed together, dark and heavy. Huber flicked the match away, his spread fingers cocking a snook; and suddenly all this magnificence seemed nothing but a trick, one half expected it to go out of focus and disintegrate leaving only Huber and the cigar.

Huber tilted his head back and exhaled; he kept his head back and watched the smoke spiral upwards in the still air.

He was waiting and he was not being subtle about it; there was a contemptuous assurance in the way he waited. And indeed he had a right to be assured! This, surely, was the opportunity for which Mitchell had been waiting. While Huber was watching the smoke, Mitchell walked past him; he did not turn his head or slacken his pace until he had reached Chillon. It was a long walk from the town to Chillon, but he was still shaking with rage when he reached the castle. He stood staring at it. He had thought he had travelled a long way since he stood in Bonivard's prison; it was a surprise to find that all he had done was to change direction. The old Mitchell remained, stubborn, conservative, and very proud. No matter what happened, this man would never deal with Huber. But it had recently become a habit to ask questions, and now he wondered whether he could afford this kind of pride.

Fortunately, it was not necessary to answer this particular question, since there was no need for him to go to Huber. He had walked along the promenade, telling himself that he must sort out the information he had gleaned from Miriam Kratz before he took the next move. In reality, he had been trying to delay taking that move. But the arrival of Huber aroused his professional instincts; he knew that the time for deliberation had passed. Automatically he turned and made his way to the Hotel du Lac Léman.

"I want Josef Novak," he said, "I am a friend of his."

They had not even exchanged names, but as he watched the receptionist studying the register he was quite sure that this was the name the man would be using. While the receptionist bent over the book, the telephone operator turned round.

"He is in Room 39." She looked at the receptionist, laughing.

"Oh, Room 39!" The receptionist laughed, too. Their ex-

pressions suggested that Room 39 was that rare phenom-
enon, a genuine personality. The receptionist looked at
Mitchell.

"What name shall I give?"

"Stephen Mitchell."

The last step had been taken; there was no going back
from this point. He felt old and tired and no longer very sure
of himself; perhaps, after all, it would have been less painful to deal with Huber. He didn't give a damn what Huber
thought of him.

Josef Novak had a room on the first floor, an end room
with a private bathroom adjacent to it. The door had been
left hospitably open and when Mitchell entered, Novak
was standing by a table pouring drinks; he was wearing a
scarlet silk dressing gown and he looked like a character
out of Tolstoy preparing for one of those wild Russian parties that intersperse long periods of introspection. But Novak
was not introspective and his eyes were particularly aware
as he handed Mitchell a Pernod, saying "A votre santé!"
After that he did not speak. Neither man felt in the mood
for preliminaries; they knew the game and they understood
each other, and that being so, the first moves could be elim-
inated. It was risky, but neither of them minded risks. Mitchell said:

"I have a problem, that I would like to discuss with you."

"A difficult one, I hope."

"For a time it seemed insoluble."

"And now?"

"I think I may have found a solution."

"Then why come to me?"

"Your views on the practicability of the solution would
be helpful."

"Why not back your own judgment? You don't appear
to be a tentative man."

"In this instance you have the advantage of me."

"Do tell me why."

"You seem to be a man who has travelled widely."

"You give that impression yourself."

"Nevertheless, I think you have a knowledge of places that I have never visited."

"I have been to South America, certainly."

"Precisely."

Novak took a packet of cigarettes from his pocket, Rothmans, not the kind to go with the flamboyant dressing gown; the Pernod did not fit into the pattern either. Mitchell accepted a cigarette, aware that he had been stopped at the moment when he was keyed to tell his story. He appreciated the move and judged that it might be best to seem slightly rattled. He lit the cigarette and said rather edgily:

"You must be wondering where all this is leading."

"To South America, presumably."

Mitchell looked at the tip of his cigarette and addressed his next remark to it.

"I am interested in someone who is in prison there. Perhaps with your knowledge of South America you can advise me . . ."

"There is no point in being interested in anyone who is foolish enough to get himself into prison in South America."

"No?"

"No."

They looked at each other and Novak got to his feet and reached for Mitchell's empty glass. Mitchell said, watching the man's back as he poured the drinks:

"I had been hoping that my friend could join me over here."

"What an amusing idea!" Novak's shoulders shook; he threw back his head and laughed until the glasses shivered and drink slopped on to the table. Mitchell waited; the

[174]

laughter was not purely for effect, the man was enjoying himself. Novak reached for the soda siphon but did not appear to make much use of it. When at last he turned and handed the glass to Mitchell the lines of laughter were still there, but they were cracks in a mask and the eyes were hard.

"You will need more than impertinence."

"So I imagined. That is why I thought that you might be able to advise me."

Novak sipped his drink; Mitchell wondered whether the mixture was as strong as his own.

"I don't specialize in advice," Novak said. "But I should like to hear the story, if it's as entertaining as the prelude."

"It's a rather dull story. In fact, that is why I feel it has possibilities." He paused, but this time Novak did not create a diversion. "This man is a doctor and he made the mistake of looking after a man who was wanted by the police. The wanted man was not of any importance—a bank clerk trying to leave the country to join his mother who lived just across the border. He was taking a little of the bank's money with him, but the doctor did not know that and had he known it is possible that he would not have acted differently. The doctor was betrayed by one of his patients. He has been in prison ever since."

"As you say, a dull story."

"But it has the virtue of being uncomplicated; the doctor is of no importance to the State."

"Had he committed any other crime?"

"He is a Jew."

"Then he is probably dead by now."

"That I should want to know, of course."

For a moment the eyes which stared at him were quite still and they seemed to have darkened. It was the only sign of real interest he had given so far.

[175]

"And what am I expected to do?"

"Find out whether the man is alive or not."

"I'm not as influential as you imagine. Nor am I interested in your affairs."

"I'm prepared to pay."

Novak stared at him incredulously; and then he laughed, but not quite so violently as before.

"Tell me," he said, leaning forward, one hand on the table between them, "What will you give me?"

"A molecular biologist named Alperin."

Novak sat back in his chair; if he had had cards in his hands, Mitchell felt that he would have tossed them down on the table. Or perhaps he would have dealt another hand, his next words made this seem more likely.

"And just supposing I wanted a molecular biologist—and I should need a lot of convincing on that point—why do you imagine that I should need your help to get one?"

"If you wanted a famous painting wouldn't it be simpler to have it handed to you by the caretaker, rather than break into a well-guarded art gallery?"

"I don't like simplicity."

"But you do like success."

"Nor do I like weak links."

"The caretaker, you mean?"

"Yes." Novak put his glass down. He looked at Mitchell, that direct glance that Mitchell had found naïve but very disconcerting when he first met the man. "Let us talk about the caretaker. He interests me more than the other characters."

Sweat broke out on Mitchell's forehead; he met Novak's gaze, but it took an effort and he felt the muscles around his eyes quivering with strain. Novak looked down into his glass, but not before Mitchell had seen the first flicker of doubt. Unrehearsed effects are always best; his discomfort

[176]

would do more to create the desired impression than anything else. No matter that he stammered a little as he said:

"This man . . . this Jew . . . he is the husband of a woman with whom I am rather deeply involved."

"Then the longer you keep them apart the better surely?"

"She doesn't see it that way."

"One can always withdraw from these affairs."

"I think entanglement would be the better word in this case."

Novak picked up his glass and took a few sips of Pernod, he frowned as though something about the drink displeased him; he was slowing down the pace now, not in order to disconcert Mitchell, but to give himself time to think.

"Why did you let this happen?" he asked eventually. "You're not without experience."

"I've never been very successful at handling women. But until now the difficulties have always been emotional and personal . . . I didn't realize this was different until it was too late."

Novak looked at him. He was dealing with a traitor and the word still had meaning for him; yet the other day, this man had seemed his equal. Novak was puzzled, reluctant to admit that he had made an error of judgment. Pride was involved, and something else, too; as he studied Mitchell's face, there was a hint of regret in his eyes. Mitchell sensed the regret and he felt that whatever people said about him afterwards, he would never be touched as he was touched at this moment; he wished that he could explain, but since he scarcely understood his motives himself this was impossible. It was best to get things over quickly. He said:

"You surely don't imagine this is some kind of a trick? Whatever else we might do, we should hardly offer you one of our scientists—particularly at the present time when there is an outcry about inadequate security arrangements."

Novak shrugged his shoulders. "One makes sacrifices."

"We are not allowed to sacrifice prime ministers."

Novak smiled suddenly. "We are more fortunate sometimes." The sally seemed to ease the tension between the two men. Novak offered Mitchell another cigarette and said pleasantly, "It is you that I don't trust."

"I don't expect you to trust me any more than I trust you. But I am still waiting for your advice as to whether my plan has a chance."

"There's rather a glut of scientists just now. Much would depend on the value of this man, Alperin."

"The fact that I am here to watch him is proof of his value, surely?"

"But as you yourself have said, your people are excessively sensitive just now; they chaperon the most unattractive creatures."

"I've no doubt that some evidence of his usefulness could be provided. Perhaps at the same time as you give me the proof I need."

"Proof?"

"I want to know that the doctor is alive, remember?"

"I'm not at all sure how that could be arranged—other than your taking my word for it, of course."

"I think we can do better than that."

Mitchell felt in his pocket and produced a sheet of paper. He handed it to Novak with an air of assurance that he was far from feeling. Whatever Novak thought of the list, his expression gave nothing away, he merely said:

"It would be helpful to have the man's name."

"Dr. Mikail Kratz."

"And he was arrested, when?"

"In July, 1962 at his clinic—the particulars are given on the paper attached to the list. For a time he was at the Nieman prison, but he has been moved from there."

The Pernod was having its effect now. Mitchell felt he could not go on much longer. Novak was sitting quietly, looking at the notes Mitchell had given him; Mitchell had the impression that he, too, would be glad when the interview was over. He finished his drink and got up.

"I shan't do anything until I hear from you."

Novak did not get up immediately. He was still looking down at the notes in his hand; he said quite casually:

"And in return for this doctor you are offering Alperin . . ."

"Yes."

"Is that all?"

Mitchell stared at him, too tired by now to think. Novak looked up.

"You must have thought about your future, surely? I suppose I can say that other transactions will follow?" As Mitchell did not answer, he said impatiently, "You're not an amateur, after all. You know that once you start on this kind of thing there is no turning back."

"Tell them there will be other transactions."

Mitchell closed the door and went out of the hotel quickly. It was a bright, warm night and there were a lot of people walking along the promenade, laughing and talking or staring aimlessly across the lake. Mitchell sat on a seat. There did not seem to be anywhere to go now.

Chapter 19

Until this moment, Burke had been very sure where he was going and why. An hour ago nothing had seemed more important than this venture; but something had gone wrong with the timing and the effects of the pill he had taken were beginning to wear off at the moment when he needed to feel supremely confident. He looked out of the lavatory window. The ledge was there all right, at least eight inches wide. It should be quite easy for anyone as small and agile as he was to climb out of the window and lower himself on to the ledge; then all he had to do was to walk along the ledge to the corner of the building, turn the corner and walk a few yards along the front of the hotel to that convenient drain-pipe. It was the corner that worried him, corners were never easy to negotiate. He could see the cars flashing along the main road; the main road was as well-lit as most of the roads in this blastedly efficient country. There was a chance that he would be seen, but fortunately the hotel stood well back with a disordered garden in front of it. Burke wished that the shrubbery extended right up to the hotel, but in fact there was an uncompromising concrete drive some

thirty feet below him. A pity he hadn't Mitchell's head for
heights. But he was agile as a monkey, surefooted as a cat,
and far from finished at forty. Yes, please God, far from
finished at forty . . . He lowered himself out of the window, gained a footing on the ledge and made his way to
the corner of the building without difficulty. When he
stopped, the pounding of his heart was louder than the throb
of traffic in the road, but that was only to be expected when
one was a little out of training. He put one arm round to
the front of the building and ran it up and down the wall,
the wall was damnably smooth. He edged one foot round
at right angles, swivelled the other so that the direction of
his body had changed and turned the treacherous corner
easily enough. He was congratulating himself on his judgment, audacity and balance, when a car came up the drive;
for a second he saw the headlamps and then he realized
that he was looking down, his heart missed a beat and his
foot missed the ledge. He landed on the balcony next to
Alperin's with rather more noise than he had intended. He
lay on his back, the breath knocked out of him, staring upwards. There were a great many stars in the sky, more than
he had ever seen before, and they seemed to be flashing
Morse signals to one another. He closed his eyes. It is always
the clown that takes the fall, he thought bitterly. Someone
was fumbling with the shutters of the window; he did not
really mind being found, provided they got him to hospital quickly. A man's voice called out crossly:

"Whatever is it?"

"That bloody deck chair has fallen over again."

A woman's bare feet went past Burke's nose, there was
the sound of a deck chair being folded; the bare feet came
towards him again and the deck chair was flung down
hard on top of him. The shutters slammed to. Burke pushed
the deck chair aside; the bar had hit him in the face, his

[181]

right eye was watering and his nose was bleeding. He sat up and fumbled for a handkerchief. He noticed that the shutters outside Alperin's window were open; to his surprise he managed to drag himself across to the railing separating the two balconies and haul himself over it. His nose was still bleeding and he did not care about anything but finding a wash basin; having miraculously escaped from his fall he was damned if he was going to die of loss of blood! He parted the curtains and stepped quietly into Alperin's room. There was a door immediately to the right, half open, and he could see the gleam of taps. He went into the bathroom without bothering to look at the bed.

It took a long time to stop the bleeding. He wondered what Alperin would make of the condition of his towel in the morning. This thought brought his mind sharply back to the purpose of his visit. He sat on the bath stool, listening. There was someone in the other room, he could hear little snuffling sounds and the occasional creak of bedsprings. He wondered what he would do if he found another man lying there while Alperin travelled East in safety. Earlier in the day the sudden realization that this, rather than illness, might be the explanation of Alperin's refusal to leave his room had brought Burke out in a cold sweat; but now he could not understand why he had been so certain that Alperin had gone. Perhaps it was the guilty knowledge that he and Mitchell had played about on this assignment that had made him so sure that it would end in disaster. One did not play about twice with Eliot. He got up, telling himself that the odds were twenty to one that no dramatic exchange had been effected.

He went into the room and felt something close to affection when he saw the thin, ineffectual face creased by the crumpled bedclothes. Burke stood over Alperin, trying to adapt his own breathing to Alperin's rhythm. This was not easy because Alperin was so restless; the thin fingers plucked at the sheet, the neat little head rolled from side to side, and the breathing was quite appallingly erratic. Burke straightened the sheet in the hope that this might calm him. Alperin said, "Dorothy." Dorothy, Burke remembered, was Alperin's sister. Alperin's fingers tugged at the sheet and twisted it again. He said, "Let go! You must let go, Dorothy!" Burke wondered whether Alperin was in love with his sister; the majority of people, in Burke's opinion, were queer one way or another. There was a bundle of papers on the bedside table. Letters from Dorothy? Burke picked up the papers and went to the far corner of the room before shining his torch on them. Lecture notes. So Alperin was still planning to put in an appearance at the conference.

Burke put the notes back on the bedside table. Now that he was here he might as well search the room. He had a talent for burglary; nature had given him an extra sense denied to most people, instinctively he would avoid the loose board, the creaking stair, wardrobe doors that had jammed for years would give quietly at his touch and ill-fitting drawers slide smoothly in and out. While he searched, Alperin writhed and twisted and made little moaning noises; he did not say anything comprehensible, but the general tone was one of protest, the whimpering, half-hearted protest of a man who expects, and perhaps hopes, to be overruled. Burke went through the wardrobe, the dressing table, and the desk without finding anything of interest. After that he sat down for a rest; his body ached abominably, his nose throbbed and one eye seemed to be gradually closing. Where? he said to himself. From the bed, Alperin said, "No, no, no, no . . ." The whole episode was rapidly degenerating into farce. Where? Burke repeated savagely, where would a man like Alperin hide anything of value? A man like Alperin . . . A man with no experience of the game, a weak man, an insignificant man, a frightened man who allowed himself to be dominated by his sister . . . He would not be original. He would copy something he had seen on television or read in a book. Burke got up and went back to the bathroom. He took out the long, sharp knife he always carried on these ventures and cut the soap in half, sliced through the shaving stick; then he examined the razor and unscrewed the top of a jar of talcum powder. He was rather surprised that Alperin used talcum powder, but a careful probe with the handle of a toothbrush revealed nothing of interest. He went back to the bedroom. Perhaps Alperin, childlike, took his treasures to bed with him? If you really knew your stuff, Burke had once said, you could strip a bed with a man in it and not wake him. It was not easy to do that when the man was gripping the sheets with all his strength, but Burke managed to raise each pillow. He found three paper handkerchiefs and a packet of Anadin tablets. He went away from the bed and shone the torch slowly round the room. An umbrella and a camera were hanging on the hook at the back of the door. The umbrella had a long, curved handle which might conceivably unscrew. As he walked towards it, it occurred to him that he had never seen Alperin take a snap although the camera was always with him.

The camera was a Zeiss, a slim, neat little job, no complications; a glance at the opening at the back seemed to indicate that there was no film inside. Nevertheless, Burke touched the spring at the side and opened the camera. There were, in fact, two films inside, both apparently used. He took one out, it was neatly sealed and the sealing label proclaimed that it was a Kodacolor film. The other was the same. An unorthodox method of carrying used films. Burke pocketed both films and hung the camera on the back of the door. Alperin was more resourceful than he had imagined —or perhaps it was simply that he himself was less alert

[184]

than he had been. A further search of the room was indicated.

It was while he was going through Alperin's clothes that he became conscious that his left hand was stinging abominably. He shone the torch on it and found that the glove was torn across the knuckles; he examined it more carefully and saw that it was not torn, but burnt. Suddenly he snatched it off; he might have been peeling off his own skin. Maddened by pain, he rushed into the bathroom and held his hand under the cold tap; the water was like liquid fire. He reeled against the wall and his shoulder caught the ledge over the wash basin, several of the bottles went over and the talcum powder jar rocked from side to side but did not fall. He stared at the jar. He remembered that after he had stirred the contents with the toothbrush, he had wiped the handle across the back of his glove. He picked up the brush; the handle was twisted as though it had been held in a fire. Burke sat on the edge of the bath, more breathless than he had been after his fall; he gripped the sides of the bath, fighting back a panic-stricken impulse to rush out of the room shouting for help. The pain was terrible, as though hot and cold needles were being jabbed simultaneously into already raw flesh. In the other room, Alperin moaned and snuffled like a sickly baby. Burke put his uninjured hand out and found Alperin's flannel, he folded it carefully round the talcum powder jar and went into the bedroom. He stood beside Alperin's bed. The world, he decided, would be a better place without Alperin; he put his hand on the stopper but the pain was so intense that he could not control his fingers. He turned away and went out of the room. The corridor was empty; he took the lift down to the ground floor and went out of the front door without encountering anyone. If he had committed murder there would have been no witness to his presence in the hotel. Later, walking in the cool night air, he was quite convinced that he would have killed Alperin if only he had been able to get the stopper out of the bottle. It would have been a gesture worth making.

He found the car, deposited his finds carefully in the glove compartment and locked it; then he drove in search of a doctor. He told the doctor that he had upset acid on his hand. It was two o'clock when Burke got back to the hotel. He went to his room and lay down. His hand hurt intolerably; after a time the pain travelled up his arm and attacked his collar bone and shoulder blades, soon his whole body seemed to be on fire. He was quite certain that germs of extreme virulence had been introduced into his bloodstream. He crawled out of bed and drank glass after glass of water. It was only at five o'clock, when fear and pain had exhausted him, that he fell asleep.

When he woke, the pain in his hand was not so bad and although his body was very stiff, he was not feverish. He ordered breakfast in his room; he also sent a message to Mitchell via the chambermaid. When Mitchell came in, Burke handed him the films. Mitchell took them without examining them; he stood by the side of the bed, his hands clenched round the films, his usually expressive eyes blank as he looked down at Burke. Burke felt his heart beginning to pound.

"What have you been up to?"

The tone was not accusing, but it was not solicitous, either. Burke told him what he had done. When he came to the fall from the ledge, Mitchell said:

"You couldn't have done something simple, like picking the lock on the bedroom door?"

"There were people about. Someone was having a party."

"What about the porter's master key?"

"I would have got that, given time. But I didn't have time."

"So there was no alternative to that ledge? A bit melodramatic, surely?"

"You sound like a civil servant!" Burke sneered, his thin face flushing at the hint of ridicule.

"But what was the purpose of this climbing expedition?"

Usually Mitchell was quick to note when Burke was nettled, but now, either he did not notice or he no longer cared. His tone was anything but conciliatory.

"I wanted to see if Alperin was there."

Burke had been so sure something was wrong; but now, in the face of Mitchell's bland incredulity, the explanation seemed very lame.

"I should have thought there were other ways of finding out . . ."

"Would you? Then why haven't you discovered one? We've enquired daily at the hotel, but the answer has always been that he was too ill to leave his room or to see anyone. Didn't it ever occur to you that he wasn't there?"

"No, it didn't. He is just the kind to run away and lock himself up when things get beyond him. As long as he stayed there, undisturbed, all was well. If we couldn't get at him, no one else could either."

He made it sound very convincing. Burke said sullenly:

"Something was achieved, anyway."

For the first time, Mitchell looked down at the films.

"Are you sure?"

"You don't imagine he usually carries exposed films in his camera?"

"He might do."

"Have you ever seen him taking a snap?"

"Oh, I'm not arguing." Mitchell put the films in his pocket. "We'll get the results soon enough, anyway. In the meantime, we're faced with a different situation now, aren't we?"

Burke, his attention reluctantly diverted from the films, said:

"In what way?"

"Alperin has been locked away, struggling with his conscience, completely introverted. Now, you've blown him out of his refuge. He'll know that he is suspected. There won't be many ways open to him."

"We were sent here to watch him," Burke pointed out defensively.

"We were sent here to stop him going East, not to precipitate his journey."

Burke lay back against the pillows. He was in the right and Mitchell was wrong; yet Mitchell was forcing his will on him, his mind seemed to work so quickly and he spoke with such assurance that Burke felt himself driven into a corner. He had not believed that Mitchell could be so aggressive. He was tired and a little frightened. He said weakly:

"What do you suggest?"

Mitchell paused, but not long enough for Burke to summon his reserves.

"Now that this has happened, he may be glad to see someone he knows. He'll want a way out, perhaps he'll be desperate enough to accept any explanation that's offered him. I'll see him and tell him that there were several burglaries at the hotel last night . . ."

Burke hardly listened. When Mitchell had finished, he said dully:

"Yes. You do that." He heaved himself up on the pillows. "But while you're dealing with the films, there's something you might like to get analyzed." He opened the cabinet beneath the bedside table and took out the talcum powder jar. He had wrapped it up carefully in polythene and cov-

[188]

ered it with brown paper. Mitchell watched Burke put the jar on the table, he made no comment, just waited; there was no spontaneity about Mitchell now. Instead of unwrapping the brown paper, Burke unwound the bandage on his hand. The flesh had burnt away across the knuckles and the bones showed. This, at least, had an impact on Mitchell. Colour drained from his face, leaving the summer's tan yellow and sickly without the substance of blood.

"Dan!" Mitchell sat on the bed. His manner had changed suddenly; it was too conciliatory now. "God knows what this could mean! Why don't you get away, right out of this place? Go back to Berlin and get Arnold at the American hospital to have a look at that hand. Leave everything here to me."

"And what will you do?"

For a minute their eyes met with an understanding too acute to be borne. Both men looked away. Burke said:

"I've got some money stored away, Stephen. If it would help . . ."

Mitchell picked up the jar and folded the paper more securely around it.

"I really think you should let Arnold see that hand."

Burke did not offer the money again; he was weary and defeated and he wanted an end to this charade. He said, "I'll think about it."

Mitchell said that he would take the films and the powder into Lausanne and Burke made no protest. He watched Mitchell putting the films away with the talcum powder jar. He said:

"I'm sorry for Alperin."

"Why be sorry for him?" Mitchell sounded angry. "He's a weak, insignificant little man."

When Mitchell had gone, Burke lay wondering what he should do. What indiscretion had Mitchell committed that

[189]

had put him so completely in Miriam Kratz's power? Whatever it was, Burke suspected that its roots were in the past because there had always been something rather guilty in Mitchell's attitude towards the woman. He was sorry to see Mitchell go down; his steadfastness, though rather tedious, had at times been comforting. He was sorry, too, that he himself was partly to blame for Mitchell's misfortunes. It had been as a result of his indiscretion that the woman had traced them to Tamaro. Why, in God's name, had he sent that card to Lottë?

The sun was shining brightly through the window. It made his eyes ache. He turned his head away, staring at the blank, discoloured wall, tracing the cracks that made it look like a jigsaw puzzle gradually coming apart . . . a return to chaos . . . What should he do? Only one thing was certain: he would not go to Eliot. He was not sure that he was a match for Mitchell, but whether he was or whether he was not, he would not go to Eliot for help. That would be a betrayal not of Mitchell, which was something he could have countenanced in the last extremity, but of himself.

Chapter 20

Alperin was in a state of terror. Anyone would have thought that there had been supernatural intervention in his affairs rather than that he had been the victim of burglary. It was the blood that had disturbed him, Mitchell gradually realized. He had not yet comprehended what the loss of the films meant and he had not even discovered the loss of the talcum powder jar. He had retired from the bathroom immediately he saw the towel. Now he sat on his bed, shaking with fear, and would listen to nothing that was said to him.

"Your burglar had a nose bleed," Mitchell told him tartly. "I should have thought that was the least of your worries."

Alperin shook his head as though it was impossible that a nose bleed could produce so much blood.

"Then what do you think happened?" Mitchell demanded.

Alperin folded his arms across his breast; he pressed his legs tightly together and bowed forward until his elbows touched his knees. He seemed to be trying to compress himself into as small a space as possible; inevitably the posture made him rigid and it was more difficult than ever to relieve the tension of his body.

"It was a sign," he said.

"A spiritual sign?" Mitchell asked in exasperation. "Spirits don't bleed."

"It was a sign to me that if I go on with this, it will be my blood next time."

This, of course, was the moment when he must dominate Alperin. Not a difficult task, God knew! Yet Mitchell found himself oddly reluctant to start the treatment.

"And if you don't go on with it? Have you thought what happens then?"

Alperin had not thought about it; so Mitchell enlightened him while Alperin hunched forward, staring at his feet as though there was something monstrous about them.

"The burglar took two rolls of film. Why you didn't give them to me in the first instance, I can't imagine. He also took a jar of powder that you kept on the shelf in the bathroom. Fortunately, I have recovered both these items. But can you imagine what would have happened to you if it had been known that you had these things in your possession?"

Alperin did not move, but his eyes roamed reflectively across the floor boards. He said in a perplexed voice:

"But you said you had recovered them."

"I shall want to know whether we are working together or not before I decide what to do with them."

"I see."

Alperin's lips quivered. Mitchell pressed home his advantage.

"Whatever made you behave so foolishly?"

For the first time Alperin raised his head. He had lately developed a special way of looking at Mitchell, his eyes expressing an odd mixture of shyness and familiarity which

Mitchell found nauseating. On this occasion, there was an added element of supplication as he said:

"Was I foolish? I'm so sorry."

"You left that powder—I shall want to know more about it—on a shelf in the bathroom. At best, I call that foolish."

Alperin said tentatively, "But I have heard that the best way of hiding a thing is to display it."

"That rather depends on the object itself, I would have thought. Suppose someone had accidentally upset a quantity of that powder over their arm. What would have happened?"

"They would have lost their arm," Alperin explained simply.

"And this could have happened to the chambermaid, for example?"

"I have instructed her not to clean the bathroom until I am better."

"The burglar, then?"

Alperin shrugged his shoulders. "There must be some penalties for burglary."

"I know you are not concerned about people," Mitchell snapped, "but you really can't afford to be quite so careless."

"Concerned about people!" Alperin was genuinely hurt. "Of course I'm concerned! Why do you think I am trying to escape from all this beastliness and destruction?"

"You care about them en masse, but not when they come too close, is that it?" Mitchell drew in his breath, aware that he was going too far. He modified his tone. "Oh well, it's over now. But tell me, have you brought any more samples with you?"

"I didn't need any more."

"You felt that you could establish your claim to usefulness simply on the contents of that jar?"

Alperin stared at him; to Mitchell's astonishment, the

pleading expression was replaced by a kind of prim outrage.

"My usefulness . . . established on the contents of that jar . . . What arrant nonsense! My claim to usefulness, as you put it, is my not inconsiderable reputation. The films will also be of value, of course; they give details of research in connection with the genetic make-up of viruses . . ."

"Save that for the scientists. What interests me is why you brought that jar with you if the contents are of no value."

"One must have some means of protection," Alperin explained in an exasperated tone. "After all, for me this is a venture into the unknown, and one doesn't go unarmed on such occasions."

"You mean that you meant to use that powder?"

"Only in an emergency, of course. I know so little about this sort of thing; but I thought that if, for example, there was some last-minute intervention—guards at a frontier—it would come in handy. The contents of that jar would account for quite a few people, provided they were in a fairly compact group . . ."

"And the wind was in the right direction!"

"I had not thought of that."

"You had better leave me to deal with last-minute interventions."

"Well, yes, I shall do that, of course. But when I set out I didn't know that you would be here to help me, did I?" Alperin's shoulders slumped and he said wearily, "I'm extremely grateful to you for everything you've done, it means more to me than I can possibly tell you. But all this has been very exhausting, and I feel that just at this moment the one thing I need is a really good sleep."

"Before you sleep, I want to be satisfied that you have nothing else hidden away."

"Nothing." Alperin's eyelids drooped and he yawned.

"No pills? You haven't prepared for another kind of emergency?"

Alperin's lids flicked back like those of a doll which has received a sharp jolt and Mitchell knew at once that this was a possibility that had not occurred to him.

"You mean, in case I don't succeed?"

"Some people lose their nerve at the last minute. But things will move smoothly for you, so you will have nothing to worry about provided you do as I tell you from now on."

Alperin said, "I will. I promise I will."

Although he appeared fairly relaxed, he no longer seemed quite so anxious to sleep and he began to ask Mitchell questions about life in Russia. Would he stay in Moscow or would they send him to a research center somewhere in Siberia? He was not, he explained, very attracted to camp life. His conversation became trivial and rather childish and the last question was surely the most trivial of all.

"Do you think I will have a housekeeper?"

"I've no idea!" Mitchell laughed. "I don't know much about Russia. In fact, I suppose you might say that I have very little experience of any place except the no-man's-land on either side of borders."

Alperin looked at him. "How terrible that must be!" He sounded as though he really meant it; there was pity in his voice. Pity from Alperin was the last thing that Mitchell had expected or wanted. He left shortly after that.

His adult life had been spent in no-man's-land and he had become so used to it that he had spoken of it to Alperin without thought. And Alperin had had the impertinence to pity him! Yet he could remember how, when the war ended and the great trek home began, he and Claus had stood apart and pitied the men about to be caught up in the web of domestic life. His own resistance had been strengthened by the realization that his affectionate wife

[195]

was extremely possessive and so he had traded the shackles of love for the freedom to travel alone. Had that been the first wrong move? Or was he the kind of man who, war or no war, would always make that choice, whose journeys would always end in no-man's land? It was too late to ask those questions now. There was no time for regret: the choice had been made. But although he told himself that he could no longer afford to look back, his discomfort was not so easily dispelled.

As he climbed the road from Alperin's hotel to the village of Veytaux his mind was more confused than ever. He sat on a seat halfway up the hill. He had not gone to Alperin immediately after Burke told him of his discoveries; it had seemed more important to see Novak and after that other things had occupied him. The day had slipped away. Now it was towards evening and the sky had thinned to a pale heliotrope, the mountains were plumed with mist and the lake was pearl grey; the whole landscape was less substantial, already resigned to night. Beyond the network of tram-lines and railway signals, he could see Chillon, bastion, keep, battlement and tower merged into one dark mass of granite indifference. For the first time, he began to think about failure.

He had been in the service long enough to know that the espionage system had its weaknesses, the chain of communication stretched a long way now and some of the links were weak. He was not afraid of immediate failure. But afterwards? He wanted to give life and hope; these were words that one used often and too lightly so that they had lost their value, but now the meaning overwhelmed him . . . life . . . hope. . . . A man broken in prison, a woman born of chaos, an abandoned child: what hope was there for them? He had wanted to work a miracle for them; but he was not God and he had not the healer's touch. He could

unlock a door, but what happened after that was beyond
his control.

He tried to think dispassionately about Miriam Kratz. It
was obvious from all that she had told him about her married life that the burden of responsibility had been borne
by her husband: now the burden would be hers and she was
ill-equipped to bear it. It had been foolish of him ever to
think that she could bear so much . . . whereas he would
demand so little. . . . The thought passed so easily across
the threshold of his conscious mind that he knew it had
been waiting in the shadows for a long time. He shivered,
more disturbed by this unguarded impulse than by his
larger treachery. Something for myself, he had thought when
he planned this, I must do something for myself, remove at
least one barrier . . . Well, that disinterested impulse to
do good had not survived long! Now, indeed he wanted
something for himself. The longing was so strong that he
was not at all sure he could withstand it. He had fought a
lot of things during his life, but he had never been conspic-
uously successful at fighting himself; the disciplines imposed
upon him by his job had been those that he was well able
to bear, they had not been the kind really to test him. Test
him! He had always hated this kind of moralizing; it was
absurd to submit himself to it now. He felt more deeply about
Miriam Kratz than he had ever felt about any woman, she
opened up a whole new territory of experience to him. One
should take such an opportunity when it presented itself;
to refuse would be cowardice, a refusal to put his feeling
to the test, a submission to the fear that he could not sustain
a lasting relationship with a woman. Miriam Kratz represented something tremendous, the last adventure . . . He
looked down the hill. It was nearly dark, but the moon had
come up and he could see the water running swiftly past
Chillon, the little silver waves breaking ineffectually against

the hard, black rocks. Perhaps the most absurd thing of all was to have imagined that Mikail Kratz could still be alive.

In Lausanne, Eliot drew back the window curtains. He, too, was depressed by the coming of evening, an unusual occurrence since on the whole night and day were barely distinguishable to him. The decision to expose himself to the neon brilliance of Lausanne at night was not a good one because for some maddening reason the scene served to remind him of Claus Hesselmann. Perhaps it was the fairy wheel high above the tall tower of a night club, which at this angle seemed to revolve a little drunkenly, that reminded him of Hesselmann. Hesselmann never did anything in moderation and during the last year he had abandoned himself to revelry. The decision to get rid of him had been perfectly justified. Unfortunately, it was doubtful whether the people in London would agree with the method adopted. They would have agreed that he should be dropped, but they would not have liked him to drop so far. And now they were making enquiries.

Eliot twisted the sash cord and peered down with eyes sharpened by pain at all the stupid, busy people crawling over the bridges, spewing out into the brightly-lit streets, eager, expectant, urgent. If only they knew the utter motivelessness to which all their bustling energy was reduced at this level! This, of course, was how God would see them, if there happened to be a God and if he ever looked down; it was ridiculous to depict him as being concerned with all those absurd little creatures. So many flies. And Eliot had got rid of one of the flies. But it was not God who would not care to whom he had to account, it was to London; and the men in London, though not particularly ethical themselves, were sentimental about people like Hesselmann who had a splendid war record and a generous, extrovert personality.

Also, far from believing that to sacrifice an agent here and there encouraged the others, London believed that such incidents were a positive discouragement. Men became nervous and nervous men became unreliable. Men like Dan Burke, for example, Why, Eliot thought wearily, why had he told Burke? Without Burke there would be no problem. He could tell London that Hesselmann had gone to the hospice at his own suggestion, that he was acting as a counter-agent. London would accept this. Any plausible explanation would be accepted, since Eliot was still valuable to London. But Burke was not the kind to keep quiet.

Even so, it was not Burke with whom Eliot was really concerned at the moment. He could handle Burke if it came to a showdown between them. Burke's sound and fury signified very little. But Stephen Mitchell was a different proposition. And it was of Mitchell that Eliot was thinking as he stared across at the wheel of light, winking, swaying, dipping, gay and foolish in the night. Mitchell. He knew as much about the man as he knew about the lure of the fairy wheel. For the first time, Eliot was conscious that to be remote from feeling was a disadvantage; for Mitchell was undoubtedly a man of feeling. This unpleasant suspicion had been growing on Eliot for a long time, it was one of the reasons why he regarded the man as potentially suspect as an agent. There was too much feeling, a softness in the eyes . . . How would such a man act in a crisis of feeling?

Eliot looked longingly at his map; he looked down at the table where he sometimes played chess. Chess was a matter of intellect; you invaded a man's mind and asked what move he would make next . . . but you had to assume that he was playing the same game as yourself. Eliot was conscious of a lack in himself. It came to him as a great revelation, full of wonder and regret, that a whole world of power had eluded him. He sat down by the window; his face was thin and wasted, the skin green, the lips mauve in the unnatural light and he looked like a vampire unexpectedly accommodated in an urban setting. He thought about the past, his mind resurrecting people he had known, some of whom he had defeated, others who had defeated him, and he realized that all of them, to some extent, had escaped him. If he had understood more about their feelings, what might he not have achieved? And it was not just the achievement, it was the exhilaration that he had missed. The pawns had feeling! If only he had been sensitive to it, understood how to manipulate it so that they throbbed, twisted and turned in his fingers, then the game would have been fantastically enriched . . . Here he became so excited that he had a bad fit of coughing and when he recovered, shaking and sweating, the exhilaration had gone and he had no energy left. No energy: but one pawn still to move into position. He hauled himself out of his chair and went across to the telephone.

Chapter 21

It seemed to Mitchell that time had lost all meaning. An age elapsed before Novak presented him with a foolscap envelope saying:

"At least we haven't lost any time." In his time, six days had elapsed.

Mitchell took the paper back to his room. He felt as though it contained a death sentence, not Kratz's but his own. His mouth was dry as he unfolded it. The questions had been typed on a sheet of foolscap and the place where the answers were to be written was indicated by a series of dots. Who had written those answers? Kratz, bending over the questionnaire in some clinical little room, blinded by unaccustomed light, watched by a guard who had been instructed not to intrude? Or had an official produced the answers with the aid of guards racking their memories for odd phrases muttered by a man long dead? It was difficult at first to gain any very definite impression. The writing was the formal, scholarly writing of a very old man who had retained his individuality at some cost. Here and there a word clumsily begun had been restarted more legibly, presumably to please some standard set by the writer rather than for any other purpose, since the answer was seldom enlightening.

The writer could remember the name of the displaced persons' camp where he had first met his wife; but the more personal question as to the names of the three people who had been present at their wedding had not been answered. Nor had the questions relating to the apartment in East Berlin where they had lived during the first year of their marriage. On the other hand, he had remembered quite a lot about the clinic; but then these were matters which were probably recorded somewhere—Miriam herself would recall only the outstanding cases, she was not interested in the small change of clinic routine. And her husband, it seemed from the long series of unanswered questions, had not been interested in the small change of life outside the clinic. Mitchell, reading slowly down the page, found himself saying, "Mikail Kratz is dead. Undoubtedly, he is dead." It was then that he came to the last question. "What names did Naomi give to her rag dolls?" In answer to this question, the man had written, "Did Naomi give names to her dolls? She seemed to me not to be interested in names, even her own." Mitchell's racing pulse missed a beat. A clever get-out? Yet the reply came across with an asperity that had a certain authenticity about it. As Mitchell sat staring down at the paper, he knew beyond reason that Kratz had written this and that he had found out something about the man that he had not known before. His belief was not shaken by Miriam's bewilderment when she saw the paper with its series of unanswered questions.

"How could he forget that gas stove?" she said.

"Probably food was not important to him."

She shook her head, unconvinced. She had been an inexperienced cook and the gas stove had been obsolete, obstinate and sometimes positively dangerous; to her, it had been a monster whose malign inhumanity was quite terrifying. It seemed incredible that Mikail should not have understood this and should not himself have been haunted by the gas stove. When she thought of their year together in this place, no visual picture of the apartment emerged. There was only the persistent smell of gas. It was because of this that she remembered so vividly every small detail of the park opposite to which they had escaped on the rare occasions when they had time to spend together. Here the smell of rotting leaves and damp grass had brought a tremendous relief which subsequently she always experienced when surrounded by damp vegetation. And Mikail had not remembered the park! He had not remembered the broken seat where they sat to watch children playing precariously on the rickety swings and ramshackle roundabouts or fishing in the stagnant pond. Even now, she could see the green slime clinging to their thin, blanched legs as the children scrambled out of the pond. And yet, to the question "Where did you go every Sunday afternoon?" there was no answer. Mitchell broke into her thoughts saying:

"Was he an impatient man?"

"Very."

"I had thought of him as being gentle."

"He was. But he was impatient, too."

"What made him impatient?"

She shrugged her shoulders. "Things that didn't matter. He was wonderfully kind and understanding over important things . . ."

"What made him impatient?"

"Messages about patients." She dismissed them with an irritable movement of her hand; one could imagine her doing this to Mikail himself. "It annoyed him if I got messages wrong. 'Fraulein Heller is worse . . .' 'Fraulein Heller is no better . . .' It is all the same, I would say; but he would not have it. When people were rude to him, he never shouted or lost his temper; but if someone expressed an idea badly, he would argue and argue and argue until he had the right words. Even if it was something that he did not agree with, he had to have it expressed properly . . . only 'properly' isn't what he would have said . . ." While she searched for the right word, Mitchell said abruptly:

"Did Naomi give names to her rag dolls?"

"Of course! There was Gretchen and Magda . . ."

"How did she come to choose a name like Magda?"

"The old woman in the room below us was Hungarian and she made the doll and gave it to Naomi. I can remember well, she said, 'What will you call it? Magda?' "

"So Naomi did not choose the name."

"But the doll's name was Magda!" she shouted, her face suddenly flushed with anger. "Mikail knew that as well as I do."

He looked down at the paper in his hands. "So you don't think your husband wrote this?"

"So this . . . so that . . . so and so and so . . . Why do you keep on with your silly questions!" She turned away and beat her fists on the window frame. "How do I know? How do I know? There is nothing there . . ."

He folded the paper carefully; when he had done this he still could not put it to one side. He said:

"Of course you can't know. But how do you feel?"

She answered through clenched teeth, "I don't feel!"

He looked at her, her head down, her shoulders hunched, the blades knife-edged beneath the thin dress. He put the paper on the dressing table and went to her, laying his hands on her shoulders. She did not move a muscle. Beyond the window, the sun was white as molten steel; in the room heat pulsed in the air. He rested his cheek against the side of her

[204]

face; he was more unsure of himself than he had ever been.

"We've done all we can," he pleaded.

"Yes."

"Will you come away with me?"

The room vibrated with heat, every nerve in his body quivered. Yet she was still.

"Please," he said. "I need you so much."

She turned and looked at him, a long, unfathomable look; he thought that she seemed much older and more assured than he was.

"Don't ask anything of me now," she warned.

"I won't. I promise I won't."

She put out her hand and touched his arm.

"You're shaking."

"It's the room . . . the heat . . ."

The room was too small to hold them apart. She seemed to understand this.

"We'll go out, then."

She stopped to pick up her handbag; he saw her pause, looking at the sheet of paper. She turned away and left it there on the dressing table.

It was just after noon. The pavements were hot and there was very little shade. It was the beginning of a heatwave. They walked down to the quayside and turned in the direction of Villeneuve. On one side of the path there were hotel lawns, velvet green dotted with scarlet sunshades and striped canvas chairs where bronzed figures reclined contemplating aperitifs in long, frosted glasses; on the other side of the path, tangled beneath tall trees, multicoloured flowers and shrubs crowded the lake's edge. The exuberant foliage of the trees screened sky and water and the trapped air was heavy with the cloying scent of flowers spiced occasionally with a smell reminiscent of ginger which must, Mitchell supposed, emanate from one of the shrubs. Although it was so hot, an occasional puff of air stirred the leaves of the trees and Mitchell felt dust in his eyes, his nostrils, his mouth. The masked sun was sullen on his shoulders. In the distance, he could hear a loudspeaker on one of the pleasure boats; the water rippled in the boat's wake and slapped against the bank with a sound that took him back to childhood excursions in the reedy waters of the Môle. He said to Miriam, "We could take a boat to Geneva." They had time to squander now. She turned her head in the direction of the lake, but said nothing. She was wearing the tangerine dress, exotic as the flowers; as she moved her head the strap of the dress pulled a little so that he saw the red line where the sun had burnt her. He put his hand on her upper arm.

"Your shoulder is very hot."

"I do not burn."

"No?"

He put his arm round her waist; she let it rest there but she did not move closer to him. But there was time for that. Ahead where there was a gap between the trees the path shimmered and every facet of stone in the curb sparked in the sun. A few moments later they came out from the shade of the trees and Mitchell felt an intense excitement throughout his whole body at the ferocious power suddenly unleashed against him. Beside him, Miriam staggered as though she had received a blow. At the point where they came into the open, there was a splendid view. He held her a little closer while he gazed at the landscape sharply chiselled in the brilliant light. Behind them the land sloped away and the lake was limitless as the sea; but ahead the lake narrowed and above the green valley of the Rhône the mountains shouldered into the sky, every jagged detail of cleft, ridge and crevasse harshly substantiated and, rising above like the highest note of a great arpeggio so pure as to be beyond humanity, the immaculate peaks of Les Dents du Midi.

"Do you like mountains?" he asked Miriam.

His senses were stimulated as though the years which had rubbed the bloom off life had been erased and he saw everything new-minted; the extravagant majesty of the mountains, the miniature precision of a delicately veined leaf, the broad ivory curve of Miriam's cheekbone with that tiny hollow of shadow beneath.

"Aren't they beautiful?" he repeated, not really thinking about the mountains but wanting her to share his delight in all things. "I'll take you there this afternoon. We could go as far as Martigny by car and then walk. There will be a few flowers in the valleys still."

"All right."

"Do you like flowers?"

"They're very nice."

He looked down at her. "You don't really mean that." Her eyes looked into his, he thought they mocked him a little. He bent closer to her so that when she answered he felt her breath against his cheek.

"They don't do anything."

"But don't you sometimes get pleasure in things simply because they look beautiful? That dress, for example."

"But the dress is useful. I can wear the dress."

He moved his hand across her hip, feeling the slight tingling friction as his rough finger tips scratched the fine threads.

"But doesn't the feel of it please you?"

She shivered slightly, but whether it was for pleasure or not, she did not say. Ahead a party of youths surged along the path towards them and he drew her on to the grass in the shadow of a tree. The branches of the tree were thick and low, they caught in her hair and she raised her arms above her head to free herself. All the magic of woman was in the upthrust line of her body. He took her in his arms and kissed her eyes, her lips, the hollow of her throat; he laughed at her helplessness as she struggled, her hair still tangled in the branches, and stopped her protests with more kisses. Only the panic in her eyes made him release her at last. She turned away from him and stood with one arm against the trunk of the tree, her head down, her breath coming in harsh gasps.

"I'm sorry," he repeated over and over again. "I'm sorry. I promised, but . . ."

She turned at last and said quietly, "Promises are hard to keep." She took his hand and led him back to the path.

"You're not angry?"

"No." She pressed his hand, but there was a heaviness in her step that had not been there before.

"I've tired you."

"A little."

After a few minutes they came to a seat overlooking the lake. There was a small inlet here, strewn with rocks over which a few children were scrambling, shouting at one another.

"We can rest here," he said.

She sat down and leaning her head against his shoulder stared up at the sky.

"Why do you like mountains?"

"They represent some kind of challenge, I suppose."

"I don't like challenges."

He laughed. The children splashed and shouted. He said, "We could swim, since you don't like mountains." He watched the children idly. Close by, a boy of about five, hovering nervously at the water's edge, fingered his penis and an older girl said imperiously, "Martin, you stop that!" She had recently been swimming and her short, dark hair was a sculptured frame for a face too agitated for the sculptor's static art. "You're a disgusting little boy. And when you grow up you'll have all sorts of horrible things wrong with you . . ." In the straight, old-fashioned costume, the girl's limbs wriggled and twisted incessantly like some emergent animal struggling to slough off an old skin. Watching her, seeing the wild, dark eyes stabbing at the little boy with an uncontrolled anger not really occasioned by his misdemeanour, Mitchell could feel the physical pain of unharnessed energy, the bewildering bodily discomfort created by unknown pressures and unreasonable impulses. He said, "Oh, the pain of being young!" This nostalgic sentiment received no answering echo; he glanced down at Miriam, his nerves suddenly alerted. He saw a dark, foreign woman absorbed in the reality of her own pain. Her voice came from a dry, aching throat.

"How old is that girl?"

"About eleven, I should think." He tried to sound casual.

"She's old for her age, surely?"

"They grow up quickly these days."

She said under her breath, "I wouldn't know how to talk to her."

"She wouldn't want you to talk to her," he said roughly. "She wants to be alone. Can't you see that?"

But it was no use trying to bring her back to him, the distance between them was already too great. The little boy was crying for his mother while the girl sat gazing unconcernedly across the water, her rage spent. Mitchell could not bear to look at them. He turned his head away and looked up at the mountains; the sun was sharp as broken glass in his eyes. After a time, Miriam said:

"I will come with you this afternoon." She might have been speaking to a stranger who had offered her a lift on a stony road.

"It's too late," he answered harshly. "It's afternoon already."

He did not want to look at her, but he forced himself to do so. There was no expression in her face and her eyes were like those of a blind person; there was no hope and there was no despair either, all emotion had been scoured out leaving an almost idiot vacuity. Only her hand moved; as though it was unconnected with the rest of her being it reached up and touched his face, the fingers traced the furrows in his forehead, the line of cheek and jaw, and rested for a moment against his chest where the shirt opened. She said in that flat, unemphatic voice, "You are burnt, too." Then she turned and picked up her handbag. She walked away, moving very slowly, but not as though she expected to be followed.

Chapter 22

"Not a first class brain." Very judicious, Professor Adlam, like a judge passing sentence. "A superb administrator, certainly, and, of course, a showman. Not that there is any harm in that."

He sounded as though there was a great deal of harm in it and Alperin wriggled with pleasure and took another gulp of wine.

"Of course, he has a first class brain!" Dr. Scunner, secure in the knowledge that his own claims were beyond question, could afford to be unbiased.

Professor Adlam studied the stem of his wine glass critically. "Yet he sent Alperin here instead of coming himself."

"With respect," Dr. Scunner smiled bleakly at Alperin, "these conferences become tedious."

"Oh no!" Professor Adlam placed his glass very delicately on the table as though the slightest jar would shatter it. "He was not a success in Bonn. In fact, he went down very badly in Bonn. The wrong approach. All right for radio—intellectual discussion for the mass audience. It's always the showman who makes the appeal on these occasions—witness

Joad, discovered not once but twice! One can imagine a similar Gethryn revival taking place some years after his death. But not the right approach to the kind of audience he had to address in Bonn . . ."

Alperin emptied his glass. He felt an imperative need to say something quite brilliant, but Scunner intervened before he could collect his thoughts.

"It would take showmanship on a godlike scale to stir those stagnant waters!"

Alperin gazed sadly into his empty glass, a little sediment lay at the bottom. The last of the wine, he thought, and felt an urgent need to cry. He also felt very sick. The room was unbearably hot and the faces of all the men around him were pink and beaded with sweat; at a nearby table he saw a woman in a tight linen dress, dark stains under the armpits. He began to think that he might actually be sick. The German professor, who had looked as though he was asleep, was ordering coffee and Dr. Scunner was ordering brandy. Everything was set for a long discussion. When they had picked Gethryn's bones dry they would feast on someone else. It had been fascinating to have his opinion of Gethryn confirmed, but he did not want to hear any more of that kind of thing; he was not good at it, for some reason he always sounded small and envious. Besides, he had had much too much to eat and perhaps a little too much to drink. He murmured excuses which, in spite of their earlier cordiality, they accepted without protest.

He still felt sick when he got outside. It was nearly midnight, but there was no crack in the heat's burnished armour. He decided that a walk would be good for him. It was a long, uphill walk from the center of Montreux to the suburb of Veytaux; noisy, too, with traffic pounding the main road to Lausanne and Geneva. By the time that he had reached the funicular station his shirt was caked to his back and his

[212]

heart jumped every time a car hurtled by on the near side. How he hated the continental roads! It was a mistake to have done so much on his first outing. The invitation to join Adlam and the others had been flattering, of course . . . He paused in the arcade beneath the Grand Hotel, staring with unseeing eyes into a jeweller's lighted window while he recovered his breath. It was wrong to be flattered by the attention of men who, with the possible exception of Scunner, were his inferiors; it was simply their greater social ease that made him feel so desperately lonely and inadequate. He began to walk again; the pavement narrowed unpleasantly and the road climbed more steeply. His mouth was hot as though he was feverish. He was glad when he reached the turning that led up to the village of Veytaux; it was a very steep road but fortunately his hotel was immediately on the left. He turned in at the gate and sat at one of the tables in the empty courtyard. The air was no better here, it was like breathing through a blanket. His room might be cooler, but he did not want to go back to his room.

He thought about Mitchell. It was time Mitchell paid him another visit. Perhaps he was up in the bedroom, waiting. The thought did not displease Alperin. It had cost him a tremendous effort to confess to Mitchell; but now that his reticence had been breached he felt a strong desire to pour out his innermost secrets. And Mitchell had a duty to listen since he was, in a sense, Alperin's guardian. A light went on in the lounge and a few people strolled on to the balcony. He felt that they were standing staring at the back of his head. He went into the hotel and took the lift up to his room. He would tell Mitchell about his disappointments and humiliations, his hopes and fears . . . particularly his fears. Mitchell was strong and the strong can cast out fear.

The room was empty except for a mosquito droning somewhere near the bathroom door. He felt lonely as the last man on earth. He sat down on the bed and switched on the lamp. His feet ached, so he took off his shoes and socks. The socks were wet and bits of wool stuck to his fingers; he noticed that there were big holes in the heels of the socks. There was also a very unpleasant smell. He wondered whether the other men had noticed it; probably not, they had been too interested in Sir Harry. Alperin rolled the socks into a ball, folding one inside the other as he had been made to do when he was a child, and dropped them on to the floor.

He looked around him. Everything seemed to be a long way away. Yet earlier in the evening it had seemed important to get out of the room because everything was closing in on him. His outing didn't seem to have done him much good one way and another. His eyes came back to the socks.

Dorothy usually mended his socks, pricking her finger tips so that the skin was hard and rough. It annoyed him so much that she would not use a thimble. He could not bear to see the living flesh pressed against the steel so hard that it seemed that at any minute blood would spurt out. "You were always a squeamish little boy," she would say and press harder, just as she had picked at thorns in her fingers when they were children because she knew that it upset him. He thought about Dorothy as he sat on the edge of the bed. He had left it rather late to think about her, but neglect seemed to have intensified feeling. The gnawing in his stomach intensified, too. It was as though some demon surgeon was trying to wrench a vital organ from the center of his being. He suddenly realized, sitting there staring down at the socks, that when he was finally free of Dorothy it would be not a release but a death.

This was odd. They lived in an atmosphere of nagging conflict interspersed with brief, weary truces; they were irritated by each other's mannerisms and were too alike in some ways to tolerate each other's weaknesses. It was odd, therefore, that it should be this one link that so obstinately held when all the other links had been severed. His meal tonight with those eminent Western scientists should have been the final test. It had not worried him, sitting there with them, that he was about to betray his colleagues, his country, to risk his reputation, even his life; indeed, he had felt a certain pride. He had passed the test. He prodded the socks with one toe. He could always buy more socks.

But how did you ask for socks in Russian? He put his head in his hands and pressed his fingers against his temples. He must put an end to these inane questions. And he must certainly put an end to the series of images which followed, absurd images, but informed with the terrible authenticity of nightmare. On this occasion he was standing in a dark, cavern-like room lit with dim Chinese lanterns; there was a man behind a counter, very old, with impassive almond eyes that gradually closed as Alperin asked for the socks until only two slits remained. Someone was laughing, but it wasn't the man. Alperin turned round and shadows moved quickly from the doorway; the street was full of people laughing at him. He was afraid to go into the street and he was afraid of the man behind the counter . . . there was nowhere to go. Alperin bit his lip until the pain forced his mind back to reality. Of course he was nervous! It was ridiculous to imagine that he could take such a step without being nervous. These absurd scenes were simply a projection of his fear of the unknown; once he was in Russia, his problems would become real, they would still be difficult but they would be capable of a rational solution. What did it matter how he would arrange his laundry, do his housework, buy the food! He would live in a hotel for a while until he had learnt to manage on his own. On his own . . . He was walking up stairs, dark, narrow stairs which seemed to lead straight through the roof; but at the last turn of the stairs

[215]

there was a corridor no wider than a shelf leading to a dim, recessed door. He took the key from his pocket and opened the door on emptiness. No, he shook his head, no, no, no! But the hollow footsteps resounded in his mind. This was no nightmare. He could not live alone, now or at any time. He could not live alone with only the incomprehensible babble of a radio between him and the ticking clock, the creaking stair. Perhaps they would find him a housekeeper. He forced himself not to think of the housekeeper, a massive woman with a beard with whom he had already become acquainted in nightmare. Bearded or not, she would be no comfort to him. It would take a lifetime to reach the state of irritated acceptance he had achieved with Dorothy. He needed Dorothy; without the friction of her personality against his, he would scarcely know whether he existed or not. There! He had admitted it at last.

Everything seemed to be moving further and further away, he felt himself gradually losing his hold. He slumped sideways and belched, the wine bitter in his mouth. He put one hand down and picked up the socks. He crouched there for a while, holding the socks tightly in his hand; then, when he felt better, he went across to the chest of drawers and put the socks away with the rest of his used underwear. Dorothy will mend them when I get home, he thought.

There was a knock on the door. Alperin remained quiet, he had no intention of opening any more doors. Then a voice which he did not immediately recognize said, "I wonder if you have your keys on you? I can't get into this room and I'm a bit worried about my friend. He hasn't been well." There was a jangling of keys. Alperin watched the door handle turn. His expression when the door opened convinced the porter that he was not well. Burke stepped lightly into the room and shut the door.

Alperin said, "What is it?" The wine was making him feel very sleepy and he wanted to go to bed.

"As I told the porter, I've been worried about you."

He did not look worried; worried was a mundane word that belonged to the day, it had no place in nightmare. Alperin, frightened, asked, "Why should you worry about me?"

Burke sat down. He spoke quietly and without emphasis. Alperin was fascinated by the white, chapped lips from which all blood seemed to have drained away; he was too conscious of the lips to bother about the words.

"You must excuse my speaking so bluntly, but there isn't much time. You probably feel that you have done something irrevocable. This isn't so, I assure you. Whatever happens you must not allow yourself to panic. You have been unwell. Everyone will understand." The long white face was taut as a mask and the eyes smouldered beneath red lids; there was no understanding in the face. "Some of the things we do assume an importance out of all significance when we are ill. A little maneuvering can often put them right and no harm done." There was a pause and then the bloodless lips moved again. "You do understand what I'm saying, don't you?"

"Yes." Alperin nodded his head; it took a great effort to do this because his head was so heavy. "Yes, I understand."

"All you have to do is to tell me everything that has happened recently and then forget about it. I will put matters right. You can go back to England after you have read your paper, or whatever it is you have to do. The incident will be forgotten."

Alperin, who intended to go back to England anyway, said, "All right."

"First, you must tell me what has happened in the last few days. You have reached some kind of understanding with Stephen Mitchell, haven't you?"

"Yes."

"I must have details."

"I don't know anything."

"Was there any question of your going to Russia?"

"No! There was no question of that."

"Did he tell you that he had possession of the films?"

"What films?"

"Don't waste time. I've seen them. Have they been returned to you?"

"No."

"It will be difficult for you if they are not returned, won't it?"

"They are copies, not originals."

"But when it becomes known that Russia has this information, what then?"

"They won't find the source of the leak."

"No? I think they may, unless you tell me what has happened to those films."

"But I don't know!" The eyes did not believe him, they were not eyes one could reason with. Alperin shouted, "I don't know!" His shrill voice made no impact. The voice went on quietly, the lips moved but not the teeth.

"What happened to them?"

"I don't know!"

"Did he give them to someone else?"

"Yes." Alperin dived eagerly down this new alley. "Yes, he gave them to someone else."

"To whom did he give them?"

God, it was starting again! "I don't know, I don't know, I swear I . . ."

"To a woman?"

Light at the end of the alley; Alperin stumbled towards it gratefully. "Yes, yes, that's right. He gave them to a woman."

[218]

The eyes seemed satisfied. There were a few more questions. Alperin answered them truthfully or made up the answers as best he could, saying what he thought was required of him. He was exhausted when Burke finally got up.

"You must not tell Mitchell that I have been here."

"No, I won't tell him. I promise that."

Burke came across the room towards him and Alperin noticed how crooked the man was, one shoulder higher than the other as though the frail body had given way beneath the weight of the fine, shapely head. The face that loomed over Alperin's was like a clown's dead mask from which eyes stared, all laughter burnt out. Alperin put his hands over his face.

"It will be all right now." The voice, with its faint Irish lilt, was quite beautiful; it seemed to come from a spirit which had nothing to do with that ill conceived body. "But you must do as I tell you in future. I shall come to see you again tomorrow. In the meantime, pretend that you are too ill to see anyone."

Alperin agreed to this readily and Burke left him still sitting with his head in his hands.

Burke went down the stairs slowly and as he moved a dark shadow hunched up the wall. The shadow was bigger than ever he had been. It was one thing to subdue Alperin; Mitchell was a different proposition. His hand, damp with sweat, slid on the banister rail. "I will put matters right," he had said to Alperin and the fool had believed him. He went across the lobby and out into the breathless courtyard. He sat down in one of the wicker chairs; it was still warm from the heat of the sun. The dust rose up from the paving stones. He could see the lights of cars on the main road; the road was only a few hundred yards away, but he was not sure that he could make it. He wasn't sure that he wanted to. If only he could wash his hands of the whole thing, stand aside and let the others play out their bitter little charade! But afterwards there would be questions, and even if he could answer them satisfactorily he would, in the process, have demonstrated his incompetence. There was no room in the service for incompetents. How would he live? He had very little money saved. His tastes were expensive and it was important that they should be gratified since he was denied the more simple satisfactions. He was forty; he could live a long time. Something must be done.

He got up and crossed the courtyard. There was a car parked just inside the entrance. He looked at it, covered in a thin, greyish pall of dust, and he thought of Eliot whom he could reach in under an hour in the Fiat. He turned away and walked down to the main road, crossed it, and took the first turning. It might be a little cooler down by the lake.

It was odd that Mitchell should have got him into this mess. Of all the men he had worked with Mitchell had seemed the most reliable, his reactions tiresomely orthodox. Perhaps one should not blame him for that; to one so well-endowed, no doubt the orthodox reactions served well enough in nine situations out of ten. Burke reached the lake and turned in the direction of Montreux. The air was hot here, too, and the shrubs smelt strongly; the water was very still and black. Burke walked on, thinking about Mitchell. The idea that Mitchell might take a fall had pleased him until he realized that he himself would go down with him. He hated Mitchell. He hated him so much at this moment that he felt he could conceivably kill him. But he could not betray him; the thought of himself sitting in Eliot's reeking room blurting out accusations revolted him. If he could make Mitchell betray himself, that would be a different matter.

He quickened his step. He had made sure before he left the hotel that Mitchell was in his bedroom, but that did not mean that he would stay there all night. In spite of the heat

Burke reached the large hotel where Miriam Kratz was staying in ten minutes. It was just after one o'clock. He stood
on the lawn, glad of the grass beneath his feet after the un-
yielding tarmac; light streamed from the main ballroom and
he could hear dance music. There were people sitting in the
chairs on the terrace and white-coated waiters moved from
table to table. Burke walked softly across the lawn and sat
at a table just beneath the terrace. After a time one of the
waiters came down to serve him.

"I have a friend staying here," Burke said. "I wonder if
you could find the number of her room for me?"

The waiter said that he was new here. Burke described
Miriam and put several notes down on the tray. The waiter
went away and soon returned with the drink and the number of the room. Burke sat at the table a long time, waiting
for the first night breeze to temper the air.

Miriam, too, waited for the breeze. She had stood at the
window for a long while as evening came. For the first time,
perhaps because Mitchell had been so insistent about the
beauty of the mountains, she had noticed the view. She was
not conscious of the lake, which was in shadow, but she saw
the mountain opposite very clearly. There was a small path
threading its way upwards towards the summit. It reminded
her of another path. She did not know the place, but she
knew that she had looked at the mountain through a tangle
of barbed wire and that someone had pointed to the dark
ridge of trees into which the path finally disappeared and
had said that the frontier was there. From the way that the
person had spoken, it had seemed that the promised land
must lie beyond the frontier. She had crossed a lot of frontiers since then. Usually she had been driven, but once she
had crossed of her own will. A tremendous decision it had
seemed, that decision to leave her child in East Berlin while

[221]

she fled to the West after Mikail's arrest. The grandparents would look after Naomi, she had told herself; it was vitally important, if they were ever to be reunited as a family, that she should run away in order to work for Mikail's release. Now, she wondered whether she had not simply run away. Whatever the answer, one thing was certain, she did not want to go back. It would be like climbing that mountain without believing that there was anything on the other side except another mountain. That afternoon, as she walked away from Mitchell, she had been prepared to accept this. But now . . . She took the sheet of paper from the dressing table and looked down at the laboured writing, trying to catch a glimpse of Mikail bending forward, holding the pen in cramped fingers. His face eluded her. And her child? Naomi was no longer a child, the girl on the rocks had taught her that. So the longed-for reunion was a fantasy, was that the answer? This one hope had kept her going for a long time; now that she questioned it, everything seemed to fall apart.

It was so hot. The heat was like a tight band round her head. The mountain, the trees, the path all blurred; there was only the reality of the barbed wire. She took off her clothes and lay down on the divan, holding the paper with Mikail's writing on it close against her body as though this was the one thing which stood between her and the darkness. She could feel her pulse beating faster, faster, faster. . . . Her mind blacked out and immediately the smell came, a smell of urine and rotting flesh which blocked her nostrils, choked her throat. Her hands began to twitch against the bedclothes and in spite of the heat she drew the blanket up to her chin.

When at last the first breeze came it was as though the world had turned to ice again. The moon was shining in the room and outside she could see a great tower like an iceberg and beyond it the land was broken into waves of ice. She was cold, cold, cold because her blood was thin and her strength was ebbing. She knew that there was a woman in the bunk above waiting, but whether it was the blanket or the sheet of paper that the woman wanted, she could not remember.

When the door opened and someone slipped into the room she was not surprised, there was often someone moving about the hut at night. The figure moved stealthily, examining the wardrobe, opening drawers in the dressing table; the drawer in the desk did not open easily but responded to the skilled probing of a long, sharp knife. Miriam was aware of these movements, they flickered uneasily through her dreams. After a time, the figure came silently towards the bed, placing the knife on the bedside table, and a shadow passed over Miriam's face as the figure bent over her. Miriam twisted her head from side to side. She was disturbed not so much by the intruder as by the moonlight which flooded the room; she tried to shield herself from it, but it was everywhere; she closed her eyes tight, but it lay like burning ice on her lids. As she twisted and turned the intruder caught a glimpse of the sheet of paper before the blanket covered it up again.

There was darkness as the figure bent forward, blotting out the moonlight. Miriam began to mumble in a strange language. The face was very close, she could feel breath on her cheek; very gently, fingers began to ease back the blanket. Miriam's eyes opened. She looked towards the head of the divan expecting to see the thin, withered arm hanging there. Instead, she saw moonlight glinting on a long, thin knife. She stretched out her hand. The intruder's head jerked up and she struck between the neck and the line of the shoulder. The knife went in clean and straight. The fingers released their hold on the blanket; the body slid sideways, for a moment it knelt at the side of the divan in a parody of prayer and then it disappeared. Miriam remained hunched forward, holding the sheet of paper. Soon, the fingers which held it began to shake, the shaking spread up her arm, along her shoulders; her thighs began to twitch. She pressed the paper against her breast. The figure on the ground made unpleasant, choking noises which she found very disturbing; she was glad when, after a while, there was silence. She leant across the divan and reached for the telephone; she was shaking so much that she could scarcely hold the receiver.

Chapter 23

"He's dead." Mitchell stared down at Burke as though in spite of this he still expected him to speak. "What happened? Why did he come here? Did he attack you?"

From the divan Miriam stared up at him. At first he thought that his words had not penetrated; then her jaw thrust upwards moving convulsively as she struggled to speak. She said only one word, "He?" She sounded surprised, and her eyes clouded. The same struggle to speak, and then words that made no sense to him. "The woman . . . the woman . . ." Death itself did not seem to trouble her.

Mitchell came to the divan and touched the fingers that clawed the blanket; in spite of the heat, they were like ice. She let go of the blanket and clutched his hand. She was shaking so much that further speech was impossible, but her eyes implored him not to leave her. He said, "It's all right, it's over now," just as though she was a child wakened from a nightmare. But words were of no help to her and she went on clutching at him desperately; the world was breaking apart and she had no one to hold to but him.

He had no clear idea of what had happened in this room.

Perhaps they had struggled, perhaps she had screamed, perhaps someone had already called the police; there was no time to lose. Yet none of this mattered in the face of her terror. Speech had failed, there remained the older, deeper communication. He lay down beside her and took her in his arms; he held her close, pressing his limbs against hers, trying to warm her body against his own. Gradually, her breathing became easier. He had no thought for pleasure, his body was simply an instrument through which pain and terror might drain away. Yet, as he felt the terrible shaking subside as she relaxed and grew heavy against him, he felt that this was the most important thing he had ever done; if the police had come and it had ended here he would not have cared. He talked to her, gently, consolingly. "It was my fault. Whatever happened here, it was my fault. He was desperately worried. I should have tried to reassure him. I owed him that much. But I didn't even bother to make up a convincing story. I drove him to turn on you." But she was not listening; her face, almost peaceful now, told him that she was drifting to a level where his voice could not reach her. Just before she crossed the borders of sleep, she whispered, "Mikail."

The word reminded him that there was still a lot to be done. He thought about Burke, calmly and without emotion; it was too late now for the luxury of personal feeling. He put grief aside, knowing it would wait for him. Burke is dead, he thought, and the body must be disposed of within the next hour while there are few people about. Fortunately there was not much blood, although it would be important not to draw the knife. He turned his head to look at the window. The moon was bright. It would be risky to use the window as a means of exit, even if it was practicable. That meant going through the hotel. When he arrived there had been one or two couples still dancing and a few people drinking on the terrace, their presence had helped him to make his entrance unobtrusively. But one could not hope to leave unobtrusively carrying a body. Could it be assumed that the dancers would have gone to bed now? He thought about the geography of the building. There was a service lift nearby which would take him down to the passage to the left of the night porter's cubicle. To reach the lift he would have to pass the linen cupboard, a lavatory, and one bedroom. The linen cupboard . . . He looked down at Miriam; she was sleeping very deeply, as though in a coma. When he gently eased away from her, she did not stir.

He went into the corridor. At this end it was dark, but there was a light at the far end, near the main staircase. The building seemed quiet now, no music, no murmur of voices or clink of glasses. He tried the linen cupboard door and found, as he had expected, that it was locked. It was not a lock that would have presented Burke with many problems, but it took Mitchell a quarter of an hour to master it. When he had the door open he was sweating and the pounding of his heart told him that it was not the heat that was troubling him. The cupboard contained the usual quantities of bed linen together with three laundry baskets and a trolley. A white overall was hanging on the back of the door; as a disguise, it seemed better than nothing. Mitchell took off his jacket and put on the overall, buttoning it at the back. He put one of the linen baskets on the trolley and wheeled it into the bedroom. It was a big linen basket and Burke was a small man, there was no difficulty there. Mitchell laid his jacket over the body and shut the lid down quickly. He caught a glimpse of himself in the mirror before he wheeled the trolley out of the room, he looked like a casualty attendant at a hospital.

Almost as soon as he started down the corridor a woman came out of the lavatory. She had no teeth, which seemed to worry her excessively; she scurried past him with averted face and disappeared into a bedroom a little further down the corridor. Mitchell rang for the lift and it came grinding up, making more noise than he would have thought possible. If the porter had been asleep he would surely wake now. The lift made even heavier weather of the journey down and the door opened with an asthmatic wheeze. The porter was peering out of his cubicle, his face puffed with sleep, as Mitchell went by with the trolley. Mitchell bade him a cheerful good night, but this ruse did not work. The man shouted "Hé!" and Mitchell heard the squeak of a stool on the tiled floor as he got up. There was a lavatory on the right of the corridor. Mitchell pulled the linen basket off the trolley and dragged it into the lavatory, locking the door. Fortunately the lavatory was on an outside wall and there was a good-sized window. Mitchell opened the window. There was another wall ten feet away; at first he thought that he must be looking into a courtyard, then he realized that this was the side of the hotel and below was a dark alley running between this and another hotel. In the corridor there was a crash followed by muffled curses as the porter fell over the trolley. Mitchell lifted Burke's body from the basket and heaved it through the window; he took off the overall and put on his own jacket before he followed.

There was no time to be lost. No time for subtlety and certainly no time for sensitivity. He had left the car on the promenade under the shadow of a tree; he could see the tree not far away. He raised Burke's body, slipped an arm round the narrow waist and forced one of the long, thin arms round his neck where it rested brittle as a twig. He walked between the tall buildings out into the moonlight, casting a monstrous shadow on the silver lawn. He swayed and laughed a little foolishly for the benefit of any unseen watcher. There was no one on the promenade, but he kept up the performance for his own benefit. He opened the door of the car and put the body on the back seat. He got in and drove slowly towards the square off the quayside. There he stopped for a while. He was in no condition to drive on the main road which was fairly busy even at this hour of the night. The breeze had died down. It was still as death. He put his head against the driving wheel. "We'll get out of this soon," he said, just as though Burke cared. "Somewhere cool, higher up."

He waited until his heartbeat was back to normal, then he turned on to the road. He drove without stopping past Veytaux, past Chillon, down into Villeneuve and along the valley of the Rhône. He took the turning that led in the direction of Champéry.

The path turned and twisted and soon on either side the mountains thrust against the sky like giants which have broken free of earth's net. The temperature dropped steadily. He had never before responded to this glacial beauty, but now he longed to reach the snow line; and when he came to it, the landscape seemed to burn with an icy fire that purged away all human anxiety. At the heart of the fire there would be stillness, always. He buried Burke in a drift beneath a climber's hut and if he felt any emotion at all it was regret that he himself could not rest there.

Chapter 24

"Not Berlin," Novak said to Mitchell six hours later. "There would be too much publicity. Kratz and the child will cross the Jugoslav-Austrian frontier near Jesenice."

"When?"

"As soon as Alperin has crossed the frontier."

"Which frontier?"

Novak shrugged his shoulders. "Does it matter?"

"It matters that I should be sure that the arrangements are honoured."

"You are afraid that we shall take Alperin and keep Kratz? Well, that's reasonable enough."

"So what guarantee have I that that won't happen?"

"You yourself. Kratz is of no value; you may be of considerable value. So we shall keep to our part of the bargain."

"And the timing?"

Time was running out, although Novak did not know that.

"First, the woman leaves for Klagenfurt. She must find a hotel there and wait."

Mitchell did not know Klagenfurt, he could not visualize

Miriam there. He suddenly realized that he would never see her again.

"But surely she could wait until . . ."

"No." Novak was quite definite. He did not understand Miriam Kratz's part in this, but instinct told him that it would be wise to get her out of Mitchell's way. "The woman goes now."

"And Alperin?"

"In two days a coach from Spain will stop briefly at Chillon to allow its passengers to stretch their legs and inspect the castle. I shall be there with another man who bears a remarkable resemblance to Alperin. You and Alperin must be in the castle before the coach arrives. I suggest that you wait in the Grand Hall of the Count—there's quite a lot to look at there—and when our party comes in, join up with it. I will do the rest. Luggage, passports, all that will be taken care of, naturally . . ."

"But this other man? Surely someone will suspect? People are at close quarters in coaches."

"My companion is unobtrusive. He will sleep most of the way from Spain. The heat does not agree with him and his holiday will have done him no good. He will wear dark glasses to protect his eyes from the sun and he will fuss about the blind which he will want drawn down all the time. And, most important of all, he will have a tendency to be sick—that always repels the inquisitive."

"Where has this man been for his holiday?"

"Tarragona. But it will not be necessary for Alperin to talk, by the time we reach Chillon it will not be expected of him."

"And when you leave Chillon?"

"There is only one thing that need concern you. It will be twenty-four hours before the coach is clear of Switzerland.

After that, nothing is likely to go wrong. But it is important that Alperin should not be missed during that time."

"It sounds simple."

"Yes, I don't think it will be an exciting trip." Novak sounded regretful. He looked out of the window at the lake, brilliantly mirroring the mountains. "In Spain it will be even hotter. Imagine, three days in a coach!"

Mitchell said, "You still enjoy this, don't you?"

"Of course." Not to enjoy life was as much as he knew or cared of sin.

Mitchell persisted, "And when you no longer enjoy it?"

"I shall stop."

He would know when to stop, the eyes told Mitchell that. For a moment, there had been some kind of communication between them and those extraordinary eyes had darkened to violet. Now, as though sensing danger, they glazed over and were still. He was curious about Mitchell, he wondered why he had acted in a way that seemed at variance with his character. But he would not try to find the answer. He was not a man to ensnare himself in the trap of pity.

"You will feel much less melancholy when this woman is out of the way."

The violent laughter welled up within him and the eyes were a vivid blue, glittering as the sun-bright lake. There was no chink in that armour now. He poured drinks and settled down to give Mitchell the details of the plan.

Mitchell left him half an hour later. Miriam was to leave tonight; he should lose no time in seeing her and making the necessary arrangements. But in spite of this he went first to Alperin.

Alperin, the girl at the reception desk informed him, was unwell and had said that he could not see visitors.

"He is always unwell," Mitchell pointed out. "It is a state of mind." The girl hesitated and he went on, "In fact, it is very bad for him to be alone. If I don't see him he may do something unpleasant. You wouldn't want that, would you?"

The girl called the porter. Alperin was becoming a nuisance and the hotel staff no longer paid much attention to his demands.

"Show Monsieur into room 15," she said.

Alperin was in bed, more firmly barricaded in than ever. The windows were closed, the curtains drawn, and the room had a sour smell that indicated that this state of affairs had gone on for some time. There was a tray on the bedside table bearing a large plate of rolls all of which had been broken although very little seemed to have been eaten; the butter was melting and a fly writhed on its back in the jam. Cold tea added to the other unpleasant odours. Mitchell picked up the tray and put it outside the door. Then he opened the window and fastened back the shutters. When he turned round Alperin was watching him with an expression which Mitchell recognized as the dread of the victim for the tormentor. It was not pleasant; but fear has its uses and Mitchell made no attempt to soothe Alperin.

"You had better get up," he said curtly. "There is a lot to do."

Alperin said, "I've changed my mind."

Mitchell laughed: laughter has its uses, too. "No doubt the groom suffers in the same way on the wedding eve. The thing that carries him through is the thought that it would be even more unpleasant to cancel the arrangements."

He pulled back the bedclothes and Alperin, who was sleeping in only a pyjama top, gave a little yelp of alarm and grabbed the sheet. When he had recovered his dignity, he said:

"Nevertheless, I should like to cancel the arrangements."

"The films have already been despatched. You realize that?"

[233]

"Already despatched!" It was obvious that Alperin had not realized it.

"But of course!"

"You did . . . did you give them to a woman?"

"A woman?" Mitchell was surprised now. "Whatever gave you that idea?"

Alperin's face crumpled, his forehead and cheeks were scored with tiny lines and his lower lip trembled uncontrollably; he looked old and ill. The truth, Mitchell decided, would be the best weapon now.

"You can go back if you like," he said indifferently. "It's not too late. But it would be advisable if you went to the authorities immediately you arrived and told them the whole story. You might get a more lenient sentence than if you waited for the leak to be discovered."

Alperin's eyes met Mitchell's. There was astonishing power in those weak, imploring eyes.

"But they won't suspect me?"

"Who else? You will be the natural suspect since you have been in contact with scientists who are known to be communists."

"But I haven't spoken to any of them . . ."

"You had supper with Dr. Scunner only last night."

"Dr. Scunner!"

Alperin flopped back against the pillows. Under the sheet his body was flat as a corpse. Mitchell hated him for being so easily broken.

"Well, what is it to be?" he said brutally. "You must make your choice and stick to it. I can't waste any more time and I am beginning to have my doubts about you."

There was a long silence, then Alperin asked that absurd question again.

"Will they give me a housekeeper?"

"I really have no idea, but I'm sure you will be made very comfortable."

Alperin did not say any more and Mitchell was glad to leave him alone. He went into the bathroom and turned on the taps.

"You must make an appearance at the conference this afternoon," he said when he returned. "When are you reading your paper, by the way?"

"On Friday. I don't know how I shall manage . . ."

"Don't worry about that now. You will feel much better by then." On Friday he would be out of the country; but Mitchell did not tell him this. "Have a bath and get dressed. We can have lunch together and then I'll take you to the conference hall. Make some excuse about the heat not agreeing with you if anyone mentions your absence. I'll come and see you this evening to make sure that everything is all right."

He left the room and went down to the lounge to wait for Alperin. He rang for the waiter and ordered whisky. When it came he drank it quickly and ordered another. While he was waiting for it, he thought about Alperin. Over the years he had bullied many weak little men; it was one of the things that had sickened him of his trade. Now, when he was dedicated to something altogether more noble, how did he achieve his ends? By bullying another weak little man. It all came down to the same thing in the end. He drank the second whisky quickly and began to feel better. He wondered why he had not tried this particular form of consolation earlier.

Alperin appeared while he was drinking his third whisky. He looked horrified when Mitchell suggested that he should join him and said in his most prim voice, "It's much too hot." He looked anxious when they got into the car: just as Mitchell was about to assure him that he drove better when drunk, he said:

"I haven't seen your friend lately."

Mitchell jammed his foot savagely on the accelerator and the car flashed through a narrow gap between a tram and an ambling Volkswagen.

"He has left the town. The heat doesn't suit him, either."

Alperin sat very still beside Mitchell. Buildings flashed by at speed, a church with a high clock tower, a big modern hotel, a post office and a row of shops kaleidoscoped. Alperin watched without seeming to register anything. But afterwards he remembered that it was one o'clock on a hot Monday afternoon when he knew beyond all doubt that there was no way back for him. He spoke only once, quite casually:

"I wonder if there would be any possibility of my sister joining me eventually?"

"It happens sometimes," Mitchell answered indifferently. "It would be up to her, wouldn't it?"

She would come, Alperin thought; surely she would come. Like him, she would discover that she could not live alone. All the time that he was eating his meal, he was trying to envisage Dorothy being unable to live alone.

After he had lunched with Alperin, Mitchell walked by the lake for a time. He told himself that he was doing this to clear his head, but in fact he was delaying his visit to Miriam. The instructions which he had to give her meant that they would never meet again; he was not sure that he could make this break. But when at last he went to her room, he found that the matter had been taken out of his hands.

Perhaps it was something about the way she stood in the center of the room with the sunlight behind her that gave her the unalterable authority of a figure in a painting, beyond argument or anguish. Her eyes met his, a level gaze, and impersonal. The desperate appeal which had drawn

[236]

him to her for so long was gone. She had finished with him. There would be no tender last words, no fond embrace; she had become a stranger with whom he could only communicate on a superficial level. He talked of trains and tickets, of passports and hotels. She listened carefully to his instructions; she did not argue and she asked no questions. When he told her that she must pack quickly she turned and opened the wardrobe door. The brilliant orange dress was hanging there; she lifted it down without looking at it, as though it did not belong to her. The bright new coat was hanging on the back of the door. She took that down, too. She produced tissue paper and folded the dress, her hands moving with the quick efficiency of a shop assistant. She did not look at Mitchell nor did she speak to him.

He noticed a small, shallow suitcase on the chair by the window. It had not been there previously; she must have bought it this morning. He watched her pack the coat and the patent leather shoes, using more tissue paper. Suddenly, he had a vision of her unwrapping the tissue paper, holding the garments up for inspection, haggling over price. He had given her money, but it would not support her for long. He wanted to say something to help her, but she did not need him any more so his advice would be irrelevant.

She made no mention of Burke. Mitchell wondered whether she had not taken in what had happened, or whether she had deliberately blotted the scene out of her mind. He suspected the latter: there was a quality of ruthlessness in her for which he had not bargained. He strolled across the room, on the pretext of looking out of the window, and examined the rug. There were no bloodstains. Behind him, she said:

"I'm ready now."

She was wearing the old raincoat over the black frock and she carried the case in her hand. He came towards her to

[237]

take the case, but she shook her head. He sensed that she did not want any contact with him, nevertheless he said:

"I'll come to the station with you, of course."

"No. I can manage."

"But you have to get your ticket, find out about the train . . ."

"I am accustomed to travel."

She stood with an abstracted expression on her face, waiting for him to release her. He loved her and he wanted to give her all the things he should have given his wife, the things he had not known it was in him to give. But there are times when one is asked not to give; it is hard, but it has to be accepted. He picked up the key to the room.

"You'll need to hand this in."

She took the key. They went out of the room and took the lift to the ground floor. When they came into the foyer, he said:

"I'll settle the bill for you."

He walked across to the reception desk. He did not look round until the bill was paid and then she had gone. Through the open doorway he could see the sun scorching the trees in the square, the leaves already yellowing. There were a few elderly people sitting on benches in the shade and somewhere out of sight children were calling to one another. A breeze stirred the trees and billowed the canvas awning over a café. Then it was still again. He stood with his hands clenched at his sides while the dust settled in the hot street.

Chapter 25

On the Wednesday morning Mitchell planned his own future. He would stay in Montreux for two days to ensure that nothing went wrong at this end; he would spend the time locked in Alperin's room, declaiming the now familiar phrase that he was too ill to see anyone. By the time that he left, Alperin would be in Russia and the exchange would have been effected. He could start his journey. He wanted to go a long way; away from all the things he had betrayed, including the old Stephen Mitchell. His present life was too much of a mess ever to straighten out again. Eliot and his kind had made nonsense of everything. There had been a brief moment of clarity when he wanted to do something simple and noble, and then Miriam Kratz had confused everything again. Perhaps he was the kind who would always be confused in the modern world. The answer was to opt out. South America was rather a predictable choice; but he had never been there and there were other reasons why it appealed to him. A man could still get lost in South America, Perhaps years hence someone would come across him on the edge of a remote forest, a white man living outside the range of civilization. A character out of Conrad.

He had been up early that morning, in time to see the Alpine glow. The spectacle had not touched him. He had lived with it too long; all the freshness had gone out of Europe. He wanted to see the sun rise over mountains whose majesty had not been diminished by man's familiarity. Nevertheless, as he prepared to meet Alperin he turned to the window again for one last look at the view. Undoubtedly it was beautiful. But in spite of the mountains, the landscape had a tamed look, dotted with comfortable hotels and villas; the imprint of the tidy Swiss mind overlaid everything except Chillon, sullen and unrelenting. Yet, most of all, it was from Chillon that he wanted to escape. One of the paddle steamers was coming from the direction of Villeneuve and he watched it, glad of a diversion. It must be the nine o'clock trip to Evian. In which case, it was time that he set out.

He walked down to Alperin's hotel. It was going to be very hot, he would not enjoy the subsequent days incarcerated in Alperin's room. But perhaps a period of withdrawal was necessary before starting a new life. The thought sent a shiver of excitement through his body; he could visualize the long, weed-infested river winding into the interior, the trees standing close on either side—"the heart of darkness" Conrad had called a similar stretch of Africa. But Africa had become very self-conscious since then; South America was more truly the dark continent now. And he wanted the darkness, he wanted it more than anything in the whole of his life.

Alperin was setting out into the unknown, too. For a man who was realizing a dream, he presented a pathetic spectacle. His face was wrinkled as a walnut and his clothes hung loose on his shrunken body; the hand that pulled ineffectually at a strap of his suitcase was knotted with veins like the hand of a very old man. Mitchell, who did not like to see him in this state, said sharply:

"What do you think you're doing with that case?"

"It won't close."

"I told you that you were not to take any luggage with you."

"But . . ."

Mitchell pushed him aside and began to unpack, stowing shirts, ties, underclothes in drawers, putting the sponge-bag back in the bathroom. Alperin seemed to mind most of all about the sponge-bag.

"I must brush my teeth," he protested in a high voice.

"You'll find a toothbrush in your new luggage."

"But someone else may have used it."

He looked sick at the thought; it was obvious that the problem of the toothbrush must be resolved quickly.

"The coach will stop somewhere for you to have lunch and you will be able to buy one then." Mitchell changed the subject before Alperin could find a flaw in this argument. "I hope you haven't done anything silly like asking for your bill?"

"Not yet."

Mitchell snapped the case shut and put it on top of the wardrobe. Alperin gazed up at it as though it contained his soul.

"Now! Let's have a look at you." Mitchell walked round Alperin studying him carefully. "Linen suit and hat, cream shirt, maroon tie, sun glasses . . . That's all right. Shoes! You were to wear brogues."

"They pinch my feet in this heat."

"You won't be doing much walking."

Mitchell found the shoes. Alperin put them on very slowly. Mitchell, who was becoming more and more uneasy, could scarcely bear to watch him; there was something about Alperin that threatened to sap all his strength.

"Can't I take the other pair with me?" Alperin asked when he had finished.

Mitchell came close to him, using the advantage of his greater bulk to the full. Alperin responded by staring at him with eyes that pleaded for kindness. It was too late for kindness now. Mitchell said angrily:

"You do realize the position, don't you? As far as the people at this hotel are concerned, you are returning here for lunch in the usual way and you will not be leaving until the weekend. So you can't take any luggage. Do you understand that?"

Alperin nodded his head, but looked incapable of understanding.

"What about your passport?"

Alperin hesitated for a moment and Mitchell, his impatience beyond control, took hold of Alperin's jacket intending to feel for the passport. Instead of backing away, Alperin came closer and grabbed Mitchell's shirt front.

"Help me! Please help me! I can't go. Oh, please understand that I can't go . . ."

Mitchell shouted, "There are more important things involved than you!"

"No, no! You can't judge that. You have no right. You're not God." He flopped on to his knees and clutched at Mitchell's legs. "I'll do anything, anything, but save me from this . . . I can't travel long distances in a coach. I've never been able to since I was a child. My sister would tell you; we went up to Edinburgh once . . ."

Mitchell took him by the shoulders and raised him, quite gently in spite of his struggles. When Alperin stood in front of him, his fists pressed against his mouth so that only little whimpering noises escaped, Mitchell said:

"It is too late for either of us to go back."

All the anger had gone from him, he felt weary and defeated. Alperin, staring at him, saw a man more lost than himself. The sight appeared to convince him of the uselessness of protest. When Mitchell held out his hand and said, "Your passport," he gave it to him without a word. He watched in silence while Mitchell put the passport in the top drawer of the dressing table. He did not argue when Mitchell asked for his wallet and he seemed quite indifferent as the greater part of the Swiss currency was deposited in the drawer with the passport. When this was done and the wallet had been returned, he said, "May I wash before we go, please?" Mitchell nodded and Alperin went into the bathroom. Mitchell said, "Leave the door open." He stood in the doorway, more from habit than because he thought that Alperin would try to escape. Alperin was broken now.

By the time that Alperin was ready, it was quarter to ten, later than Mitchell had planned. He took the key of the room and put it in his pocket; then he led Alperin out, chatting to him as they went down the stairs. Fortunately the staff were accustomed to Alperin looking sick, so no one took much notice of them. Outside a hot breeze blew dust in their faces; there was no cloud in the relentless sky. Alperin turned his ankle on the steep path down to Chillon; he gave a little sob and caught at a railing to steady himself. Something stirred in Mitchell as he watched him, not so much pity as an awareness of its absence.

He looked at his watch again. Five to ten: Novak's party was due to arrive in just over half an hour. It was difficult to see what could go wrong now. Nevertheless, when they came to the bend in the path and the castle rose ahead of them, he held Alperin back. It seemed safer out here in the sunlight. "There are supposed to be traces of a thirteenth century gallery at the top of one of those towers," he said.

Alperin stared at the castle bleakly. Mitchell decided that it would be wise to reduce the time spent in Chillon to a minimum. Every man is a prisoner in such a place as this, he thought, remembering Bonivard with only the sound of water on stone to break the long introspection. He could visualize Bonivard, hunched against the pillar; the features were familiar, although he had never seen a picture of the man—the blond type of Jew with a sad mouth and eyes that still believed in the human race. It was strange how well he seemed to know him; he had the feeling that after all the confusion of the last weeks this man was the one person to whom he could still be true. Beside him, Alperin said fretfully:

"What are we waiting for?"

"We have a little time; it's more pleasant out here."

"I'd much rather go in." Alperin dabbed his forehead with his handkerchief. "It will be cooler."

Mitchell was the more reluctant of the two as they crossed the bridge. While they were paying for admission a coach drew up in the road and he turned eagerly. Of course, the coach might be early! He could leave Alperin here and walk back into the sunlight. But the people who were clambering out, stretching cramped limbs, shouting to one another, were unmistakably English. Mitchell moved into the shadow of the postern gate. Beyond, in the first courtyard, Alperin said, "That's better! I couldn't have stood that heat much longer."

The coach party surged forward and Mitchell and Alperin were caught up in its midst. The party was led by a cadaverous, lantern-jawed man who regarded himself as a natural comic. He herded his companions through the underground vaults, bunched so tight together that they might have been in one of those interminable corridors in the London tubes for all they saw of their surroundings. When a young couple stopped to read Byron's name on the pillar in Bonivard's prison, he shouted, "Move along at the front there!" They climbed stairs, went through the second courtyard, the Grand Hall of the High Bailiff, the Coat-of-Arms Hall and the Duke's Chamber, borne on a ceaseless tide of patter. Alperin kept his eyes fixed on the lantern-jawed man with the half-repelled fascination of a child at a Punch and Judy show. Mitchell, content to be inconspicuous, held to the center of the group with the result that he was unaware of the people moving on the periphery until he reached the Grand Hall of the Count. Here, he broke away, drawn by the sunlight to the long windows overlooking the lake. It was then that he noticed Huber. It was like being confronted with a piece from a jigsaw that has already been completed.

It was important at this stage that there should be no pieces unaccounted for. There was no place in the discreet, unemphatic pattern for Huber, flamboyant in saffron suit with deep violet shirt. Mitchell lingered in the Grand Hall of the Count while the English party went on; he talked to Alperin about the tapestry hangings which were thirteenth century. Huber followed the English party into the next room. Mitchell cursed the pride that had made him dismiss Huber as someone beneath his attention.

"Why don't we go with them?" Alperin asked, uneasy now that the vacuum was no longer filled by the lantern-jawed man.

"I'm getting bored with that fellow. We'll give them time to get ahead of us."

When the last murmurings of the English party had died in the distance, Mitchell and Alperin went into the bedchamber adjacent. Huber was reading a guidebook. He was as conspicuous as a leopard in the empty room; there was something of the sour smell of the cat about him, too. Alperin's fingers tugged at Mitchell's arm.

"I can't go with that man!"

"You're not going with him." Mitchell hustled Alperin through the gloom of the latrines to the somber loftiness of the Hall of the Scribes. Alperin protested:

"You didn't tell me that he would be here."

"Because I didn't know. It's pure coincidence."

But it was no coincidence. As they caught up with the English party, Mitchell saw Huber strolling after them. A woman said, "What's a chevron?" and the lantern-jawed man said, "Don't be vulgar!" His stock of repartee was running out and the laughter of his companions was on the ebb. Huber was standing near one of the windows, plainly idling. So Novak does not trust me, Mitchell thought; he has sent Huber to ensure that nothing goes wrong. Was that the answer?

The English party were moving across to the windows, the recesses of which bore traces of old paintings; the group studied them, drained of laughter, beginning to be bored. In contrast, Huber seemed to find something obscenely amusing in the faint marks on the wall. And suddenly, watching that dark face, Mitchell, too, saw the joke. He remembered that Eliot had once said, "The gods have deserted us, but we can still learn from them. Hubris, for example, is dangerous and deserves to be punished." And what better punishment for a man he had always considered too proud than that a check should be kept on his movements by the man he most despised? It was funny, very funny indeed; a pity, though, that he had not seen the joke earlier.

The English party headed towards the museum, the lantern-jawed man had become morose and one of the women was complaining that her feet hurt. Mitchell looked at his watch. Ten-thirty. Novak's party would be arriving now; fifteen or twenty minutes later, depending on the speed of their tour, they would reach the Grand Hall of the Count;

[246]

and half an hour after that they would leave in the coach. Mitchell pushed Alperin to the front of the English group. The doorway to the museum was narrow and Huber, at the rear of the party, was not making any effort to shoulder his way through; he was standing on one side lighting a cigar. Huber had time on his side, he had only to watch and report; Eliot would do the rest. Mitchell hurried Alperin through the museum, past the models of the castle at the various stages of its long existence, towards the treasury. Here, he stopped at the foot of the wooden staircase leading to the keep. He said to Alperin:

"It's important that we shake off Huber, you understand?"

Alperin did not understand what was happening, but he was in favour of shaking off Huber.

"There is a courtyard beyond," Mitchell spoke quickly, "Go out there and wait for ten minutes; then come back and make your own way to the Grand Hall of the Count—straight through from room to room—it's the large hall with the marble pillars and the big windows, remember?"

Alperin nodded his head, staring anxiously at the doorway to the museum.

"When you get there you will join up with the German party. Someone will take care of you. You must trust him completely."

Alperin nodded, looking pitifully eager. Huber's intervention might prove useful, after all; Alperin would entrust himself to Novak now. Mitchell waited until Alperin had disappeared through the passage leading to the courtyard before he began to ascend the flight of stairs. He waited at the top of the first flight until Huber came into the room below; then he called upwards, "All right? I'm following you." He began to ascend the next flight, calling upwards occasionally. A couple on their way down waited for him to pass them on one of the narrow ledges; they gave him an odd

[247]

look as he went by talking to himself. It was a long climb, and dark, like climbing a chimney; he did not hurry. He did not look round, either, but the smell of cigar smoke wafted up and he knew that somewhere below Huber had begun to follow him. So far, so good. But what happened when they reached the top? It was not going to be easy to keep Huber immobilized for the next half-hour. And even supposing he did succeed, how was he to keep Huber quiet for the next twenty-four hours while the coach was still in Swiss territory? He thought about it while he climbed the last flight of stairs, but no answer presented itself.

There was no one at the top, he was fortunate in that. Sunlight came in dusty shafts through the eastern windows; but there was no air in the tiny room and the sloping roofs seemed to bear down on his shoulders. He felt trapped, as though it was he and not Huber who was cornered here. He went to one of the windows and looked out. Sunlight glittered sharp and merciless on stone, and, far beyond, the lake and the mountains pulsed with heat. He was weary of this endless assault on his senses. Only above, the unfurrowed blue of the sky looked tranquil and undemanding and he felt that this elemental beauty was the most desirable of all. He wanted to shoulder aside the wall of stone and step out into that blue void. An this, he realized, when Huber at last came into the room, was all that he had left to do. But it was not quite as simple as that, because Huber struggled a lot. Mitchell managed easily enough to force him into the narrow recess of the window—he was a small man, the last of the small men —but he clung to Mitchell with all the strength of his wiry wrists. There were steps on the stairs, a man's voice, a girl's nervous laughter. Time had run out. Mitchell forced Huber back and for a moment Huber's shoulders blotted out the blue sky; then Mitchell thrust forward with all his strength and the glass splintered. Huber at least was free. He swayed

[248]

on the edge of that desirable void; but still he clung to Mitchell. There was a breeze now; Mitchell felt it soft as a promise against his cheek as he yielded to the pressure of Huber's encircling arms and let his own body swing forward. The grey walls of the castle came up to meet him; then the world tilted and for a moment it was all sky and sunlight.

II

"Mitchell landed in a courtyard a long way below," Eliot said to the man who had flown hurriedly from London. "He was dead when they reached him. Huber was impaled on one of those spikes on the roofs of the towers. Astonishingly, he didn't die at once."

"Did he talk?"

"He screamed a lot apparently. Nothing interesting. He wasn't the kind to gasp out a last message." Eliot found this amusing, he coughed and a little saliva ran down on to his chin.

"How did Huber come into this, anyway?" the other man asked.

"It's sometimes advisable to have a situation covered from all angles."

"It doesn't seem to have worked in this instance, does it?"

Eliot clawed the blankets closer round him and edged his chair nearer to the fire. The man from London, sweating in the over-heated room, regarded him distastefully.

"And Burke?"

"Burke has disappeared. It doesn't matter. He wasn't of much consequence."

The man from London shook his head, like a dog with canker in his ear.

"What made Mitchell do it?"

Eliot took the brandy glass from the table beside him.

[249]

Brandy was not good for him, but in some obscure way he felt that he had scored a victory over London and victory should be celebrated.

"What made him kill Huber, do you mean?" he asked innocently. "To stop him interfering with their plans, I suppose."

"But what made him turn traitor, a man like that?"

"Money, I imagine. He was seen with the Kratz woman on several occasions. Perhaps she blackmailed him, or perhaps it was simply that she was expensive. Who knows?"

"I would never have thought it. Of all men, I would never have thought it of him."

Eliot smiled. "Oh, the weakness was there all right." He took another sip of the brandy, it was going to kill him, but he did not much care. "You can always tell a real agent by the eyes. There's something there at the back of the eyes, behind the soft film of civilization, something that he didn't have."

"He had a fine record."

Eliot shrugged his shoulders. "He and Claus Hesselmann came into the service during the war. In those days, they took in a lot of people who weren't really suitable."

Epilogue

The light was an enemy pressing hot steel against the rims of his eyes. Everything was white, the dusty road, the high mountain wall, the sky from which the sun had scorched colour. The strong air tore at his lungs, strained his heart. The child drew her hand away, probably his coarse fingers had held too tight: he was unused to human contact. He looked at her, the thin body hunched in the corner of the car. She stared back resentfully. To begin again . . . so many beginnings in his life, he was not sure he had strength for another. What was it that Camus had said? One must suppose that Sisyphus was happy? While he had his strength, perhaps.

The man beside the driver turned and saw that he was exhausted. He said, meaning to be kind:

"Not long now. Your wife is waiting for you at the police post outside Klagenfurt. There will be a lot of formalities to go through, but you will have a little time with her."

The man in the back seat closed his eyes. The flesh fell in seamed grey folds over the sunken cheeks, the mouth drew inwards. It had taken all his resolution to bear himself with some sort of dignity for the child's sake, he had nothing left to give his wife. He longed for the undemanding darkness of his cell. But he had learnt over the years that it was better to accept the future than to reject it; so he sat quietly, trying to accustom himself to the light and to the constant stabs of speech from the two men in front. Perhaps by the time he arrived he would think of something to say to them. If he was to live in the world again, he must learn to trade in words once more. There was so much to learn. If only he knew where the strength was to come from.

The car reached the top of the ridge and the valley lay before them. It was a long, wide view; his heart fluttered and gusts of panic shook his body when the sheltered mountain wall was left behind as the car began the long descent. He closed his eyes again. The child, frightened by the steep drop to one side, edged closer to him and put her hand in his. This time, he let it lie there without any pressure from his fingers. At least that was one thing he had learnt. But his wife? How could he expect her to understand, after these empty years, that she must ask for nothing now? For her, it would have been better if they had not come.

The car twisted slowly downwards, turn and turn and turn again like a corkscrew boring into the valley below. It grew hotter, dustier. There were fields on either side, green in spite of the sun, a passionate green that hurt more than the dust and the white mountain walls. Where the mountain road at last met the valley road there was a farm; then a long straight stretch ahead, houses in the distance, a church steeple rising above, a compact world, people living close, making demands on one another. The car stopped in front of a low bungalow with neat window boxes and a woman in a black dress waiting in the porch with something in her stance of the mute, endless patience of the peasant. He frowned, not understanding. Then he saw two men in uni-

form behind the woman, standing back, tactful but watch-
ful. He had not recognized her! She looked so enduring, as
though she had put down roots in suffering since he last saw
her.

The car door opened. The driver and the plainclothes
officer helped him and the child out. Then they, too, stood
back, waiting for some rite that must be performed in the
square patch of ground lying between the two parties. He
took a few steps forward and then stopped, knowing that he
had reached his limit.

She came to him, unhurried, but as though she knew what
must be done. She put her arms around him and held him
steady against her; her arms were strong. She used the words
he had used often when she had a nightmare.

"It is all right, my dear. I am here."

The child held back. The woman called to her by name,
but the child made no movement.

"We mustn't expect too much yet," he said anxiously.

"Yes," she said. "There will be time for that."

She sounded as though time was her gift. Behind her he
saw the green land rolling away into the distance and the
road, twisting and turning, hot, dusty and uphill most of the
way. The men who had been standing by came closer and
the party moved into the police station, the man and the
woman holding to each other, the child following behind.

A Note About the Author

Mary Hocking was born in Acton, London. After attending the Haberdasher's Girls' School, she served in the Women's Royal Naval Service with the Fleet Air Arm during World War II. Miss Hocking is a local government officer and makes her home in London. ASK NO QUESTION is the first of Miss Hocking's novels to be published in the United States.